MW01675283

Sherlock Holmes

THE BAKER STREET UNIVERSE

By John Pirillo

Copyright 2024, John Pirillo

"Dark the thunder, bright the light, may this evening not bring you fright."

--Lord Dunsany

Lightning Strike

"Blast it, Holmes!" Watson shouted, striving to drown out the pounding rain that was smashing against the carriage's roof and the blasts of thunder that rang out with each burst of renewed lightning strikes. "Why do we always seem to be in the very last place any sane man would ever desire to be?"

Holmes puffed several curls of smoke out the window, watching them blow away in the crisp winds outside, and then turned to his stout companion. "Surely, we do not take cases that any Constable in his right mind could solve with a few quick questions?"

"Most assuredly not!" Watson responded, pride touching his voice. "What would be the point of that? Men of our intellect need to be challenged to exist."

"Indeed, Watson. Indeed." Holmes said with a slight smile and then turned back to browsing the landscape as their carriage continued along the rain-beaten road.

Watson was about to comment again when he suddenly realized that Holmes had quite neatly turned his question around on him. No further insight into his first question was possible since he had answered it himself.

He was close to commenting on the turnabout when a bolt of lightning struck.

Drear Mansion

Watson lowered his forearm from his eyes.

The flare of light was gone, but he could still see dancing blue bolts of light in his vision.

And he could also see they had arrived.

He didn't know which was the more shocking to him at that moment, the bolt which had narrowly missed them, or this home which looked like some drear mansion taken from one of the Frankenstein books written by Mary Shelley, that splendid authoress that Watson had met on an outing with Holmes after a wonderful rendition of her play in the old Global Theater.

The mansion of that theater had been all dark and crooked, with gargoyles hiding in the nooks and crannies, peaks, and valleys of its gables, overlooking the grounds below, waiting for their next victim to pounce upon.

It had given Watson nightmares for nights afterward, remembering those ghastly creatures that clung to that stage prop, and yet it had also introduced a kind of excitement into his somewhat mundane life at times. Being a doctor, and a man of the investigation, Watson was becoming increasingly worried about his and Holmes's future. Now that they were nearing their middle years, he and Holmes were losing friends and comrades by God's Grace or more nefarious means to another world, leaving them with fewer and fewer good minds and gentle souls to enable their intellects with.

But the Frankenstein play had enervated Watson once more, leaving him with a sense of disturbing purpose, which when he took the time to think of it, meant he was not just a doctor, but a voyeur of sorts when it came to the macabre and the wicked. And that thought made him somewhat moody and bellicose when he considered its implications.

Their driver tapped the door outside Watson's side. "O'Brian residence, gentlemen."

Watson stuck his head out and for reward was stricken by sheets of rain that poured into his eyes and nostrils. "Wait for us!"

The Driver, used to the rather nasty weather of that time of year, merely shrugged, and huddled down into his overcoat and hat, as both Watson and Holmes climbed from their carriage and scampered as quickly as dignity would allow for the rather dark entrance to the home.

Before Watson could pound on the door with the handle of his umbrella, it flung open and a rather drear older man stood there, like a creature from one of the Bram Stoker novels, a creature of the night held captive by the moon and prisoner of dark desires.

Without a word, both Watson and Holmes stepped inside, as the butler took their soaking overcoats and umbrellas to store them.

The yellow light cast by tall candles in sconces about the entryway caught Watson's attention. He noticed they weren't real candles. But some kind of fangled invention that gave the electricity a flickering motion like one, causing the bulb shape to seem like a flame.

He had just come to that conclusion when a huge crackling sound deafened him and every light in the house went out, plunging him and Holmes into pitch darkness.

Nasty Night

"Sorry, sirs," the Butler said, his voice not giving Watson any sense of comfort or safety. It only added to the enigma of this horrid place and the sinister feeling that seemed so thick about it.

The lights went off again.

"Drats!" Watson cried out angrily. "Either stay on or stay off!"

The lights came back on.

Holmes smiled at his anxious friend. "Come now, Watson, you've been pounded by enemy artillery in the Chinas, surely this is not worse?"

"At least they didn't plunge one into the darkness of a crypt!"

Holmes arched an eyebrow.

Watson cleared his throat. "Sorry."

The Butler hadn't reacted at all. Not to the sound, to the lights out and on again, or to Watson's outburst.

The rain pounded the rooftop like demons striving to break in. The night was dark and dreary. Not a single soul in the house slept. Could ever sleep through such a terrible deluge.

The whole home shook from the violence of the

Thrashing and bashing of shutters. The swishing and slapping of curtains over opened windows. The sound of rain pelting the glass of the windows was like a million hungry creatures trying to get in.

Windows rattled in their frames. Doors slammed shut by sudden breezes that came through open windows.

The Butler looked upwards. "The second-story windows are still open, I'm afraid. The Master prefers that. I apologize for the fright."

Watson nodded.

The lights went out again.

Home of Wrong Ways

"Oh!" Watson cried in genuine surprise and disappointment. "Dratted storm anyway!"

No one replied.

It stayed dark.

A hand gripped Watson's shoulder.

'Oh!" Watson cried out yet again, but this time in fear he was being attacked, but before he could move the hand let go.

"Just stay close," the Butler advised and entered the house properly, his blob of a shadowy form passing before Watson.

"Carrots, John."

Watson turned toward the voice of Holmes. "I can't see a bloody thing, but blobby shadows!"

"Carrots."

Watson snorted. "That will be the day."

Watson watched Holmes pass him next.

Holmes looked back. "Watson?"

"Nothing. Nothing. Coming."

Watson stayed close. It was worse than the inside of a Pharaoh's tomb, he thought.

"I hate carrots!" He told nobody.

Holmes chuckled.

"I do."

Flashes of light struck through the heavily curtained windows inside the mansion, giving chairs and lamps grotesque, fearsome shapes as the two men made their way cautiously from one room to the next, following the silent Butler, whose shadowy form would become revealed in one flash of lightning and then doused in the following thunder, then lit again as the new barrage of light and sound began.

They finally entered a large room, judging by the depths of shadows within.

As Watson wound his way about the furniture in their way, and not always in a comfortable manner, but sometimes with a poke to his ample stomach and a nudge to his side by some heavy furniture or a smash of his toes when he accidentally struck something too low to see, his siege of sudden discomfort and pain finally ended.

Not once had he complained of the pains.

He was used to such in his many adventures with his taller friend, but carrots? Now that got his gall.

Finally, he stopped, but not until he had knocked against Holmes, who had stopped already.

Several matches were struck by the Butler and then an antique candelabrum with five hands reaching upwards of fine silver with thin candles was lit.

"Oh!" Watson exclaimed.

What he had thought was merely another piece of furniture opened its mouth to gnaw on a side of lamb.

They had stopped before a large table where a heavy-set man sat, whittling away at a side of the lamb with a fork and knife was finishing his late meal. He was a brutish-looking man with a dour expression and beady eyes that darted constantly about as if they were about to orbit his skull entirely. He cocked an eyebrow up as his attention caught Watson's full attention and gave him a once over.

He rose.

Not smiling.

His face was as death masklike as the Butler's, but even more intense. His hair fell to his shoulders like snakes of a medusa and his eyes didn't so much look at you as through you.

Watson shivered.

"Sir, this is Mister Sherlock Holmes and his partner, Doctor John Watson," introduced the Butler, who promptly left them, vanishing into another opening of darkness that branched from the larger room. It was if he and the darkness were one of a sudden, when before they just appeared to be two. And he was no longer of flesh and blood anymore.

Watson couldn't help it. He shivered yet again.

"Disgusting!" He uttered, despite himself.

Both Holmes and the man turned to look at him.

"The weather, of course," Watson pointed out, forcing a smile to his lips, which he felt for certain would surely break every muscle in his face.

"True," the man finally acknowledged after another once over of Watson. "Nasty night."

"Rather," Holmes said politely, but his eyes were on Watson, who took the hint and looked away, trying to find something that wouldn't put further chills into his bloodstream.

Holmes nodded, and then looked back at the man. "Most unexpected."

"Weather, that, we have no control over," the man commented.

Holmes nodded, feeling no further comment was needed or expected.

"I don't know whatever happened to the electricity," the man volunteered with a frown. "This has never happened before," he commented without much emotion.

He took the silence of Holmes and Watson as enough of a reply, took the candelabra from the table, and headed towards the same darkness that the Butler had vanished into.

Into the Darkness

"Stairs to the second floor are this way," the man cautioned, flicking a handout of the thick darkness for Holmes and Watson to see. Even with the help of the barely surviving glow of the candlelight, the hand was more ghostly than physically appearing.

"Well?" He asked, a touch of irritation in his voice when they didn't follow.

"Our apologies," Holmes replied, having finished evaluating the room they stood in. He nodded and headed for the way out. Watson followed closely to his right. Not an advantageous position when there were so many articles, as this house seemed to have to grab and snatch a man painfully, but necessary. Even Holmes, he could tell, was feeling the oddness of the place.

Holmes was silent, but his eyes were taking in everything as they traversed the long room to the stairway.

Watson whispered to Holmes. "I do not like this place on whit!"

Mister Warner chuckled. "The house is a bit convoluted. Constructed to resemble a puzzle for some odd reason. The Mistress has odd tastes."

He stopped to look back at Holmes and Watson. "But who does not, hey? He smiled, revealing perfectly white teeth for a moment, and then looked away. "I am her Assistant. Was it my home, I would have it remodeled. So much wasted space. But I am not. So..."

"Holmes, I am not liking this one bit."

Mister Warner stopped and looked back at Watson. "Nor do I. But it will do. And I have quite good hearing."

Watson winced. He wasn't sure if he had just been reprimanded or the man was evincing displeasure with the home as well.

"Mister Warner, I presume," Holmes finally said.

"Yes. I would have told you before, but being the detective, I assumed you already knew that."

Holmes nodded.

Mister Warner began walking again. "I'm sure she shall be more than happy to know you two are coming to protect her." Mister Warner went on, oblivious to the storm outside.

Even when the mansion shook as if struck by a huge fist, he didn't falter for a moment in his ascension of the winding staircase, which, carpeted step by step, was leading to the landing above. Barely lit in the ghastly glow of a candelabra laid on an exquisite antique piece of furniture that had been recently polished and cleaned, as Holmes noted as he touched a finger to it the gloom of the place was not ameliorated in the slightest by the glow of the candles.

More so the gloomier it was, casting so many dancing shadows from the bizarre armor that lined the walls, swords, and lances, maces, and shields, old paintings of lords and ladies dancing, children frolicking next to ponds, knights in battle, astrological signs spun from gold and ruby red cloth that draped the spaces between the paintings and armor.

"You do all the cleaning?" Holmes asked.

"I and several house cleaners with the help of the Butler, of course. This home is rather…how shall I describe it properly? Cumbersome, if not overly large."

He turned to Holmes. "Sure, you saw them scampering about in the darkness searching for more candles after the lightning took away our electricity?"

"Does this happen often? Holmes asked politely, avoiding the question. He had not noticed anyone at all.

Watson noted the avoidance, which was not comforting to him at all, but he remained tight-lipped and said nothing.

Mister Warner replied. “I’m not sure why the power has gone out; our Lady hired the best that Edison could supply to wire the home.”

“Accidents happen,” Holmes replied cheerily.

Mister Warner turned with his candle to investigate Holmes’s face as if searching the paths on a map. “If you say so, sir.”

“You think not then?” Holmes inquired almost a bit too casually.

“I think not.”

Holmes nodded.

Mister Warner ignored him and continued to walk along the second floor to a distant door. "She's been nothing but worrisome since the first incident."

They reached the door and Mister Warner opened it to reveal a new staircase rising to a third landing.

For some reason, the windows on that floor suddenly banged open and the wind came charging inside, roaring like a wounded lion angry and ready to tear someone apart.

It blew out all of Mister Warner’s candles out.

The Oddness Continues

A match is struck.

Holmes guides the match to Mister Warner's nearest candle and lights it.

"That should do us for now," Holmes said.

"I agree. Don't worry, you won't get lost if you stick close."

"Quite interesting architecture, Mister Warner."

He nodded. "You haven't seen anything yet. It goes on like this quite a bit and then branches out. The original architect supposedly had secret entrances and exits built into the structure."

"For what reason?"

Mister Warner shrugged.

"I see," Holmes replied. He adjusted his collar to allow more air to reach his chest. For some reason, the home was like a furnace, even though it was cold outside.

The sudden burst of wind into the home had subsided.

For a moment, Holmes noted by the one candle that no windows were open to their right, where the side of the house was closest. He frowned but said nothing.

He glanced at Watson, who was having a terrible time of it. His weight increased his body temperature much more than that of Holmes.

“You all right, Watson?”

“I will be,” Watson replied, not elaborating.

"I'm sorry about the temperature, but it’s part of the problem, you see." Mister Warner told Holmes and Watson, once more ignoring Watson’s remarks.

"How so, my good man?" Watson asked.

"Because we have neither heating in this house, nor fireplaces. The Madam is deeply afraid of fireplaces. Something dreadful to do with her childhood I’ve heard.”

“From whom?”

Mister Warner fell into silence.

"What about the kitchen? Surely you have fire in there?" Watson asked, perplexed by the answers the man was giving as well as his sudden silence.

"Oh, not at all." Mister Warner replied. "The kitchen is merely a nice presentation for visitors. The real food is prepared off the grounds and delivered each breakfast, lunch, and dinner hour by a hired cook, who lives nearby in Westwick."

He began climbing the new stairway.

Watson and Holmes carefully followed.

It was claustrophobic. Tight as a womb with barely enough shoulder room for the two of them together, forcing Watson to fall back some or force Holmes to hurt himself. The man was ever so kind and would not complain unless Watson forced him to.

Mister Warner suddenly vanished as the one candle's light quit.

"Holmes!"

"Steady, Watson."

"Easy for you to say. You have the eyes of a cat."

Holmes chuckles.

"Carrots."

Watson bridled. "I hate carrots!"

Staircase of Doubts

A new light came from above and Mister Warner turned towards the two below. “Not much further now.”

Mister Warner continued climbing towards a dark opening above.

Watson glanced at Holmes. “I don’t like this one bit, Holmes.”

But Holmes refused to comment, he hurried after Mister Warner, a determined look on his face, as if he had seen something Watson had not, and it was important for him to reach it.

Above Mister Warner became front-lit, while the back part of him remained in darkness.

“Ah!” He said in a pleased voice. He turned about to look at them, an odd smile on his face. “Everything is perfect now.”

“I doubt that,” Watson commented and rushed after Holmes to follow him through the opening.

The Third Landing

Watson stepped onto the third landing and froze for a moment. It was as if he had yet again walked into a different world. One as uniquely different here as the last had been on the second landing.

This hallway was strewn with antique tables and chairs along the walls, each with a single lit candle on top and a single red rose in a vase.

"Interesting," Watson noted. "Lit, freshly evidently, yet no sign of anyone who might have done so."

Holmes nodded but said nothing.

Mister Warner eyed Watson in a manner that made his skin crawl. "The Mistress loves candles. Love roses. So…" Mister Warner left the sentence hanging as a fresh flash of lightning outside lit up the hallway, causing all the furniture to leap into a grotesque kind of life as their shadows played about each other and upon the walls.

The lightning flashes also revealed a huge window at either end of the new hallway, both with baroque wooden frames seizing the glass between antique woods, and both windows wide open.

"Holmes…"

Holmes gave Watson a slight shake of his head and Watson shut up.

The walls of the hallway were the more notable because they had a large white canvas on all of them with tiny wicker birds pinned every several feet. They had blue eyes and white feet.

Watson liked the look of these things. He sighed with a kind of relief, not even realizing that his whole body had been as tight as a coiled spring ready to break. "Beautiful!"

"She also liked doves," Mister Warner commented, a slight smile curling the right side of his mouth.

"Why blue eyes?" Holmes asked.

Mister Warner looked at Holmes, then away. He continued up the hallway.

"Strange," Watson commented.

Holmes again didn't respond.

Watson felt frustrated but managed it.

Barely.

Mister Warner led them through a door and another long hallway. Huge knights stood on both sides, each clasping a mace or a bludgeon in their hands. Both weapons were raised over their heads in a threatening manner.

"Very friendly," Watson observed.

Mister Warner laughed. "This is the hallway she has her bill collectors pass through. Few of them ever return after having passed through here."

"I wonder why," Watson replied with a hint of sarcasm in his voice.

A new burst of lightning outside, then another and another. As they walked deeper into the hallway the weapons of the knights along the walls seemed to move with them menacingly, as if waiting for them to pass and then strike.

Watson felt shivers up and down his spine. A new burst of lightning struck, and the entire building shook as if two giants had struck it from opposite directions.

Then something large lunged at Watson from behind.

Death Beckons

Watson felt something tackle him to the floor and roll him away as an ancient suit of armor with an outreaching hand clutching an ancient battle-ax struck the space he had just inhabited.

He rolled over onto his back.

Holmes was alongside him.

"If you wanted to play on the floor, you could have asked, Holmes."

Holmes chuckled. "But then it would not have been quite so fun."

Holmes jumped to his feet and gave Watson a hand up.

"I could have been killed," Watson uttered, as the shock of the incident finally settled into him, noticing how the battle-ax was buried headfirst through the carpet and wood of the floor.

He raised a shaking hand to smooth his hair and then noticed his missing hat. He stooped down and retrieved it and then Holmes's cap.

"Not likely, Watson," Holmes replied, accepting his cap. "Not as long as I'm with you."

"And that's what worries me, Holmes?"

Holmes gave Watson a grin and then looked away.

Watson nudged the battle-ax with his right foot where it lay on the floor and it fell apart, revealing it to be made of cloth and a light wood frame.

"Impossible. This could never have cut the carpet and wood like that!"

"The Mistress is said to have some articles of magic. Perhaps this one."

Holmes eyed Mister Warner thoughtfully. "Perhaps."

Watson glowered at the man, his dander firmly up now. "Well, even so, my dignity is shaken, if not my body, which came close to being detached from my head, thank you!"

"You're welcome," Mister Warner responded.

Watson glared at him, not sure if that was a joke or not.

Mister Warner looked away. "Well, I am glad you were not hurt all the same, Doctor," Mister Warner said in a remarkably impersonal voice that carried not at all of emotion to it.

Watson cleared his throat. "There's the rub of it, my soul and body are intimately intertwined. And right now, they both are quite sore!"

Holmes laughed at Watson's joke.

Mister Warner did not.

He opened a new door. Went inside.

Holmes started after him.

Watson held back.

Holmes looked at his friend. “What?”

“Magic axes. Windows open but not open. Wind from nowhere. What’s next? A werewolf?”

Holmes smiled. “My dear Watson, you and I both know there are no such things in our world.”

“And that’s what worries me most, Holmes.”

“What if we were not in our world any longer?”

Yet More

Holmes and Watson followed Mister Warner up yet another flight of stairs. This time the walls were even narrower, such that only one man could ascend at a time.

The tiny light there was, seemed to almost choke on the darkness clutching at the narrow space.

They finally emerged onto a fourth landing.

Mister Warner walked several paces and stopped. "Here we are." He flung open a door that had a used look to it. A single portrait of a flower was nailed to its front. There were scratch marks beneath the portrait. Deep ones.

"Does the lady also have a pet lion?" Watson asked jokingly.

Mister Warner turned to face Watson. "Once."

Watson's face paled.

Mister Warner smiled, then said, "This is my Lady's office and...bedroom."

"Finally!" Watson sighed with relief as he moved to follow Mister Warner into the room.

Then he froze midstride, made a face, and began to cough.

"It smells like death!" Watson complained. He glanced at Holmes, who remained unreadable.

"Death beckons and we must enter," Holmes uttered poetically.

"You knew already?"

"Quite obvious, old man. Lady O'Brian is famous for taking her guests into town when they visit. The Inspector came earlier, which is why we are here. And why I knew something was wrong the moment we entered this house."

Slumped over an ancient antique maritime desk taken from what must have been an old merchant ship was the Lady O'Brian, departed. And recently, judging by the still streaming flow of blood at her feet.

She wore a simple white starched blouse and a long black cotton skirt. Her blouse was bloodied, hands splayed across the top of the desk as if she were trying to embrace it. Her eyes were bulging outwards, as if in sudden horror.

Watson crossed himself.

"Death is neither pretty nor desirable," Holmes uttered.

"Especially when it deprives one of a longer life," Watson noted, a twinge of sadness at its edges. Death was never a sight he enjoyed, even though it was a regular part of most of his work these days, in the office and on their missions.

"Life is tenuous at best, Watson. This is why the good Lady O'Brian preferred roses and candles. Both are symbolic of the ephemeralness of life."

Watson gave his friend and partner a glaring look of disapproval. "This is not the time to wax lyrical, Holmes."

"Oh, but it is, "Holmes replied.

He took out a pair of surgical gloves from his jacket and put them in his hands, then went to the desk, passing Mister Warner, who stood there, no expression on his face, as if there were just one more unremarkable thing among many others of the day.

Holmes gently turned Ms. O'Brian's head to reveal her still open eyes looking into the darkroom, open wide in horror and fear. "I suspect that our Lady O'Brian might have thought poetry an effective manner of describing the current state of her affairs, as she was said to have quite a sense of humor, correct Mister Warner?"

"Humor depends on one's point of view, sir," Mister Warner replied.

Holmes nodded, glanced at Mister Warner briefly, and then returned his attention to the Lady. He circled the desk, touching this and that. A feather pen. An inkwell, which he lifted and examined closely for a moment, then the bit of scribe she had done on the paper before her.

Watson watched quietly as did Mister Warner, who didn't budge an inch from his position, as if the man were more of a statue than a human at that moment.

Holmes examined the floor where the blood still dripped, then the desktop, gently tracing a course of blood until it stopped at the woman's right breast. There, something dark was protruding, still quivering.

He straightened up and examined Mister Warner's face for a moment. "You did not know of this?"

"I did not mention so."

"But you were just with her before the Butler brought us forth?"

"I was eating."

"Then how did the Butler know to speak with us?"

"I told him earlier to expect you."

"When did you last speak with the Lady?"

"Just before I descended to eat."

"And what was her state of mind at the time?"

"Busy."

"She had you sort out her expectations of us?"

“She had.”

“Then why were you eating and not preparing for us?”

Mister Warner gave Holmes a long stare, and then said, “I was hungry.”

“And no one else was in this home but you, the maids, and the Butler?”

“No, sir.”

“Then how do you explain this?”

“I don’t. “She was right as rain before I went downstairs to eat and wait for your arrival.” He replied, his body beginning to shake.

“I see,” Holmes said with a nod.

“At least her death was quick.” Mister Warner finally managed to mutter.

Holmes scrutinized Mister Warner’s features closely as he walked toward him. “Oh, I concede that would be a happier thought to think than my current deduction, Mister Warner. But I do not agree at all. Lady O'Brian did not die so easily, or as quietly as the storm outside."

Holmes pointed to the window near the desk. A slight drizzle of wetness pooled at its base. “That window has been recently opened and closed.”

"Likely the Mistress was urgent to catch sight of you upon the sound of your arrival and looked out."

"The water is not from the outside, Mister Warner, but the inside. That window has not been opened at all; the wind outside would have blasted the floor with moisture."

"And this..." Indicating a line of blood on the floor. "It comes not down, but up. Notice how even now, it does not spread further but instead collects upon the desktop."

"Holmes, you're frightening me!" Watson declared.

"Indeed. But fear not Watson, the solution is at hand."

Holmes turned to point at the quivering object in the breast of Ms. O'Brian. "And that...it still quivers. Even now."

"But that's impossible."

"It would be if she were quite dead," Holmes replied.

Ms. O'Brian sat up and smiled at Holmes. "Congratulations, you are hired. I knew you were brilliant, but this surmounts even my wildest expectations."

She turned to Mister Warner. "You chose well Mister Warner."

"Thank you, Mistress." He told her. "Will that be all?"

"Yes. You may retire now. I have much to speak with Mister Holmes about and…" She smiled at Watson. "Doctor Watson, I presume?"

Watson took his hat off and nodded. "I am sometimes called other than that, but yes, that is appropriate."

She laughed and began scrubbing with a handkerchief she pulled from her top right desk drawer at the blood on her desk.

"Now that we've met each other so nicely, let me explain what I need from you."

Writer's Block

Arthur set aside the paper he had been scribbling his latest story upon and looked out his window. It was another wintry, blustery day in London. No wonder lightning and storm played such a big part in his latest story. It was no different here and now than in his mind.

He watched as some of his neighbors rushed from their front doors to their carriages, striving to keep their top hats, scarves, and caps on against the force of the biting sting of the freezing northerly wind.

The Atlantic cast bitterly cold winds across London this time of year.

His ears perked up when he heard Jane practicing her piano in the back of the house. It was a fine piece from the later years of Mozart. Quite simple and complex at the same time. He recognized it from the Movement of Blue, an opera that Mozart had composed, but never released, based on a lost tale of Shakespeare. He had happened upon it quite by accident when he met a traveling adventurer from the Germanies, who was a lover of both history and music. Something which he and Jane had in common as it turned out.

He sighed and wearily set his pen to the paper once more. Work at hand came first before useless musings. This last story would be the crowning glory of his works to this point in time. He had killed Holmes and brought him back. Now he had a much larger mission to fulfill with his detective friend. Ascend him. Link him to his life mission of proving that there was indeed life beyond this life. Meaning to existence. Not fallacious discouragement and futility, mourning and bereavement. That man should look forward to going beyond the present into a much wider, more loving world where man's true spiritual purpose was no longer veiled from his discovery.

It was teaching he had picked up from his studies of the occult and the spiritual arts. They had led him to the teachings of Madame Blavatsky, but also the much older writings of the Bhagavad Gita and the writings of both Plato and Confucius. An odd set of twins in philosophy if ever there was one, but both men had an enlightened outlook on life. One which he found both energizing as well as challenging.

He continued writing after he scratched out several pages. He pulled his mustache angrily for a moment. He had so little time left to complete this work and it must have been perfect.

More so than his last piece or any other before that. This was to be his masterpiece. And nothing must fail him, either time or his state of health to get it done!

He began writing furiously once more, striking out the mistake in thought he had made, and continuing from there.

He was fortunate enough he had someone who could take this mess he was making and put it all back together nice and neat for publishing, otherwise he'd be truly pulling his hair out, instead of figuratively.

A Clue Emerges

"Wait!" Holmes cried out.

Mister Warner did so as well as Watson, who hadn't a clue what had made Holmes stop now.

But Holmes knew. His eyes were as sharp as a hawk's and like that famed bird, had spotted some clue others might have missed. He dropped to a knee at the top of the landing. He carefully traced a finger across the rug that lay upon it, observing it spring back after he had tracked through it as hard as he could. He repeated that process, and then stood up.

"Carry on," Holmes told Mister Warner, who hadn't bothered to look back to see what Holmes was up to.

This mystified Watson even more than the fact that Holmes had found something in the least likely of places. For Holmes that was his trait of genius, but for Mister Warner, it was both aloof and troubling at best.

They proceeded to the library, which was quite a large room, with an exceptionally beautiful concert piano whose piano white piano keys stood out even in the subdued lighting of the place. Huge vases filled with fresh tulips are mounted on every available flat surface. Enormous windows of stained glass that had heart shapes in them that resembled swans peered from the right and left walls. The tulip vases, upon closer inspection by Watson, were obviously of Asian origin, as they had very delicate golden scrolls of Chinese sayings along their heights. And the center of the scrolling text was beautiful and erect carved hearts of gold upon them.

Mister Warner noted the direction of Sherlock's attention which had turned the same direction as Watson's now and pointed to several shelves. Sherlock's eyes followed his gesture. "I see. She loved hearts."

"Absolutely, sir. Everything she purchased had a heart in it, around it, about it, on to it, or within it."

"She had to have searched far and wide to find such authentic oriental Ming Dynasty vases with that upon them."

"Oh, not at all, sir. She hired excellent forgers."

Watson made a face.

Mister Warner eyed him. "Every talented artist must forge someone's identity in their work. Greatness is borrowed from those who came before. We all create upon the history of others who have trod the path before us."

Holmes smiled then. “With that, I must agree, sir. I would be nothing without the prior works of many before me.”

Watson coughed a chuckle. “That I suspect is a bit of a stretch.”

Mister Warner ignored Watson’s remark.

"She often told me, sir, before she crossed over, God bless her heart, that her death would arrive neatly dressed on the day there were no new hearts in her life."

Holmes gave Mister Warner a weak smile. "I surmise that day arrived sooner than she had expected."

Mister Warner's face, which had lit up somewhat, well dead once more, his expression vanished as quickly as it had come.

BANG!

Shutter, Shutter on the Wall

Arthur jumped up from his chair, his heart palpitating and hurting.

He thrust his hands over his chest and pushed at his heart as if that would make everything right again.

The pounding slowed.

His pained expression became gradually one of resignation and relief. He had been so shocked by the sound that it felt like a gunshot.

It was not.

It was merely the window shutters that he had opened to allow more light that was banging against the window frame. He sighed with relief, but the pain he had felt in his chest remained. He shrugged it off, turned about, and went to the double windows behind him and pulled the shutters outside shut, latched them, then shut the glass windows and locked them. He drew curtains across them, and then returned to his desk.

The light was close to being complete darkness.

But he knew his writing world well.

He pulled a candle from his top right-hand desk drawer, set it into a candle holder he kept for occasions such as this, and then lit it with a match from a box that had sat next to the candle holder.

In moments, the room was bright and cheery again, if shadowy now.

"Good!" He sighed. "Not perfect. But good."

He sat back down.

"Back to work."

And work it was. This was...he felt a growing certainty...to be his last story and so many interruptions were taxing his strength, as well as his memory which had been troubled of late.

He rubbed his forehead, trying to sharpen his memory further, fully knowing it was a useless gesture. He was a doctor. He knew there was no easy cure for what ailed him.

He grits his teeth in consternation for a moment, then took a deep breath and eyes his paperwork again.

He wanted to get through this last story while he still could. He hadn't spoken to Jane about it yet, but his doctor hadn't been helpful in his attitude towards Arthur's condition, warning him that he must slow down or there would be consequences.

"Drat consequences!" Arthur swore so loudly that he feared Jane might hear him, but her music didn't even falter for a second as she continued playing her piano.

She would often play as he wrote. It was soothing for him and helped him to concentrate listening to the sweet melodies her wonderful hands wove with the help of the splendid piano she played every day.

He looked out the window again. "What would Holmes have done had he been stuck in his study, and had to solve the crime from there I wonder?"

He almost cried at that moment. He knew that story would never be given birth. So, his thought would have to be its only monument.

Arthur's forehead creased in thought for a moment, then he put pen to paper once more, ignoring the sound of some children outside playing loudly in the brewing storm of hail, water, and snow.

In his mind, he could see what they did.

He had watched them do it eve after eve.

He loved children.

They gave hope to the world.

One that he feared adults would never give fruition, they were so busy at war with each other so much of the time.

In his imagination he watched them kick the black stone they used for a ball from one side of the street to the other for several long moments, a faint smile touching his lips. Children were so innocent of the cares of their parents, and especially of those so close to death's door…or life's…he suddenly reminded himself.

An idea came.

He began scribbling furiously once more when something hard struck the shutters outside.

He stopped a moment, smiling at the sound of young voices crying out in alarm, fully expecting this old man to come charging from his flat in alarm and anger and to bring down the wrath of God upon them.

He grinned at the sound of their fleeing footsteps, and then returned to his task of writing once more…feeling a lot better.

Accidents Happen

Holmes shrugged a blanket over his legs and stared out the window over Baker Street. He cursed himself as a fool for slipping on the icy walkway below earlier. He had just returned from the examination of the home where Mister Warner had insisted that no foul play had been involved, despite the insistent and repeating waves of extreme cold and heat that passed through the home.

Holmes cringed at the idea of the possibility of ghosts or poltergeists, which Mister Warner hinted at. He didn't believe in the impossible, only the probable, and the impossible was merely a lack of details, missing information.

He tilted to the right a bit to get a better view of the street and streaks of bitter hot pain raced up the tendons of his damaged right leg. "Curses!" He uttered; his voice intense with frustration. He had a murder to solve, but now he was stuck. Paralyzed by his carelessness. Even Moriarty was he alive to this day, would consider him a fool for being so stupid as to hurt himself in such a careless way when only a smaller step to the right would have spared him the tumble that pulled his right leg.

Despite the sharp pains of recrimination and doubt he momentarily felt, he went back to the crime scene once more in his mind, reconstructing what he needed to continue with the case.

He was stuck in this dratted room, which usually he loved with great affection, but because of his injury, it felt more like a prison to him, even with the warm care bequeathed upon him by dear Ms. Hudson and his good friend, Watson.

What was it about their inspection that still bothered him; undermined his peace of mind?

He shifted again to get more comfortable, and his leg reminded him that comfort was not going to be his for a time.

"Drats!" He swore this time.

Then he remembered what was missing from what he had been structuring in his thoughts.

At Death's Door

A wave of freezing air struck Holmes and Watson as they entered the bedroom of the late Lady O'Brian.

Watson had shrugged his overcoat tightly about him. Even his breath had become chilled. Exhaust rings of smoke puffed from his mouth as he opened his lips to speak. "Holmes, this is, definitely, not normal! I'll be damned if I'm not freezing to bloody hell by just standing here in this room. No breeze. No northerly winds tearing at my face. Just a blasted room is all." He cursed.

Holmes had ignored the remark and instead gone about the room, searching its drawers, closets, and windows.

"Watson, could you be as kind as to take samples from here for me?"

Watson stopped swatting himself to keep warm, and then rushed over and noted a bluish fluid seeping from beneath the closed window paneling Holmes stood next to. "That's odd. "He took a vial from his black bag, unstoppered it, then a swab and drew it across the bluish fluid. He dropped the swab into his vial, stoppered it, and then waited for Holmes to say more.

He did not. He could not. Literally. At that very moment, as he stood next to the last window where he had hoped to open it to look outside for further clues, he had become immobilized. He felt a fear unlike any he had ever known before clutching his heart, mind, and soul, freezing him in place.

Holmes tried to move from the spot he stood upon, but it was as if his feet were nailed to the floor. Even trying to move them was causing him utter misery as burning shots of pain surged up his ankles, his legs, and then into his chest, which now felt ablaze with a fire that was not physical, but somehow felt that way.

He tried to reach for Watson but could not. Something was holding him back. Something intangible. Something...evil!

Holmes ordered, "Watson, Mister Warner must be removed from here at once. Do not let him return!"

"But!"

"Now!" Holmes ordered.

Watson started to protest again, but when he saw Mister Warner's eyes, he was quite alarmed. Where iris and pupils had been a thin veil of pure white snow shrouded the eyes. Only the fluttering of the eyelids offers any sign of life. He took the man by his right arm and headed for the hallway corridor outside. Mister Warner came effortlessly but was as silent as a rock. Something about the stiffness of his walk set off alarms in Watson's mind as a doctor. This wasn't just fear or reluctance going on.

Watson left the room, but Holmes was still unable to move a single muscle. He tried to move, but still could not. Finally, he closed his eyes as he had been taught some time back by a practitioner of yoga. He felt comforting darkness begin to absorb his thoughts as he slowed down his breathing and heartbeat. As he did so, he felt this warmth begin to permeate his entire body, as if the windows had opened, allowing the warmth of the afternoon sun to light upon him. Of which there were none now.

When he opened his eyes again, he could move. He did so. Promptly. He rushed out of the room to find Watson on the carpeted landing, overlooking Mister Warner, who laid there on his back, his eyes were pure white as snow, unmoving.

"Watson?"

"A stroke, Holmes. Most dastardly, cunning, and devious. No time to administer any kind of relief. It happened as if a light had suddenly been turned off," Watson explained.

"That makes no sense whatsoever, Watson," Holmes replied.

Watson looked about them, peering into the leering darkness of the landing, then back at Sherlock. "Does any of this?"

Then the windows on that landing all opened at the same time and a howling, piercing, freezing chilly wind struck inside, chilling them to their bones.

Frozen

"Indeed!" Holmes whispered to no one in particular, his eyes still on Baker Street below.

The memory of him and Watson fleeing that bizarre place lingered for a bit on his mind, and then shattered as one of the street urchins outside let out a familiar cry and ran to a constable. "Coins, sir! My family is starving. We have nothing for Christmas. Our home is freezing."

"For a freezing lad, you surely love the snow and ice," the constable replied but handed over several coins.

The boy did a very touching thing next and hugged the constable warmly, then ran off screaming happily at the top of his lungs.

The constable, who had seemed a bit doubtful and reluctant in giving his coin, broke into a smile and then began whistling a happy tune to himself as he continued to patrol his beat, heading up Baker Street.

Holmes smiled.

Kindness still flourished in the world.

Even if not so frequently as it might or should.

He shivered when a sudden shift of the wind outside cast slurries of snow and wet ice upon his face and lap.

At that moment what had been bothering him surfaced.

“By Jove I got it!”

“Holmes?”

Watson came running up the stairs into the room. “I heard you scream.”

“Happily, John. Happily.”

Watson smiled at him.

So, he explained. “Remember Lady O’Brian’s body had been found as rigid as if she had frozen to death. There were no marks on it, and yet not a single ounce of blood remained within her veins?”

“I do.”

Watson sat next to Holmes to listen as the man unveiled his deduction.

“I verified later on in the forensics lab at the Yard what you just said.”

“Frozen.”

“Yes. Her blood had frozen solid in her veins. She had perished from a heart attack when the frozen blood reached her heart and brain.”

"The Case of the Frozen Damsel." Holmes almost whispered

Ms. Hudson came into the room, carrying a tray with a fresh pot of steaming tea.

"Well, I can tell you this, Mister Holmes, which is exactly, exactly what I would become if I went outside at this moment. I've had to shut every window to keep out the freeze."

She smiled warmly at the two of them, and then set the tray on the table.

Watson got up and poured a cup of tea for himself and Holmes.

"Thanks ever so much, Ms. Hudson," he said.

She gave him a nod and departed.

Watson watched her depart. "She must have been a truly lovely young woman."

Holmes eyed Watson. "Time does not always depose to our favor those we embrace in our lives, Watson."

"Indeed, indeed."

Watson brought a steaming cup to Holmes, who took it with a smile. Watson set the pot on the side table near Holmes. "More if you want."

"Not drinking?"

"No, I had more than my share of coffee downstairs with Ms. Hudson. She was regaling me with tales of her youth and a lovely young man she had wanted to marry, but who died at sea."

"Tragic," Holmes commented.

"Indeed."

"Anyway, Holmes. Thanks. At least the tea should help stave off any chill you might be having."

Holmes glanced at his arms. He had chill bumps on them.

Watson shut the windows and sat next to him.

"I doubt it will help much, Watson since it is of the soul, the spirit, and not of the flesh and bone that my chills abound."

"Nevertheless, drink," Watson insisted. "Doctor's orders, you know."

Holmes eyed his friend and smiled. "Do I indeed."

Holmes cradled the warm cup between the palms of his hands, rotating it lightly, eyes on the surface of the tea as it washed about, plumes of milk that Watson had put in it surfacing. He frowned for a moment.

Watson was just sitting down when Holmes exploded from his chair, spilling the tea on the floor as he did so. "By Jove, Watson, I have the body of it by the tail!"

Watson choked for a moment on his tea. He was so surprised by the sudden outburst that he had sucked some tea up into his nose by accident. He blurted out, "What in God's name has gotten into you?"

"I have why Lady O'Brian was frigid like ice, bloodless, and yet with traces of frozen blood in her," Holmes explained, his face warm with the smile of certainty.

Watson waited.

Holmes grabbed Watson by both shoulders. "Don't you see, dear Watson? It's as clear as pure snow on a Christmas day!"

"Honestly, I don't," Watson replied, waiting for the inevitable clarification Holmes was dying to reveal now. The man reveled in mystery and kept his audience on the edge of their chairs until he deliberated his usual, succinct, and to-the-point deduction.

Holmes opened his mouth to speak, "Dear...?"

Watson glanced at Holmes as if he had gone mad. Holmes's voice had become feminine.

Holmes gave Watson a shocked look, and then tried to speak again, "Dear!" Once more, a feminine voice!

The Little Death

"Huh?"

Arthur woke up, his face laying on top of his manuscript, ink splattered to his left, and the ink well on the floor from where his tumble into sleep had struck it.

"Arthur!" Jane's alarmed voice sounded.

He sat up, rubbed his eyes, noted his mess, and then looked towards the source of her voice.

"Dear, you there still?" She called from the door to his study.

He must have been sound asleep for her voice to have jarred him so much.

He frowned.

Glanced at his manuscript. He hadn't written down what he thought. It must have been all in his imagination while he dreamed. He groaned.

"Arthur?"

"I'm here. Come, please, come."

In his dreams, he had emerged into a clear realization, just like his most famous character, Sherlock Holmes, of how to solve the riddle of the frozen woman. But now in the stark light of reality. It had fled from his mind just like shadows do when light is thrust upon them.

This reminded him the candle was low.

He reached for a new one to replace the old one.

In his heightened sense of reality, he sighed inwardly as he lit the new candle and placed it into the candleholder, the once clear idea of how to reason Holmes out of a very incredible plot into a realistic deduction of the truth had fled like a thief in the night, leaving both him and Holmes bereft of completion.

Yet again, his sleep had deprived him of the advantage it had also brought.

He thought back to some of the occultists he had mingled with. Madame Blavatsky was the foremost of the lot.

And the only one he had found to be genuine, if somewhat frightening to him. The things she spoke about...higher worlds, higher consciousness, life after death...were not part of his usual world. Though he did find them to be fascinating topics.

Dear Madame Blavatsky

"You look for truth everywhere, dear Arthur, but within yourself," she told him.

He eyed the cigar in her hand.

"I see only a cigar."

She smiled, barking with laughter.

She stubbed it in a silver bowl shaped like a pentagram with small ruby eyes about its rim. Finished, she looked up.

"What do you truly want from life?"

"To stop all the charlatans who are plaguing London and robbing the grieving of a peaceful period of mourning."

She snorted. "Come now, Arthur, we both know that grievers do so, not because of the loss of their loved one, not because of the pain they no longer feel but has now been healed. No, they grieve because they no longer have that person to depend upon, to use in small or large ways, or to gain some kind of physical satisfaction. Rarely, do those who mourn do so for anyone other than themselves."

"Still..."

She reached across from her large chair, which was

plush with thick pillows to bear her weight. "Still, you persist in blaming them, when it is the mourners you should blame, for they have so little faith in their Creator, God."

He gave her an exasperated look.

"Madam, they are not all charlatans!"

"Most certainly not. Some truly do miss their loved ones because they will no longer be able to talk with them, to share and love with them. But most mourn death because they fear it."

"I do not."

She smiled.

"A card laid on the table is only a card until it has been picked up and turned over.

"What in the devil is that supposed to mean?"

"That it's easy to say what one will do before one is faced with the action required."

He sighed and investigated the palms of his hand.

"I fear I will be turning that card over soon enough."

He looked up and saw a tear in her eye.

"Why are you crying?"

"Because I love you, my dear friend, and I will sorely miss you."

She rose from her chair, which she seldom did, and

he rose from his chair, uncertain if his time was over with her.

But she surprised him. She enfolded him in her arms and held him tight. "When your card is turned; do not be afraid, dear friend. God never closes one door, but he opens another."

"How can I not be afraid? Here I go about scolding all these fools for patronizing the weak of heart with lies and confabulations to get money from them, and I, myself, face the same drear path of my extinction, knowing what I know."

"Arthur," she said, letting go of him and pinching his right cheek gently. "You punish yourself too much for too little. When your time comes you will know what to do."

"I pray so."

She gave him a beatific smile.

"I know so."

Jane

He shook the memories off.

Madame Blavatsky was right of course. She was always in her way. He admired her for her intellectual prowess, and more than anything else, for her grand heart. He had few friends who could come within an inch of the heartfelt joy she brought to him.

But then his thoughts returned to the manuscript on the desk before him. At first, he was dismayed and disappointed. This was to become the penultimate adventure of the greatest detective and the crowning achievement of his lengthy career. A career of one man's journey using forensic science to stop the criminality of man from overthrowing common decency and love amongst the innocent.

Yet now his thoughts were so scattered, so frozen with blocks he could not begin to understand, that he had to admit that the man who had brought him so much fame and fortune, and the man he had tried to dump at one time, were now fighting within him for dominance.

He could give neither that.

So, he just smiled and laid down his pen. He went to his study door and opened it for his wife. She gave him the sweetest of smiles.

Then he realized Jane hadn't entered. She had to be quite worried about him. He was always on time. He got up from the mess on his desk. During his short, but powerful nap, he had knocked over the inkwell. It was too late now to do much about it.

The damage was done.

He would have it cleaned later.

For now, he was just grateful his Sherlock Holmes story had not been the victim of his brief sojourn into the land of dreams...and nightmares.

He hurried from his room to Jane's piano room and good thing he did, because she was about to lock the door, which meant she had given up on him coming and that she would indeed be quite hurt by his lack of attention.

He took her shoulders in his hands. "I beg you, dear heart, this was not planned. I assure you. I was so deep in my work and the strain so great that I lost consciousness and slept through our appointed time together."

She looked into his eyes. "I forgive you."

He smiled back. "I am here. I am humbly yours to do with as you choose. To reject me for my brutish oversight or to enlighten and uplift me with the chorale of your music that always refreshes my heart and soul."

She giggled.

He grinned.

"You writers are all the same. A few pedicured words and you're off and running from any harm you've done."

She gave him a light kiss on his cheek. "And I have to admit, I love you for it."

"Come, Arthur."

She put a hand to his face and stroked it lightly. After she did his fatigue and sense of frustration vanished like an eraser removing chalk from a blackboard.

He smiled as warmly as he felt at that moment. "I am yours to do with as you please, my dear. I truly mean it."

"She gave him a smile that duplicated the one that Madame Blavatsky had done in his memories. For a moment he felt a Déjà vu sweep over him as if this moment were ordained and meant to be.

But whatever this moment was, surely it was one of the best decisions he had ever made, for writing is only a fleeting gift, but love is enduring to the souls who are lucky enough to have it bestowed upon them. And for Arthur, there was no greater love in his life than his wife, Jane.

"Dratted Holmes can find his way home," he sputtered as she took his hand and reopened the door to her piano room.

"I'm sure Doctor Watson will take fine care of him, my dear," she said, playing along with his jest.

He nodded.

She sat him on the comfortable chair that was his when he visited to listen to her exquisite music. She gave him a coy look. "Now, I haven't polished this piece yet..."

He smiled. "I'm sure I will love it regardless."

She gave him a look that made his heart leap and then began playing her a new melody. He listened to it and as she played, he felt as if he were living and alive inside his own stories. She rushed through melodies that evoked Sherlock Holmes and Watson...mystery, the game that must be solved, their profound respect for each other; their friendship; their adventures; the enemies they fought, and then she launched into a bar of music that made his hair stand on end.

"Professor Challenger," he roared, despite himself.

She nodded but kept playing. This was Professor Challenger he thought as he listened. Her music exuded a sense of exoticness like the man himself and then it embraced a series of sharp turns and thrust him into his first encounter with the great Madame Blavatsky.

It was quiet, subtle, and provoked images of worlds beyond worlds, of angels divine, of a loving God, of life in all its variations being led gently to an end that was both mysterious and wonderful.

When she had finished, she left her fingers on the keys of the piano.

"What's wrong, my dear?" He asked, fearing he might have inadvertently said or done something of which he wasn't aware.

But he hadn't. She turned to smile up into his face. "I'm sorry, Arthur. I don't know what just got into me."

She swiped at the tears in his eyes. He got up and sat on the bench beside her, then gently pressed a handkerchief against her moist eyes and face. "What got into you was Divine. I have never heard anything so beautiful before."

She gave him a doubtful look. "You think so?"

"I do, with all my heart, I do."

What do you think of it? I composed it all for you. For your lovely stories, all the wonderful feelings they evoke in me, and I'm sure all your readers."

She looked at her fingers, which still rested on the piano keys. "For some reason, I couldn't keep going; not because there's no more to follow, but..."

She gave him a mysterious look. "It's as if my fingers had taken on a life of their own. As if they were waiting for you to commit to the rest of your story."

He laughed. "My dear, how much more could there possibly be?"

"Oh, so much more," she said, meaning it with all her heart.

He didn't say a word. He just smiled. Holmes and his grand revelation could wait. His wife, dear heart that she was, had just written an ending that he could never in a thousand lifetimes have ever produced.

"You are wonderful!" He told her.

She smiled.

The Bedroom

This night was like a honeymoon for both. She stood there in her dress, which she was carefully undoing and he in his suit, tie, and jacket, slowly taking off his shoes, then his jacket, tie, and shirt.

Neither looked at the other. That would have been wrong at that moment.

It was like they were newborn, embarrassed lovers, as they prepared for bed.

Finally, she hurriedly slipped beneath the covers. He did likewise.

The warmth of her body drew him to her like a magnet.

He crushed her to him and gently began kissing about her throat, then her earlobes, her nose, her eyelids, her forehead, and then her lips.

He stopped. "I will always love you. No matter what!"

She shut his mouth with her lips.

The next hours were a blur to him as they clasped each other's naked bodies the way that all lovers do, satisfying their needs and sharing their warmth, satisfaction, and love as best they could...slowly, carefully, tenderly...taking as much time as they could to allow the building passion to explode into a panoply of delicious intimacy that only heightened their sense of closeness more so.

When the penultimate time came, they both gasped in pleasure, letting out long sighs, and held onto each other for what felt like hours.

That night would become a monument to their friendship and love.

As they lay side by side, holding each other, he felt that persistent twinge in his heart once more and he knew that the thought that had just blossomed was something he must do before it was too late.

Tomorrow!

If he had one.

A pain struck him.

He ignored it for Jane's sake, but gently let go of her. She slid next to him, her nose against his chest and he put an arm about her shoulders, but he did so more to protect her from what he was feeling...pain. So much of it.

Just when he thought he might die from it, it released.

And then he swept away into a gentle but sweet sleep with memories of the two of them in better times.

It helped to soften the dull, aching pain in his chest, which had earlier felt like a devil's pitchfork stabbing him.

As painful as it had become, it vanished, replaced with a soft and gentle warmth that immersed his soul. Softening the pain and erasing it as quickly as it had come.

But even as he dreamed, he had a vision of a certain man. A proud and even quite arrogant man with bristly red hair that poked all over the place and an itch for adventure only matched by his bravado.

Then he vanished into those heavenly realms where pain cannot touch or remorse.

The White Light

"At the dawn of realization, one quickly learns that everything that came before was only preparation for what is to come after. The Creator is quite clever in how our life lessons are learned. And of course, during the after...that's when true patience begins, and truth becomes our long-enduring friend."

--Sherlock Holmes

Before him, was a huge tunnel.

Pitch black.

But at its far end was a brilliant burst of white light, whose fingers reached towards him vainly. He wanted so badly to run into that tunnel, forget about this world, his pain, his sorrows, his ever-growing sense of loss and remorse, but he was stuck.

It was like two gigantic hands holding him in place. No matter how hard he ran, he got no further. It was a miracle he could not comprehend, though he should have been able to. He was certain this was not the first, nor would be the last time he would have such an experience.

But knowing that did little to mitigate his dissatisfaction at that moment.

So, he did the only thing a reasonable man with a modicum of self-awareness would.

He groaned.

"Arthur?"

The tunnel shot away from him, growing ever deeper, and brighter with the brilliant white and peaceful light becoming only a dot in the distance. A sudden flare of brilliant golden light struck his eyes.

"Drat it all!"

He lay there stunned as if someone had struck him in the gut so hard all his air was gone. The morning light was shattering the darkness of their bedroom. Jane stood away from the curtains she had drawn open to admit dawn's light, a worried look on her face.

"I can close them again."

"No, no, my dear. You did the right thing. You always do the right thing," he added, though, at that moment, his words rang a bit hollow as he was so close to reaching that white light. If he had just had a few more moments…

Then he struggled to sit up, groaning again. Jane sat beside him and fluffed his pillows behind his back so he could get comfortable. He brushed a hand through her hair, his eyes taking in her breathtaking beauty. Every line, every curve of her cheek, her neck, her eyes, her ears, her gentle bosom which he had clasped so tightly the night before, then he looked into her eyes.

"You are the light of my life," he told her.

She broke into a sob and threw her arms about him, holding him so tight he almost couldn't breathe. Then she wept for a long time.

He didn't try to stop her.

He had learned by now to trust a woman's intuition. It was always right. It was just crusty old chaps like himself that did not fare so well with that dratted insight device.

He scowled at himself; glad at that moment she couldn't see his face, or he would have felt like such a cad for feeling sorry for himself when she was exploding with grief and a sense of loss that was not with them, but she feared soon would be.

He could sense it in her last night when she had given herself to him more completely than he could ever remember. So much so, that once was not enough.

At the time he had felt like a satiated lion that had had more than its share of a kill. Bad comparison, but what he had felt. Proud, defiant, and possessive.

But the more he had striven to possess her body last night the more hollowed he had felt inside of himself until they were both spent again, and he could look back on those feelings and realize it was not the physical touching that had caused this feeling of remorse, but his fear he would never experience it again.

Jane finally sat up, pulled back, and smiled at him like the little girl she seemed sometimes when in her better spaces. "I seem to have wet your poor pajamas dear Arthur."

He smiled. "Wet them where you will."

She gave him a playful slap on his face. "You brute!"

"And you loved every moment of it."

Then she burst into tears again.

He put his arms around her and cradled her against him until she subsided yet again.

She said nothing.

At first, he thought she slept; but she had not. "Arthur…"

He looked down.

Her eyes were searching for his face. "I had the strangest feeling earlier. Which is why I threw the curtains open."

"Oh, and what was that?"

"That you were about to leave me."

And that did bring regret to his heart. He felt tears begin to stream from his eyes. 'You are the last thing I would ever want to leave behind, dear Jane. Ever, ever, and ever."

He smiled brightly, holding her chin up gently with his right thumb. "You are the game that is always afoot and the one game I feel shall never reach an end of, nor would ever desire to."

She giggled like a little girl, causing his heart to spike with sudden compassion and warmth.

"You writers, you're so full of…"

"Words?"

She laughed.

"Time to face the new day," she told him, then slipped from his embrace with a soft peck on his cheek, then dropped to the floor and padded towards her boudoir where she began searching for the new day's wear.

She gave him a last lingering look. And for a moment only, he was sure she was going to fling herself on him like a ravaging tiger, but either his look of surprise or hers at her own sudden need shook the feeling off and she laughed, and then departed to see to breakfast.

Monster

"Doctor Jekyll, you must pull yourself together," Arthur told him, as the poor man wrung his hands pitifully in front of himself over and over as if to get something horrible from them. Something dark and loathsome.

"I saw me. I saw me like I truly am," Doctor Jekyll insisted.

"And?"

"I was..."

Doctor Jekyll turned away to hide the piteous look on his brows. "...A monster."

Arthur chuckled warmly. "Come now, Doctor, surely you are wrong. All the time you've spent, all the years, those moments you sacrificed to make this mastery..." Arthur pointed out. "...Surely, they were not for waste."

Doctor Jekyll spun about. "No, they were not!" He growled.

Arthur recoiled in horror.

The young professional doctor and friend that he and Challenger knew so well were going through a horrible change. His body was sloughing off like that of a caterpillar shedding its skin to become a butterfly. Only his friend was not becoming bright and beautiful, light, and airy. An angel of the light.

He was shifting off his flesh and becoming this terrible beast of energies like electricity attacking itself, trying to lash out and destroy itself at the same time it reached out to destroy others.

"Doctor, what have you done to yourself?" Arthur cried out.

"I have become..." Doctor Jekyll smiled through the energies, revealing a ghastly countenance that caused Arthur to wet his trousers. "...Death!"

Then the Doctor rushed Arthur.

A Nightmare Only

Arthur gasped in terror, reaching his hands out to ward off the demon his friend had become. But it was useless.

Then he grunted.

His chest hurt so bad, he felt like he was going to explode.

His eyes shot open.

He was still on his bed.

He had fallen asleep.

What had struck him was the vase his wife usually kept on each side of their bed, filled with fresh flowers, to help them sleep and add a more pleasant fragrance to the room.

The vase, somehow, he couldn't understand how, how flung from the side table into his chest. He carefully set it back on the side table, allowing his feet to touch the cold wooden floor. He felt about, found his slippers, and tucked his feet into them.

He got up.

His pajama top was wet where the vase had struck him. He turned to the bed. It was soaked and flowers were all over it. "How in the devil am I going to explain this to Jane; let alone myself?"

He headed for his dresser, where he kept a pair of pants on a portable rack by it. He pulled them down and shrugged out of his long, white pajamas.

Then he saw his reflection in the mirror. He had what looked like a handprint on his chest.

"Impossible!" He uttered but shivered in horror, nevertheless.

He shook his head. "Must have been the way the flowers struck me."

Giving it no further thought he finished dressing and headed for his office.

His chest still ached from the blow he had been struck. And the vision of that creature smashing at his chest with its outreaching hands did nothing to help his sense of terror at that moment.

His research into the afterlife had shown him many things. One of which was that there were energy beings who were just some kind of powerful emotional substance that could cause dishes and loose items to fly.

He looked back towards his bedroom and frowned. "Or a vase?" He asked himself.

"Is that you, Arthur?"

He smiled, all thoughts of terror fleeing from his mind at the sound of her bell-like voice.

"It is indeed."

Then he smelled the aroma of the food she was making for them. The cook was off for the day as well as the butler. So, they had the run of the house without having to worry about appearance.

He tightened his tie in appreciation of that thought, then, smiled brightly. Today was going to be a good day!

He passed his office.

He saw his unfinished manuscript lying on his desk, begging him to come back and finish it. He almost went inside, and then shook his head.

Into the Light

"Go into the Light, Conan," a voice urged him.

He struggled to open his eyes. But they wouldn't do so. The black tunnel loomed before him, but at its end were utterly brilliant and dazzling shades of white, dancing and spiraling towards him with tendrils that almost seemed like welcoming hands, hands that wanted to embrace him in their welcoming folds of splendor.

"I can't. Not yet. I have too much to do."

The voice droned at him from all sides.

"It's already done. Wake up to the greater reality."

"I am in the best one already," he replied, meaning it with all his heart.

Confusion and Doubt

Arthur recoiled as if struck. "What in God's name?" Then he felt growing anger inside himself. Not at anyone so much, but at his lack of consideration for so much in his life. For wanting to put so much before what was the most important. For seeking to fill a hole that was impossible to fill.

"Holmes be damned!" He uttered, not meaning it at all, but enough so that he could justify passing what he was certain now would be his last body of work.

"Writing be damned!" He uttered.

Jane rushed from the kitchen; her eyes wide open in fear for him. "Arthur?"

She looked the wrong way and then found him. "I heard you yell."

"I didn't...yell," he told her, surprised that he had done just that. It shook him up even more than the vision he had just had.

That kind of vision he knew from experience and talking with many who had near-death experiences were usually given before death. Most came back. Or they could never have spoken about it. Others told their experience from the other side if you believed the charlatans who claimed their voices were those of the recently departed.

He had debunked many of them, but some were borderline, and he had found it to claim them liars, but still had not enough evidence yet to prove otherwise than what they claimed…they spoke for the dead.

Jane touched his arm.

“Arthur.”

He snapped out of his thoughts. Again, time had passed, and he had no idea where he had been, except in a jumble of thoughts.

He shook his head to clear it. “I'm fine. Just the sleep fogging my damned brain is all.”

She laughed and took his arm. “Then maybe that big brain of yours needs some food to stoke its fires so that it may burn the more brightly.”

He stopped her and looked into her eyes for a long time. Then he pulled her to him. “Have I ever told you that I love you?”

“No, so keep on saying it.”

They both laughed and she pulled away and led him into the kitchen.

He didn't regret their meal. Such as it was. He couldn't remember one bit of it, his eyes never left her face, even when he was eating his toast with marmalade on top.

They ate their breakfast in a congenial silence. Both still have quite fond memories of the night before. He hadn't realized how long it had been until that moment. No wonder she seemed brighter than usual. But why he felt so miserable and dull; that he couldn't explain. But even with all that, he still felt like a young man again.

His eyes slipped to her figure again.

She giggled.

He blushed.

This snapped him yet again out of thoughts that were strapping his mind down and causing him to lose his focus.

He wiped his mouth with his napkin, and then rose.

"Dear, I need to do a bit of shopping. Would you mind if I were gone for a time?"

She gave him a surprised look. "For what? We could have our man fetch what is needed."

He patted her hand warmly and then smiled. "Remember, he is off for the day and..."

He gave her that look he always did when he didn't want to discuss the object of his journey. She got it immediately.

"Oh!" She spoke.

They knew each other so well that a look could convey that much. A luxury and wealth found only in a well-tuned marriage, he thought. One of deep love and union of purpose.

She knew then he was up to something for someone special.

Her.

She looked away; her face sweet with love for him. And a bit embarrassed. She was that. Always. She never expected a thing from him. And that's because for so long he had given so little at times. But he was determined now to turn that part of his character around and admonishing himself for lost time, made for the door.

He hated to leave her at that moment.

But he felt a sense of time running out.

That sense of urgency drove him to rise. He wiped his mouth with a napkin and then headed for the door.

"Don't worry about me. I'll be back soon enough."

Something about the way the words came out felt wrong. She gave him a look he had hoped not to see blossom on her face.

Fear!

But for what?

A sad note to leave her upon but leave he must. He took his wallet and walking stick from their places, and then stepped outside, pondering what he had seen on her face.

It was not old.

It was not new.

But it was something he wished never to have brought to the woman he loved.

Fear.

A carriage was coming his way.

He hurried to the sidewalk and waved his walking stick.

The driver jumped down, opened a door for him and Arthur climbed inside.

He told the driver where he wanted to go, and the carriage began to move as the horse trotted off.

He sat there enfolded in his thoughts, reliving those moments before.

The Ride

Fear.

Not for herself.

But for him.

She had lost the flush of happiness that had suffused her smile and face. Suddenly, she looked small, drawn, and weary as if the world had collapsed about her.

"Arthur? What aren't you telling me?"

He looked away. "I'm sorry. I didn't mean it to come out like that."

She nodded and walked him to the door, lifted her chin and he kissed her for the first time in a long time fully on the lips.

They both stared into each other's eyes for a long moment, as if new lovers who had just tasted the wonder of their souls merging in an ecstasy of love.

She breathed heavily into his face and whispered. "Love does not need to hide, my beloved Arthur."

He opened the door and left.

He paused a long moment at the door, regathering his senses. "Love does not need to hide," he repeated.

A bump in the road shook Arthur out of his nap.

He shook his head.

Why was he so dratted tired?

Magnificent words. The words of his waking dream came back to him. "Love does not need to hide."

The writer in him surged forth and grasped the words. He straightened up. It was that kind of moment we all have at some time or another in our life. A moment of such clarity and certainty that we no longer doubt what we must do next. What must be done, must be done without hesitation.

He knew how to end his last story.

Holmes must say those very same words to his beloved friend Watson before it was too late to do so. How could two such close souls, such fearless companions tread through so many nights and days of danger and hardship and not have an enduring bond that was both special and unique?

Yes, he felt much better now. This is what all his experiences to this point were leading him to. To cap off his Holmes series with a bright moment. A gentle moment, which to this point in time, Holmes denied not only himself but his dear and trusted friend, Doctor John Watson.

Now he felt better. He had a mission to accomplish for his love and another for the man who had inherited so much of his time and life: Sherlock Holmes.

Holmes had to finally and once for all tell Watson that he loved him.

Not as a physical source of desire, but as a friend and companion.

Every man needs to hear that from their friends as much as any woman might from her lover. It was the crème de la crème of life. The cherry blossoms of happiness that should never be avoided.

As all of that dawned upon him, he felt more love for his wife than ever before. Yet again, she had elevated his consciousness, guided him onto a loftier path. One that was filled with the truth that all men need to follow and embrace. That we do not just offer friendship to each other. But love. True, divine, and special love.

The physical was just God's way of allowing us to feel that love on some kind of level until we were ready to experience pure love.

"Sir!" His driver called from the curb.

He looked out and nodded.

They were there already.

Had he been lost in his thoughts that long? Something about the way the driver was looking at him spoke volumes of unspent words. The man was laboring to be polite and not say more than what was necessary. And he had that kind of look that Jane had before he left her.

Fear!

"Splendid!" He answered his driver, as the man smiled at him with a nod, and stepped aside to open the door for him.

He got out, his thoughts still whirling about him like tiny flower fairies distraught from having their flowers picked and taken away.

Then he realized where he was.

"Oh!"

"Sir?"

"I meant another jeweler."

"No problem, sir."

He climbed back inside, and once settled down properly, his driver shut the door shut.

He sighed happily. Today was turning into such a remarkable day for him. A tremendous burst of inspiration from his wife and a chance to gift her with something from his heart that was tangible. As the driver leaped to his seat and then urged the horses into a gentle canter, he stared out the window. Observing women with the latest fashion of umbrellas...lavender, pink, yellow and blue...that were imported from the French across the channel. The ladies twirled their umbrellas gaily above their shoulders as fine gentlemen in finely pressed suits and shirts marched alongside them, engaged in conversations he could only begin to imagine.

All worries and concerns about his condition, his failing memory... flew away as he admired the state of humanity about him.

He laughed as owners would groan when their dogs chased his carriage, merrily wagging their tails and barking to let the driver know they were there.

And the children. He didn't know why, but it was like every child that had ever existed was suddenly outside. Kicking balls. Jumping in the air. Chasing ribbons. Each other. Waving at him. Smiling and laughing.

He sighed.

How long ago those years seemed now.

It was a pleasant day, unlike the prior night's storm activity, today was settled and peaceful.

The night had been a sweet one.

The sweetest.

But even the sweetest of moments on this earth has a beginning and an end.

And here he was now; engaged in what he hoped would not be a selfish mission, to show his beloved a better side of him.

He was silent on the way to Sir Charles Jewelers in South Hampton. Barely noticing any of the views he passed.

He had a lot on his plate; much to arrange; much to accomplish and finish.

Before...

He felt a twinge in his chest.

Not the warmth of love.

Worse.

He shut his eyes and waited until it diminished.

He sighed with relief and allowed his thoughts to pursue more pleasant things as the miles unfolded.

A beautiful necklace with a sapphire crowning its glorious pearls. These days he could afford such trinkets, even though a part of him still felt pinched at doing so. Having come up from extremely poor to extraordinarily rich, so to speak, he still tended at times to restrain his purse, hold back on his spending joys, for fear of not having enough. He knew that was foolish, especially now of all times, but habits rule strongly in a man's patterns of behavior. And unlike Sherlock Holmes, he was simply a man with the ability to convey his thoughts on paper. He had no remarkable powers of deduction, other than those any writer might assume who knew how to write his thoughts on paper.

And the brilliance of Holmes was no more than properly executed lines of thought in the right order of occurrence on paper.

His thoughts were not as orderly as he drifted off yet again into a kind of daydream. But this time it was soothing. Not alarming.

Well Done

Watson sat next to Holmes where he lay on his bed. His friend didn't look well. He hadn't for quite some time. Holmes began coughing violently.

Watson held Holmes's right hand tightly as the man stiffened from the exertion. He finally relaxed, but Watson didn't let go.

Holmes smiled at Watson. "Here we are, two old, silver-haired men, ready for one last adventure, but now I fear it must be postponed."

Watson would have none of it.

"You'll get well. You always do."

Holmes patted Watson's hand and squeezed it warmly.

"Watson, after all these years…"

"Decades really."

Holmes smiled. "Decades. Seems like only yesterday."

Watson smiled, doing his best to hide his pain. "But they were good yesterdays."

Homles laughed weakly. "We're lucky to be alive !"

Watson chuckled. "Indeed."

Holmes coughed several times more.

Watson got up, went to a large bowl he had put on Holmes's dresser, wet a washcloth, then came back and wiped Holmes's mouth for him.

"You're always being so good to me, Watson."

"And you to me, Holmes."

The two men stared at each other for a long time in silence, allowing the sudden warmth both felt to endure as much as humanly possible.

"When I'm gone…" Holmes began.

Watson put a finger to his friend's lips. "Shhhh. Let's not talk tomorrow."

Holmes laughed. "Watson, you're a doctor. You know that's a euphemism at best and that tomorrow is a day I do not have."

Holmes began coughing harder.

Blood spewed forth from between his lips.

Watson pressed the cloth to them to soak it up.

Holmes took Watson's wrist in his bony hand and pressed it gently.

"I love you, Watson."

Watson gave Holmes a distraught look. "No…"

Holmes's eyes began drooping shut. "After all these years of companionship, I have never told you the depths of my feelings for you."

"Now's not the time."

Holmes's eyes snapped open.

For a moment, the clarity in them was astounding.

He said in his usual almost distant voice. "Well done, Watson. Well done!"

Then his eyes shut.

He let out a long sigh.

Then passed from our mortal realm.

Watson sat there a long time, holding onto his friend's hand, and then began to weep.

But not for himself, but for the loss to the world of a man who gave so much to those about him, who cared so deeply, but could never allow himself to speak those words openly.

Watson put his head on Holmes's chest and shut his eyes.

"Farewell, old friend. "I love you as well."

Sir Charles's Jewelers

"We're here, sir!" The carriage driver announced.

Arthur snapped out of his daydream and realized he had been crying. It also took a moment for him to realize the rude sound had been merely the sound of a door being shut.

When he slept every sound became extremely magnified. His hearing was that good.

His driver must have moved something forward from where he sat.

He glanced at the open door and the shop before him. He smiled. The man was good. Again, he had that look in his eyes, but this time it was tempered somewhat, for he seemed to realize that Arthur was not distressed at all, but radiant.

That's what he felt.

Radiant.

He had finally closed the last chapter of Holmes's life with Watson. And it was wonderful!

He wiped his eyes.

"Must have gotten something in my eyes with the open windows," Arthur commented as he got out.

"Windier than usual, sir."

Arthur nodded in appreciation. He knew full well that there was no wind. He was being kind. Something he hadn't been able to commit to Holmes's character or his own, it would appear.

He intended to rectify that.

"Please wait for me, I shan't be long."

The man nodded, the hint of a smile on his lips.

He didn't have to say anything; he knew Arthur well. He had been serving him for years faithfully. *Shan't be long* could be a few minutes or hours. Didn't matter. He was paid to wait as well as to do other things.

Arthur turned to face the store. Smiled. The lobby of the store was open, but not the main part. He shrugged, then straightened his tie and shirt and entered the lobby.

For him to be standing in the lobby of one of the most expensive jewelers of South Hampton was totally unlike him. He would have gone to Carnaby, but the jewelry he sought was not there. He had been informed by a particularly good friend that what he sought was not to be found in that upscale area, but here at Sir Charles Jewelers in South Hampton. So, he had called for his carriage and rode the morning through dawn and gathering mists to arrive just as the doors were opening.

Several others were also gathered to enter as he stopped before the large ornate doors that fronted the interior of the store. White and gold dragons embossed the door handles and sheets of lightning bolts hurled by ancient gods hovered above his head on a canopy that had a small sign which read: *Welcome to Sir Charles Jewelry.*

Above all that was an exquisite, embossed painting of King Arthur holding up the mighty Excalibur, preparing for battle.

He paid for the sign and his fellow buyers no more attention than it took to notice them. However, the image of King Arthur struck him more deeply than he was willing to admit now. He saw something in that man that he found lacking in himself to this point. Selflessness.

Some of the gathered customers recognized him, but he abruptly turned away from them, not wanting to get into another one of those hounding autograph sessions where everyone talked so foolishly, including himself, from embarrassment.

No one bothered him. He sighed with relief. His heart had enough to deal with lately without the added pressure of pursuing readers. Speaking of which, a slight pressure was building again. He almost panicked, but then it subsided.

He decided to shut his eyes.

Bang! Bang!

The Birth of Ms. Hudson

His eyes snapped open to see the Shop Manager catching the huge door on the right where it had slammed into the base of the wall where a large metal drum had been inset to keep it from damaging the wall.

The Shop Manager caught a sweep of iron at the bottom of the door and swung it out. It caught and the door remained in place.

He repeated the motion on the other side, all the time smiling happily at his waiting clients. He knew them all and greeted them by name as they clustered eagerly forward to get inside.

Arthur wondered if the smile was genuine or just the man's anticipation of extra wealth, he would accumulate this day from sales.

Arthur shrugged off that niggardly idea. It wasn't kind of him to think such. It was that Holmes side of him; the intellectual part that had to dissect everything and put it neatly in a box so it could be found again.

Labeled and set aside as his wife, Jane, would sometimes remind him when he spoke outwardly what he thought inwardly.

He swept inside with the others.

"Good morning, Mister Doyle," the Shop Manager greeted him.

Arthur nodded but didn't smile. He was only thinking of the huge amount he had taken from the safe at home to spend this morning.

Also, he still harbored a suspicion of the man's motives. It was sparked when the man checked out Arthur's bulge, where he usually kept his wallet. It was much larger than usual.

Arthur knew the type. He didn't believe this man was such, but he knew of a type that would do anything for money. Much like some of the criminals, he wrote about...or rather, had written about. He sighed with a sudden kind of relief.

Holmes was at his end.

At last.

Once and forever.

At that moment and before, and probably after, he never considered the possibility that his hero would become so well-loved that others would take the man on further adventures.

Holmes had been hard for him to let go of, but he had to. A man needed to find other things to do than writing about the same thing over and over with slight variations. Then he frowned. Here he was out to please his wife, and instead was scolding himself for killing off an imaginary character with no proper explanation in sight.

Well, Damnit it all! He thought. *At least I have put him to bed in a way that will touch everyone's heart. It certainly touched mine!*

Then he felt guilty and annoyed at himself because he hadn't truly killed him off. Just give him a rest and now he was stuck with a story that was so melodramatic in its ending that surely the Queen would once again beg for more, as well as his readers.

Lately, he had begun finishing a new series of novels about a powerful teacher and explorer who discovered a Lost World. He still had no titles for the novels, but he knew they would come in time. If he reminded himself, he was able to live that long. Professor Challenger was the kind of man he sometimes wished he could have been. An explorer who traveled far and near accomplished great adventures. Always went somewhere and did something magnificent. But...

"Excuse me," he said to a lovely mature woman standing behind the nearest jewelry counter. "I was referred by Sir Cedric of Yorkshire. He said you had an especially handsome piece of jewelry that my wife would adore. Something with a sapphire in its crown?"

"Why surely we do, sir," she replied, her sparkling eyes smiling at him. *This was a woman he could enjoy*; he thought for a moment and then shoved the thoughts from his mind. It was not gentlemanly to think about women as objects of desire...even if they were sometimes considered that way...a naughty part of him added. And then he realized he recognized her. He smiled, even as he growled at himself and his impertinence at allowing such lesser thoughts to seduce himself, a moral man into realms he would not gladly have gone.

“Ms. Hudson, I presume.”

A Chapter of Gentleness

Watson eyed Ms. Hudson sternly. “I cannot start my day without tea and cakes.”

Ms. Hudson shook her bob of dusty brown hair as if disagreeing, but instead said, “No problem, Mister Watson.”

Holmes said, “And I prefer not to be interrupted during my meditations. Unless our home is on fire, of course.”

“Of course,” she replied.

“And I insist on clean silverware,” Watson demanded.

Ms. Hudson’s kindly face turned quite frigid.

“Sir! You insult me; I would not even serve myself on such, let alone my tenant!”

“But...” Watson began.

She got in his face, and Watson backed off. The first time any woman had ever intimidated him so much, frightened him to the very core of his being. This woman looked ready to cut his throat by the look in her eyes.

“No, but...I will do everything I have been hired to do. You can expect your rooms to be clean on Fridays. Fresh linen every morning. Breakfast as six...”

"Nine," Watson cut in.

"Six," Holmes agreed.

Watson looked at him. "You know I can't get up any earlier!"

Holmes smiled. "Perhaps it's time to wear a new hat, Watson."

Watson glared at him. "Wear a new hat? What in God's name are you talking about?"

Ms. Hudson laughed. "I think I'm going to enjoy having the two of you here."

You offered an arm to Holmes, who took it. "I assume you will be managing the money."

She glanced over her shoulder at a fuming Watson. "You appear to be the more rational of the two."

Holmes nodded. "Yes. Rather. Come, Watson, don't doddle back there like a whipped puppy."

Watson stared at holes in the backs of Ms. Hudson and Holmes as they entered the flat.

Then a whiff of freshly made food caught his nostrils. His eyes widened.

Ms. Hudson came back out. "Well, are you coming or not? I prepared breakfast in advance of your coming, knowing you probably hadn't time to dine yet."

Watson almost ran up the stairs.

The Real Ms. Hudson

"Mister Doyle!" She said, her face lighting up. "I haven't seen you since you begged for permission to use my name in your splendid series of stories about that Holmes character. I'm sorry I never read them, but someday I shall, when I have some free time."

Arthur flushed with embarrassment. How do you respond to a compliment with a veiled insult in it? "Uh, I'm sure you will. No rush. The books aren't going anywhere."

"I should hope not, or I'll have a fit," she replied, her cheeks dimpling with humor.

Arthur stared at her for a moment in thought. This woman was every bit, Ms. Hudson. She was exactly what he had visualized in his mind, then included in his stories. How could he have forgotten she was the source of his template for the property owner?

Then he remembered she had been a widower and raising a family of five by herself. He also remembered another person then. It was all coming back to him now.

"And that remarkable man you worked for. What was his name...?"

"Olmes Sherland." She told him, smiling warmly. She winked. "I fancy the way you twisted his name about to produce your detective's name. Quite clever that. That much I did learn, at least from your book titles."

Arthur blushed. "Well, had I never met your Mister Sherland and seen the remarkable feats of intellect he performed, I might never have produced a proper name for Mister Holmes after all or his overall disposition. I'm amazed I forgot about him until now. Funny how aging sips the teacup of our memories and leaves them filled with the remains of shredded memories like used up tea leaves."

“They were quite remarkable,” roared a man behind him.

“I beg your pardon, Sir” Arthur bellowed.

The voice had spoken directly into his right ear. Expecting to see a callow man standing beside him, or behind at the worst, he found none standing anywhere close at all.

Ms. Hudson ignored his rudeness and even his perhaps touch of odd behavior. The man was known for having some temper at times, but he had seemed so even when he greeted her.

"Well, that makes us both happy then. Not that you have forgotten, but that you did remember at one time," Ms. Hudson hurriedly explained.

"How so?" He asked her, truly perplexed by her statement, but still nagged by the strange voice. He continued to survey the store for signs of some man who might fit the voice that blasted his ear drums so thoroughly.

"Why? Because with your good words to Sir Charles, I was promoted to his better store. This one. I can now feed my children quite well...our children that is." She leaned closer and whispered, "Sir Charles asked for my hand within a month of being hired. He is now my husband. And a good man he is too. Took me and my five children into his home and treats us properly he has."

Arthur was at a loss for words at first, his mind still trying to piece together the odd bit of business he had just experienced, but finally, her words clicked together and made sense enough for him to respond.

"I am truly happy for you," he told her and meant every word of it. He even revised his opinion of the shop manager, who was her husband, Sir Charles, from the way he kept glancing her way. Perhaps he wasn't half as bad as Arthur had thought earlier. It was at that moment of regret for his earlier judgments, he found himself assailed by a fresh bout of extreme dizziness.

He staggered against a display case, fumbling to recover his balance. Everything began to go black.

"Mister Doyle!" Ms. Hudson cried out in alarm.

Crashing sounds shattered the shadows he collapsed into.

The Chase

"Bloody Hell, Challenger, we'll never get to the top of that monster!"

Challenger eyed his shorter companion, Conan, known in our world as Sir Arthur Conan Doyle, but whom Challenger had rechristened as Conan for the ease of speaking.

Conan was sweating so badly his jungle outfit was wet through and through. The pure white straw hat he wore was just as soaked as his pure white shirt and pants.

"I should never have listened to you about wearing these clothes and this hat," he blasted at Challenger, then tossed his hat into the air and watched it sail off into the tropical leaves high above and vanish.

Challenger fixed him with that usual stoic glare he made whenever he was about to pontificate to Conan and tell him about the meaning of life as Challenger saw it.

Challenger didn't seem to notice even for a moment that his face was dripping wet, his hat wet as a fresh pond, and his clothing clinging to him like some exotic dancer from a foreign country.

Challenger pulled his hat lower over his eyes and then stared through Conan.

Here it comes! Conan thought and steeled himself.

"You need to shed some of those pretty pounds you wear as proudly as the Queen of Sheba."

"She was not fat!" Conan complained."

"Then why did it take ten slaves to carry her?" Challenger countered.

"She liked men?"

"You're impossible!"

"And you're, you're…annoying."

Challenger eyed Conan's pot belly. Conan bristled at the stare. Again, he knew what was coming next. He even said them at the same time as Challenger spouted them. "They are not pretty!"

Challenger smirked.

"Rattled, hey?"

"I mean, I mean," Conan stuttered. Flabbergasted. He could never get the best of this man. He was like one of those idiotic mirrors at a carnival that distorted everything you looked like, no matter which direction your eyes traveled.

Challenger softened.

Conan sighed a breath of relief. He also knew what was coming next with this new aspect of Challenger. *I'm a good guy, you know.*

"I know. I know." He clapped a hand on Conan's shoulder. "You've got to look at this climbing as a necessary part of your life if you intend on continuing to accompany me on these adventures."

"They're not adventures. They're tortures conjured by the most diabolical mind in creation."

"Whose?"

"Why yours, of course!" Conan insisted.

Challenger grinned. "Well, a compliment at last."

"I'd rather chase Hyde through the gates of hell than climb another monolith! Or pay you a compliment!"

"You have done both," Challenger assured him.

Conan shook his head. He just couldn't win with this man. But when Challenger gave him a knowing wink, he saw a glint of the man he had come to admire and love as a friend and companion. Challenger said softly now, "I value your friendship, Conan. I truly do. And I never, ever, never have drawn you into anything I feared you would fail to be able to overcome."

"What about the Lion's Oven in Africa where we had to fight three lions with our feet and hands tied?"

“Challenger, they were just old lions and pets. They just licked our faces.”

Conan made a face.

“I hated their breath.”

Challenger sighed. "As I, but what must be done, must be...done."

Challenger eyed the spire of the mountain, which was sheathed in a myriad of hands of cloud that squirmed and shimmied like bowls of liquid oil, colored with snow. "From what I can see if we start now, we should get halfway to the top by nightfall."

Conan gave him a look that could kill. "You said it'd be a piece of cake!"

"I did, didn't I?" Challenger agreed, and then he smiled. "Would you have come had I said otherwise?"

Conan said nothing.

"I rest your case."

Challenger put a hand to the rocks above him and began climbing. "Oh, and I wouldn't wait for me to come back, as the only way out of this part of Fairie is up there.'

"You stinking, rotten Tosh!"

"Come now, Conan, sticks and stones and butter do not mix, you know."

Conan was so frustrated he could punch a hole in the mountainside, but upon looking at the hardness of it in the light of reason, he pocketed that thought for more consideration when he got back home. Where, it was safe. Then he would tell Challenger exactly what he thought of him while he clubbed his brains out with his knuckles.

He chuckled at the image a moment, before reaching up to follow his friend.

"I heard those thoughts, Conan. Killing me won't help you one bit."

Conan raised a fist. "Is there nothing of me you don't know?"

Challenger paused about ten feet up and looked down. "Never gave it much thought, but I suppose not. Oh, and by the way, there's something you might want to notice before you decide to play stubborn much longer."

"WHAT!" Shouted Conan, his face reddening with anger once more.

At the precise moment Conan finished his angry question a horrendous bellow shattered the quiet behind him. Conan spun around and felt his heart sink into his stomach. It was a prehistoric beast from the worst of his nightmares.

It stood at least fifteen feet tall, had a twin tail with each end sharpened to a point, razor-sharp rows of teeth set in three heads with ruby red eyes that blazed with both intelligence and hunger.

"I'd suggest you climb, Conan. Fast!" Challenger sternly suggested.

Conan was about to curse Challenger when the monstrous beast which had been eyeing Challenger first, turned its attention to Conan now.

Conan leaped for the highest handhold he could reach and began climbing frantically. The beast behind him was quite sizable. If he didn't get at least another ten feet up and fast, one of those nasty heads would surely be snacking on his best parts.

Challenger scrambled as well, moving swiftly, but carefully at the same time. He had the better lead, so wasn't worried about the beast's reach, but he was worried about his friend. Though stubborn and hotheaded at times, he was truly a remarkable man with great writing talent and a genius for forensics, and imagination to die for. He looked back and saw Conan wasn't going to make it.

"Hurry, Conan. Hurry!"

Conan scrambled as fast as he could, but the beast was faster. Its huge mouth, filled with rows of razor-sharp teeth and a ghastly stinking breath opened to envelope him. Now it was ready to seize him from the mountain wall, a rope coiled over his backpack and tightened, and he swung away from the wall, screaming like a madman.

The beast's jaws slammed into the mountain wall, nearly knocking Challenger from his precarious perch above, but he managed to hang on, then resituate himself so he could swing Conan higher and out of the monster's reach.

Conan became a dangling carrot for the monster, who would swipe at Conan to eat him, shortly before he was jerked away and a bit higher.

"Damn you, Challenger! Either feed me to him or get me out of here!" Cursed Conan.

Challenger strained Conan's weight. He was almost equal to Challenger's body mass, even though shorter by a foot, then he grunted and made a Herculean effort and just as the beast launched itself upwards to seize Conan, he pulled him the rest of the way up and into his arms.

The beast's three heads snapped their jaws just inches from Conan's bottom before he was safely out of reach.

The two men eyed the beast below.

It bellowed its rage and frustration as both Conan and Challenger gasped for air and strength.

The beast paced below them, looking for a way up it could traverse.

"Just think, even if you could have managed to escape its mouth, those front feet, which look an awful lot like hands would have caught you."

"Don't remind me."

The beast suddenly looked at its front hands.

"You and your big mouth, Challenger."

"Not my intention at all."

Conan gave Challenger a sour look.

"It's not happy to have lost its meal, Challenger."

"Would you be?"

"Yes. I think I'd extremely poor eating."

Challenger laughed and helped Conan to a better grip on the mountain. "I suppose you would with that salty attitude of yours. Too much salt in a meal can be very disheartening."

The beast below looked to be going away, just looking back now and then at them, as if mourning for its missed meal.

"I don't like the look of that creature's gaze upon us, Challenger."

"Nor I."

They both began climbing upwards as fast as they could, almost recklessly, but just short of that, sending sprays of rock off the mountainside to bounce down below, where the beast turned around, then stormed the mountain wall with all its strength. At the last moment when it looked like it might smash into the side of the mountain, it made a tremendous leap. Its upper clawed feet, which resembled hands shot upwards as it sprung into the air.

Incredibly, it caught hold of the mountainside, with a roar of triumph began scaling the edifice below the two humans, its mouths open wide, saliva drooling between its enormous teeth and lips in anticipation of the meal it expected to obtain.

"Blast it all!" Conan cursed. "You said we were safe now."

"I said no such thing!"

"What?"

Challenger looked down. "Conan, please this is no time to be jesting. Our lives hang in the balance. The bloody beast is climbing after us!"

"Challenger, your boot is on my right hand."

"Sorry."

He lifted it and then began climbing again, this time more recklessly. Conan followed as swiftly as he could below him, urging every ounce of strength from his body. In minutes they'd managed to maintain their lead, but the beast was close behind. So close that both men could smell its foul breath on their heels.

Challenger paused once to pry at a stone, to pull it free and send it tumbling at the beast, who only flicked it away with one of its snouts, not slowing down for a second.

"Oh, Tosh!" Challenger cursed, and then pushed upwards, struggling to keep his aching muscles from giving out.

Conan was doing a little better, and much worse. Challenger could hear him gasping for air. He knew his friend would never make it. What could he do? What could he do?"

Then an idea flashed in his mind. He immediately dismissed it, but when he looked down, he saw that

Conan had fallen further behind and the beast was almost upon him.

"Oh, Bloody Hell!" Challenger cursed, then shrugged off his backpack and flung it at the beast, which was so intent on Conan the beast didn't see it coming. The backpack struck its left eye and blinded it. The beast let out a howl of rage and let go of the mountain face with one front paw, almost tumbling away.

Challenger crossed himself quickly, then let go of his handhold.

"Challenger no!" Conan cried out as his friend fell past him, arms out.

Conan turned about to look as Challenger fell, not to the earth far below, but upon the beast's middle snout. It roared like it had been violated in the worst conceivable way and with its remaining free paw broke it free and swung at him, at the same time as Challenger leaped for the mountainside.

The beast roared in rage and anger as it lost its grip on the mountainside and fell head over heels towards the ground below.

Challenger caught hold of the mountainside, but barely. The rock he held onto was crumbling beneath his grip.

“Challenger!” Conan called out to him.

Challenger felt his grip loosen more. He tried to strengthen it, but more rocks crumbled away. He began to slowly slide down. The rock below his grip was shattering. Soon, the whole thing would give away.

He wouldn’t survive a fall this far.

The grip gave way when the stone parted in three different directions.

He hollered angrily as he began to fall.

But before he had fallen an inch, a strong hand grabbed his arm and swung him back to the mountainside.

He looked up. Conan, red-faced, his eyes wide as small moons, smiled into his face. "You're not getting away from me that easily, you old gasbag!”

“If I’m a gasbag, what does that make you?” Challenger roared back.

“The man who is saving your bloody life!”

Challenger was lifted just enough and managed to grip the mountainside again. He righted himself properly. He swiped a hand across his forehead, which was bleeding.

"You're hurt." Conan pointed out.

"No, just my bloody pride, being rescued by an overweight sausage."

Conan burst into laughter.

Challenger grinned up at him. "I apologize for my former behavior."

Conan grinned back at him. "You saved my life twice. I'd say we're even."

"Hey!" Challenger hollered at him. "That's just today I'm counting, you bloody idiot!"

Conan smiled warmly and then reached a hand down.

He helped Challenger reach the first piton that Conan had hurriedly pounded into the mountainside and then as Conan climbed above him, driving fresh pitons into the mountain, he followed.

Conan laughed and then began scrambling up the mountain faster as more handholds, small cracks in the side of the mountain came into reach. He ignored his friend's curses below him.

It had turned out to be a good day after all. An exceptionally good day indeed. And now if only he could get home in time for a warm meal with his beloved wife.

"Jane!"

The Invisible Man

"Jane!"

His voice seemed empty and hollow as a pair of strong hands gripped his armpits and steadied him.

He opened his eyes, but the vision of his wife still hovered before him and of a man he had written. Professor Challenger.

The mountain climb caused his heart to pound in his ears. Beating to the tune and thrill of the adventure. The near capture by the monster.

How could it all be so real and yet be just a...*What?*

"It was so real," he exclaimed as he regained his balance once more.

He found himself stumbling forward.

Again, a pair of strong arms steadied him. He could smell perfume. And then he realized where he was again. And what his head was against.

Ms. Hudson.

Her bosom.

He immediately pulled back, almost falling.

She grabbed his hand to steady him.

He held on, but reluctantly.

"Mister Doyle!"

He looked up. He had to. But he couldn't face the impurity of his actions. He had placed his head against the bosom of another woman! It was humiliating!

"I am so sorry. I didn't mean to take advantage of you," he pleaded.

She grinned. "Believe me, when my husband returns from the pub, he leans against me much harder than that, Mister Doyle."

He gave her a relieved look. "I feel like such a cad for doing so."

"Give it no more thought."

"I'm so sorry to give you such a fright. I'm afraid I didn't rest much last night."

She gave him a look that told him she didn't believe a word of it. "You're sure? I can call a doctor for you."

He smiled patiently. "I am a doctor."

The crowd that had gathered about him burst into laughter and he then realized he had been the focus of many for the moment he had his incident.

He smiled at Ms. Hudson to soften her worried look. "I'm fine."

The other customers, who had begun to fret about his sudden stumbling, looked away and returned to their jewelry shopping. He felt both relieved and ashamed of the public performance he had just given. Now he knew how the Conan of his dream must have felt when intimidated by the rascal Professor Challenger.

His blood stirred at the thought of writing down such a story, but then he realized he didn't have that luxury of time anymore.

This last incident only pounded one more nail into the coffin of his future.

He returned to his mission this day, "About that piece of jewelry..."

"She's going to love it," that man's voice roared from behind him.

He felt a sudden surge of anger. He let out a short growling sound. What kind of cad would butt into a man's private conversation? And then vanish!

Ms. Hudson backed up in alarm.

Once more Arthur felt a wave of anger pass through him, and then subside. Who was this invisible man who kept irritating him?"

He turned around but saw no one.

"You are expecting someone?" Ms. Hudson asked. Her eyes were wide with fear again. He had to calm her down or this mission would fail miserably, just like his damned heart was doing.

"No. No. Not at all." He said in an almost apologetic voice.

He gestured towards the glass case they stood next to.

She caught his intent. "The jewelry? Are you sure? Perhaps you should rest some before..."

"No, no, no. I'm so sorry for frightening you, but yes. Yes, I would love to see it. Forgive my rude behavior. I have not been feeling well of late."

"I'm so sorry to hear that."

She gestured to her husband. "Charles!"

He came over.

Arthur could see the relief on her face when he did. He hadn't realized how much it had bothered her when he growled as he had. Or maybe she just didn't know what to do with the dying man in front of her.

He shivered at that thought.

Not yet! He thought, *Please God!*

"Please fetch Mister Doyle a comfortable chair. He is feeling a bit out of sorts."

Charles, her husband, gave her a warm smile and departed.

"You needn't have bothered," he growled before he could catch himself.

She backed up again.

He gave her a weak smile. "I am so sorry. I don't know what's come over me. Please forgive me. It shan't happen again," he said. He hoped! *God, no wonder I've written Watson so poorly. He reflects my emotional side. As Holmes does my intellectual.*

She held a hand up. "Don't apologize. Please." She gave him a knowing look, which for a moment reminded him of his wife, Jane, who knew what he was going through at any given moment and what to do to deal with it. It was as if she were peeling back the layers of what had been going on since he came into the shop and weighing them carefully on a scale of understanding. But it wasn't a cruel or unjust look, just a thoughtful and concerned one.

He respected that.

No wonder he had created Ms. Hudson in his stories after this woman. Even back when he first met her, he realized she was something special.

Charles returned with a chair. "Here you go, Mister Doyle. And I must say, it's a pleasure to serve you." He offered his hand after Arthur sat and Arthur shook it.

"Thank you. Your wife speaks well of you. And now I can see why."

Charles gave her a quick warm smile, Arthur a nod, and then departed to help another client.

Arthur returned his attention to Ms. Hudson, who laid a beautifully embroidered black box with golden threads lining it and a beautiful ruby swan on its top. “I believe this is the beauty you were warned about.”

He chuckled. “A kind warning at the worst.”

She smiled and then opened the box. He gasped. Inside was a beautiful pink pearl necklace, laid against a red velvet swatch of material. "This is called The Victorian Crown."

It was stunning. Pure, naturally pink pearls, rare and beautiful, were poised together along a golden wire, and silver wires twisted about it. Which opened at the crown to clasp a star-shaped sapphire of the greatest clarity and brilliance his eyes had ever fallen upon. He immediately knew he must have it.

He fell in love with it as deeply as if it were a mortal woman like his beloved Jane. It filled his heart with a glow it hadn’t felt for a long time.

"This is even more beautiful than the one that Professor Challenger found in the Caves of Destiny, the story where he travels to China to discover the truth behind the legends of snake dragons," he gasped without thinking.

“Sounds like a marvelous story.”

“Haven’t finished it yet.”

“Oh.”

“But I intend to…or...”

“Or?”

“No matter. I’m rambling.”

"Oh, I rather doubt that old man,” a strange, but familiar voice roared from behind him. “I know you quite well and this is not rambling, though you are quite well suited to it at times.”

A Mystery of Sorts

Arthur stiffened.

Arthur ignored the comment. He refused to be baited by this Invisible Man.

Ms. Hudson gave him a searching look, but he recovered quickly and with a smile said, "I am interested."

Another idea sprouted in his mind then. About a man who could walk anywhere and not be seen. An Invisible Man.

"Fascinating."

"What is, Mister Doyle?"

"Oh, nothing. Nothing at all."

But he was lying. He already had the idea for a story about an Invisible Man. A man who terrorized people as a way of building his self-confidence and proving his self-worth. The man would be loud, arrogant and most of all…annoying.

He smiled, and then glanced at the beautiful necklace once more, his eyes tracing its delicate beauty hungrily.

"Nice enough."

"I would love to wear it. I suspect any sane woman would. She would be the toast of society, and everyone would be adorably jealous of her good fortune," Ms. Hudson replied.

He looked into her eyes, and he knew she was quite aware that in his mind the sale was all but over. Still, for the good of appearances, and to hide his manly pride, he blustered, "The price seems somewhat..."

"High?"

"Yes, definitely that."

She smiled. "Perhaps we could manage to take a few pounds off the price. I would have to speak with Charles, of course."

"Of course."

She pulled a sales associate aside. "Please ask our manager if we can offer a discount on this fabulous piece of jewelry."

The sales associate nodded, was about to leave when she saw the necklace. "Oh blimey, that's the most precious and beautiful piece my eyes have ever laid upon!"

Ms. Hudson gave Arthur a "See, I told you so!" look and nodded.

The sales associate took off.

“Lovely weather,” he ventured, trying to salvage what dignity he had left. The sales associate had just blown that to kingdom come and back.

“Quite so,” she replied, a merry gleam in her eyes.

“I suppose it could rain before the day is over though.”

“Yes, it could.”

“She wasn't going to relent to him. He could see that. She knew he was in for the purchase, hook, line, and sinker. She was just giving him the courtesy of salvaging his manly pride.

God, she was so much like the Ms. Hudson of his stories, he thought.

“The pearls seem a bit more opaque than usual.”

“None like them.”

“I’m not sure about the wire.”

“It has been tested for strength. It would take two grown men tugging at both ends to snap it.”

“Rugged, hey?”

“Quite so.”

He was saved from the savage verbal beating she was giving him, by her husband, Charles.

“I see you are enjoying our splendid piece my wife has shown you?”

"It is quite lovely!" Arthur commented, trying to sound not quite sure, even though his voice trembled with enthusiasm.

Ms. Hudson nodded and gave her husband, Charles, who was nearby, a knowing smile.

Arthur couldn't stand it any longer. They both knew he wanted it; they were just waiting for him to say it aloud.

Arthur finally managed to blurt out his thoughts. He was determined to design his path through this purchasing decision. "Of course, the price must be right as well."

"Naturally." She told him, her smile warning him that it must match the quality of the necklace.

Charles nodded. "We would expect no less on such a perfect piece of jewelry priced at such a profoundly fair price."

"Five hundred pounds."

Charles reacted as if struck in the face, his eyes widening in horror.

Ms. Hudson turned away to hide her smile. She knew this was just a manly game between her husband now and Arthur. The deal was done between them. Now they only had to agree and shake hands.

Arthur, however, felt his heart pounding in his throat. Five hundred pounds!

It was scandalous.

Never in his life had he paid so much for a piece of fine jewelry.

He felt like a sailor stranded on a desert island for a moment.

"Just do it, you old windbag!" The invisible man roared at him.

Arthur was so startled that he blurted out, "I am prepared to place in your hands in the next thirty seconds five one hundred-pound notes. Not a shilling more."

He crossed his arms over his pounding heart and grimaced. "That's my final offer!"

Ms. Hudson appeared shocked at his outburst. She glanced at Charles.

"Perhaps we should consider his...umm...offer?"

Arthur smiled triumphantly, "But of course, speak with your husband," he replied with a smile, smelling a victory in his grasp. Knowing that the manager was already but a few feet away was comforting, as well as disconcerting. Perhaps he had bid too high on the piece.

But something inside him told him otherwise. He waited patiently for the arrival of the man.

"You did the right thing, old man," the invisible man told him.

"Shut up!"

Ms. Hudson and Charles, who had been walking away, turned back, questions on their faces.

"I'm sorry, rehearsing an idea for my next story."

They nodded and walked off.

"She's going to always remember this day, Conan. I'm proud of you," the invisible man said in a much quieter voice.

"I don't need an invisible man to prop up my ego, sir, wherever in the hell you may be or from?"

"Oh, I'm real enough."

Arthur swung around.

No one was even close to him.

Though some of the clients were examining him as if he had gone quite mad. He had been speaking quite loudly.

So, he did his best to be patient, bide his time and hold his tongue, though it unnerved him to do so. He kept feeling like someone was quite near to him and chuckling at him. Though why he should have felt that way he couldn't say for certain.

He took out his pocket watch and glanced at the time. He repeated this a bit later. Ten minutes.

Even the invisible man was silent and that unnerved him even more for some reason. Maybe he was losing his mind.

As time continued to go by, he began to doubt himself, feeling that perhaps he had overplayed his hand.

He glanced about but couldn't see the couple anywhere. This time his heart was pounding for another reason. Fear. Fear he would lose his bid. And strangely enough, he truly did not want to lose this precious gift for his wife.

Maybe he had been too rigid. Perhaps he should have offered more. After all, his time was extremely limited in this.

He quickly quashed the next word that had begun to explode into his min...*World.*

Then he heard Ms. Hudson and Charles chatting warmly as they approached him from a direction in the back. Approaching. But slowly. Her husband was responding, also in muted, but soft tones. They were respecting his offer at least, he thought. And not dismissing it outright.

He pondered the beauty that lay before him again. He allowed his right forefinger to caress the beautiful jewel crowning the necklace. It was so remarkably radiant. He felt almost as if he were gazing into the eye of God for a moment.

He held up the necklace to peer through the crown jewel.

He gasped.

He shut his eyes to stop the turmoil and dizziness he suddenly felt.

For a moment, he saw the outline of a very tall man next to him. And a smile. No face, just a smile. Blast it all, what was going on? But he didn't have time to answer his question; he lost consciousness of the jewelry store entirely, the sound of the approaching manager and Ms. Hudson fading away, along with the voices of the other customers.

He could no longer feel the counter he was against or the floor he stood upon.

A brilliant white light engulfed him, and he was spun off God only knew where!

Mount Sinai

Professor Challenger wiped at his bushy beard, and in the process swept about twenty nasty little flies that were huddled there sucking at the sweat that had accumulated there. He swore when they flocked away, then focused again on the tablet set in the stone of the mountain cliff face he was hanging from, secured by several large ropes that descended from above.

"Anything?" Conan asked from above him.

He shook his mangy hair and grimaced. The blasted tablet was indecipherable as far as he could tell. It wasn't Aramaic, though it should have been as it was from the same time, and he was hanging from Mount Sinai, which was about 7,497 feet high. He and his companion had ascended from the eastern side, to skirt the Egyptians who were guarding that area at the time. They had been very protective of the mountain for some time since the last Religious Wars of the Twenties.

"The blasted tablet keeps changing every fifteen minutes, just as I'm about to decipher it." Challenger roared at his colleague above, Conan. The famous English Arthur whom he had rescued from death in his original world so that he could be a part of the real-life he had written so famously about.

"Shall I come down?"

"No!" Challenger shot back. "I'm going to take a rub, then return. Drop my satchel to me."

A moment later a satchel descended on the end of a rope. He clasped it to him, then reached inside and pulled out a sheet of clay paper. He very firmly pressed it into the tablet's face. Smoothed it over with a palm, and then gently eased it free, so as not to tear its delicate surface.

"Drat!" He cursed. The paper had two sets of languages imprinted into it.

"Something wrong?" Conan asked, peering over the edge that Challenger dangled from.

"The damned tablet changed as I pressed it."

"Oh," Conan said, not sure what else to say.

Challenger dug into his satchel, after stashing the first paper into a pocket of his jacket, then reached for another paper. The rope tying the satchel to it slipped free and the effort of opening it again caused it to fly outwards. He grabbed for it so vigorously that Conan screamed in surprise above, as he had been helping to anchor Challenger's weight.

Conan flew downwards, barely holding onto the other end of the rope as Challenger ascended the other direction on his section.

The satchel flew into the distant abyss of space below them.

"Oh, buggers!" Challenger cried out as he flew upwards, madder that he had lost the satchel, then the fact that his and Conan's lives appeared to be in danger.

At the last possible moment, when it seemed like he would fly over the edge, and Conan flies free, He dug in his boots with the iron spikes in them and caused them both to stop. Conan swung outwards from the cliff face, his face pale as a ghost and screaming.

The British Museum

The Curator examined the length of metal laid upon the examination table before him. Oxford had a very elaborate forensics laboratory. One that Holmes had availed himself of many a time in the past and probably would again in the future. He and the Curator, Sir James Avery, were both puzzled by the metal. James because it defied his chemicals, and Holmes because it defied logic.

James grabbed a vial of yellowish liquid and looked at Holmes, who nodded.

"This should separate enough of the metal for me to be able to put it into a spectral analyzer. James intoned, as he delicately swabbed a portion of the vial on the tip of the metal. It began to fizz like crazy.

James clapped his hands. "This is the last resort, and it usually works when all else fails."

"Hydrofluoric Acid, I resume," Holmes commented.

"Precisely."

The fizzing stopped finally, and James raised his magnifying glass to examine the surface of the metal. He made a distressed sound and then said with a tone like a child who has lost his favorite plaything. "It's perfect."

"How so?"

James looked at Holmes. "The metal. It's perfect. Not a flaw. The acid didn't disturb a single molecule as far as I can see."

"That's impossible, isn't it?"

James nodded. "No known metal to man can resist Hydrofluoric Acid entirely. None!"

Holmes nodded, and then picked up the medical bag he had carried the metal in for the examination and placed it on the tabletop.

James put a hand on the bag. "Leave it!"

"The bag?"

"No, the metal. I must find out what this is made of."

Holmes hefted the metal and slid it into the bag, resealing the bag afterward.

"Perhaps another time."

He headed for the door at the back of the room.

James hurried after him, like a little child pursuing candy. "When?"

Holmes stopped and looked at James. James' face fell. "Oh."

"Sorry. Sir James. But I'm not authorized to give out such information."

"The Queen again."

Holmes said nothing. He opened the door, then gave James a fleeting smile and exited.

James sighed, then rushed to the back of the room and picked up a telephone. Its receiver glows bright Tesla red and he spoke into it. “Give me the Ministry of War. What do you mean, who is this? It’s Sir James Avery, that’s who. Now give me the Ministry, you dolt!”

221 B Baker Street

Watson found Holmes perched in his favorite chair by the fireplace, a lap blanket across his legs, reading a book when he returned home from his meeting with Inspector Bloodstone.

"Holmes," he greeted.

Holmes nodded but kept reading.

Watson, knowing Holmes' propensity to get lost in himself when doing research, headed back downstairs to the kitchen where he found Ms. Hudson pulling out from one of the Royal Line of stoves, which are heated by bright red Tesla Coils, a tray of scones. "Evening, dear." He said, giving her a light peck on her cheek.

She smiled at him, then laid the tray on the tiled counter to her right and began scooping the scones off onto a large silver platter. "How was your day, John?"

"Simply..." He sighed. "Boring. Utterly. Utterly boring."

She laughed. Came over and gave him a big hug from behind. "You big Teddy Bear. You always say that and then go back for more."

He sighed again. "Some men are just a glutton for punishment, I guess."

She laughed, then plucked a date from the bowl beside the scones and held it in front of his lips. He looked at her. "I don't like dates."

"Open wide."

He was going to refuse until he saw the look in her eyes. And like the good man he was he recognized defeat knocking at his door and let it in. She pushed the date into his mouth, and he took a bite.

"Sherlock's not in the mood for playing, I take it." She asked with bemusement.

He shook his head and was about to say something when she popped the rest of the date into his mouth.

"You need it." She told him.

He gave her a quizzical look. "Your work is starting to sour your disposition."

He scowled. "I'll have you know I am not in the least bit sour about anything!" He exclaimed.

"John, I know you better than that."

He shrugged and she handed him a new date. "Eat it!"

Without questioning, he ate it. It was quite good, he thought to himself, and then reached over for a third. She slapped his hand. "Don't want to spoil your supper."

He shook his head and then had to laugh. "Sometimes I don't know why I put up with you."

She pinched his cheeks and gave him a light kiss on his forehead. "But of course, you do."

She opened the oven door, where a sizzling pot of stew was about to boil away its contents. The aroma struck Watson and he knew immediately that it was time to eat. It smelled wonderful.

"Beef and broccoli, just like you like it." She told him and then used two oven mittens to retrieve the pot and place it on a large silver tray. She placed some slices of bread around its base, then sticks of carrot and celery. "Take that up for me, will you, dear?"

He nodded and lifted the tray carefully. He had no intention of spoiling this meal or any other. Ms. Hudson's meals were the highlight of each day, and of course, her wonderful personality, which caused him to smile.

She grabbed the tray of scones, set it down on the opposite counter, where a teapot sat. Sat that on the tray, then a small pot of honey and spoons, she swept up the stairs after Watson. She caught up with him as he set his tray down on their dining table in the sitting room. It was clustered with notes that Sherlock had been making, but he deftly removed them into a stash which he tossed onto an empty chair and helped Watson set the table alongside Ms. Hudson.

"It almost feels like Christmas." Ms. Hudson said cheerily.

"That's because it is.... almost Christmas," Watson told her.

She giggled.

Holmes smiled, but after he averted his face. At times like these, he sometimes regretted not having a wife, but also at times like these he didn't. He still had the hope that someday he might have a child, but for now, the work was enough. And his friendship with John was not to fill the empty times since he no longer fell back into his chemical misuse anymore.

Though at times when he did his research and was exposed to the chemicals again, he felt the devil of a temptation at such times to try it once more, just to see if it was what he remembered, then he'd remember John's pleading voice in his head, asking him to stop destroying himself, to lean on him instead or anyone, but that dratted drug and then he would smile and let it go. But sometimes...

He didn't care what any rich man or crime lord thought about wealth and its comforts; the true comforts of life were friendship. Nothing else even came close.

They sat down to eat.

When they were finished, Holmes gathered his notes to study again.

"I say, Holmes, any word yet of Challenger and Doyle?"

"Not as yet."

Almost as if on cue, the front door below gave a loud rapping sound.

Ms. Hudson sat her tea down to get to the door, but Watson stopped her. "Let me. Enjoy your tea, my dear."

She gave him a sweet smile and sighed with pleasure as she continued to sip her tea. It had been an especially long day because she had been knitting a sweater for both John and Sherlock and had to do that between her normal duties, which left her precious little time to complete the knitting. But they still had a few days until Christmas.

"Ah, Harry!" Sherlock cried out before he stepped into view from the stairs.

Harry paused. "How did you know it was me?"

"Your steps. You step two, pause one, step two, pause one, then stomp your left foot."

Harry gave him a surprised look. "You have remarkable hearing, Holmes."

"News of Challenger, I presume?" Asked Holmes.

Watson sat next to Ms. Hudson as Harry pulled up a chair next to Holmes.

"May I?" He asked Ms. Hudson as he reached for a teacup.

"Oh, where are my manners?" She asked herself, then jumped up and poured him tea. "You must be famished what with all the cold…?" She paused.

He smiled gratefully. "Actually, I hadn't time for dinner, but if…"

She touched his shoulder lightly. "Harry, no indisposition at all, I'll be right back John, would you like something as well?"

Watson looked across at Holmes, who held a hand up to indicate he wasn't interested. "No, dear. We're both fine."

Ms. Hudson was heard descending and then the sound of her footsteps vanished.

"Thank you!" Harry said to Sherlock.

"Something untoward has happened?"

"You know it is so. They would never stay out of communications this long."

Watson eyed the Christmas tree in the corner with its Tesla light bulbs twinkling. "Ever the Christmas, never the joy." He rose. "I'll see to transportation."

Holmes nodded, and then looked into Harry's eyes. "Foul play?"

"I can't tell. My magic blocked."

Sherlock grimaced, his thoughts assigning worst-case scenarios and best case. "We need a strong party."

"I agree. I'll take care of it."

He got up and began descending the stairs just as Ms. Hudson was ascending with a warm meal. "But I just got your meal prepared, Harry."

Harry grabbed half a sandwich, nodded, then smiled at her and hurried down the staircase.

"Sherlock, whatever happened up here while I was...."

Watson came into the sitting room with a rifle. "John!"

He blushed. "We're ah..."

Sherlock rose and helped Ms. Hudson with her tray. He sat her down and investigated her face. "I'm sorry, dear Ms. Hudson, but we have a bit of an emergency. Can you make sure that whoever calls for us while we're gone gets our message?"

"Certainly." She gave Watson a panicked look. He looked away, not wanting to get into it just then.

Holmes quickly scribbled a note with his ink and pen, dusted the paper off, then folded it and sealed it. "I expect you'll see more than one visitor anxious to find us. Once the seal is broken you may give them the information verbally."

This was his way of saying that he couldn't discuss it at that moment, but that all would be revealed in the note.

Watson came out again from the back with a heavy coat, a traveling bag for himself and Holmes. Holmes took his cape and hat, and coat, then went for the stairs. "See you downstairs?" He asked Watson.

"In a minute," Watson replied.

Holmes nodded and descended from view.

Watson set his rifle and bag down and put his hands out. Ms. Hudson stood her ground, scowling at him. "I won't budge until you let me know what's going on!" She demanded.

He sighed. "My dear, I'd love nothing better, but for your safety and your sanity, I dare not."

She looked hurt. He went to her and enfolded her in his arms. "I'm sorry. You'll understand once this is all over. We need you to hold down the fort."

He pulled away. She wiped an eye. "Don't I always?"

He gave her a quick kiss on the forehead, then grabbed his rifle and bag, and descended after Holmes. He closed the flat door and stepped carefully to the sidewalk, making sure he didn't move too fast on the icy pavement, or he'd fall.

Holmes glanced over at him and then nodded. A moment later a Tesla Cab came down Baker Street and pulled over. Harry was already in the back, a huge black case in his lap and a wand attached tucked into the inside of his jacket.

"Prepared are we, Harry?" Watson asked with a somber smile and sat next to him.

"Always," Harry said with a grim look as Sherlock climbed in opposite him and sat down.

Harry knocked against the back of the cab, and it sped off.

"I just pray we're in time," Harry said.

Both Holmes and Watson gave him an alarmed look.

Train Station

The Tesla train slid into its berth beside the Train Station as quietly as a mouse, slipping out from its hole to sneak some cheese from the kitchen. The only thing that alerted Watson, who was napping with his hat over his eyes, was the sound of the doors opening with a loud SWISH.

"What?" He groaned, pulling his hat back to look.

Harry, seated beside him, still had his eyes closed. He was meditating, or so he said, but Watson suspected that he was sleeping too as he could hear a light snoring sound coming from his friend.

As he stood Holmes stepped into his view with a flask. He held it out for Watson, who thanked him and took a swig. He made a face and spit it out! "Bollocks, Holmes! That's not Sherry!"

Holmes smiled. "You need to wake up, not go to sleep."

Watson shook his head, wiped his mouth, and then handed the flask back. "Tea is for crumpets, biscuits, and scones, not to wake up with!"

Harry yawned, stretched, and then stood up. He looked bright and eager to meet the day. "Watson giving you a tough time again, Sherlock?"

"Always," Sherlock said with a gentle smile.

Watson made a sound of disgust and headed back into the station. "I'll be back with a proper wake me up in a moment."

A Conductor stepped onto the passenger platform. He raised a bullhorn. "All aboard for the Direct. All aboard for the Direct!"

Watson cursed, then to the smiles of his two friends, picked up his travel bag and followed them onto the train. They went down several compartments until they reached Section C. Harry opened a sliding door and they scooted inside, storing their bags in overhead hampers with straps to hold them down.

Harry settled in next to the window and Holmes on the other. Watson didn't sit down."

"Sit down, Watson. We'll be leaving soon."

Watson shrugged. "Not until I have..."

The Direct gave a loud whistle and then began to move, at first slowly, then swiftly picking up speed. Watson sat back down and crossed his arms in front of his chest. "Some days just weren't meant to be."

Harry laughed.

Sherlock took out a map and spread it on a table that folded out from beneath their bench. He leaned over it and dabbed a finger on an obvious mountain. "Mount Sinai. Our destination."

"Why in the world did Challenger go to that God-forsaken place in the first of it?" Watson demanded.

"Excalibur," Sherlock spoke lightly.

Watson looked up; his attention caught. "Isn't that what the metal was you were investigating, Holmes?"

"Indeed. But I have only the blade. The pommel, the grip, and the guard are there."

"Why?" Watson demanded, genuinely interested now.

"Because they are too powerful when brought together," Harry answered instead.

Watson looked at him. "And just why in the bloody hell would that be? It's just metal."

Holmes made a sound of dismissal. "My dear Watson, nothing about Excalibur is ordinary or just metal."

Holmes explained what his forensics study had revealed and even Harry was entranced.

Watson rubbed the stubble on his face and then yawned. "Okay, I'll give you that, it's not that ordinary. But the ancient Brits had some surprisingly good metal workers."

"Oh, and more," Holmes commented drily, an amused smirk on his face.

"What more?"

The door to their compartment swung open and Lord Graystone stood framed in the light pouring in from outside. “Am I too late to join the party?”

Watson jumped up and grabbed his hand. “It’s so good of you to come!”

Lord Graystone smiled. “My pleasure. Lady Shareen is busy with a charitable event in the India Isles with Captain Nemo, so she won’t be joining us.”

Lord Graystone shook everyone else’s hands, but instead of sitting down on a bench, he elected to drop to his heels and sit on those. When he did his very white highly starched shirt popped its lapel buttons and top button and his bronzed chest came into view and its muscles.

They ignored the view, as they’d seen him unclothed before, which was often when he was in his homeland of Fairie.

Holmes gestured to Lord Graystone. He stood up and jabbed the map where Holmes had touched it earlier. “Mount Sinai is a ley line focus for that area of the world. It holds great mystical forces within it, hence Moses and other biblical wonders of that area.”

Harry agreed. “Furthermore, a splendid entrance at almost any point into Fairie.”

“This brings us to the crux of this problem.” Lord Graystone added. “Here.” He stabbed the India Isles. “Here, is another rather large focus and one that has been exposited quite recently, I’m afraid, by a not so wonderful guest.”

“Moriarty.” Harry burst out.

“Exactly.” Holmes agreed. “But not just the one.”

Lord Graystone nodded. “Since our failure to retrieve James, the parallel worlds Moriarty’s have been rebuilding their strength.”

“And you know this how?” Watson demanded, fearing he already knew the answer.

“Because I have seen the three.”

“Three!” Watson exclaimed. “But I thought one was eliminated.”

Harry waved his hands and Watson looked at him. “It was a homunculus. A duplicate made of clay and imbued with temporary life and personality. Merely a chess piece for the masterminds in their plot.”

Holmes templed his fingers in thought and nodded.

“It would seem that the game is far afoot from what we thought.”

"But what I don't understand," Watson asked. "Is how this is having anything to do with the disappearance of Professor Challenger and Arthur?"

"Everything." Holmes declared. "You see, my dear Watson, when we dealt with only the one mastermind, his chess pieces were of a lesser scale, but now that we are dealing with a far great consortium of such brilliant minds, then we are dealing with a problem of a much larger magnitude."

"In other words, we're about to have our arses handed to us!" Harry said with a smirk.

Lord Graystone laughed and clapped Harry on the back. "Leave it up to Harry to find the upside of things."

Watson sighed. "More like the downside in this case. But still, I don't understand what Fairie has to do with Mount Sinai other than it being a nexus for entry there."

Holmes leaned forward and looked into Watson's eyes. "I believe, Excalibur is an excellently laid trap to acquire our services."

"What?" Harry and Watson cried out.

Lord Graystone's eyes narrowed. "You think they're playing us to get hold of the full sword."

"Exactly." Holmes agreed. "Furthermore, by having the two hostages, we fall into a very difficult trap of morality."

"Which is?" Watson asked.

"Whether we sacrifice our friends for the greater good of the Empire..." He paused. "...And the world."

Professor Challenger

Challenger groaned when he awoke. His back was killing him. He rolled over and gained great relief and then realized he was lying on a stone floor with stone walls, no windows, and a single door with no window as well.

"Arthur?" He demanded of the empty cell.

Nothing. He stood up, and then almost fell again. What had happened? He thought, as his senses struggled to regain normalcy. He had been helping his friend with their discovery when everything had gone crazy. He remembered falling and falling and hearing his friend's scream of dismay, and then nothing.

He leaned against a wall, gathering his strength. *"Where am I?"* He mused.

He heard a kind of slithering sound near his feet and dropped to his knee. He saw a tiny crevice in the wall and an exceedingly small head peeking out. It was a mouse. When he didn't attack it, it bravely came out a bit further and eyed him thoughtfully. "Well, who do we have here?" He asked the mouse.

The mouse squeaked in alarm, frightened by Challenger's harsh voice.

Challenger sighed. "At least he…has a way out."

"Psst." A voice came from the crevice.

Challenger thought he was hearing things.

"Hello, anybody there?" Came the voice again. It sounded familiar, but different somehow.

Challenger dropped to eye-level with the opening. "Yes. I'm here."

"Challenger?"

"The only one." He blasted back, getting annoyed at the little game going on.

"It's Conan!"

Challenger sighed with relief. "You're alive."

"Abundantly obvious, wouldn't you say?" Came Conan's retort.

"Are you alright?"

"Again, abundantly…"

"Yes, I know obvious. But are you hurt; I remember nothing of what happened?"

"We are in Fairie."

"How do you know…?"

Challenger froze as the wall before him extruded outwards and the mouse he had seen earlier investigated his face but now made of stone and whiskery barbs of granite rock. "This is how." The face said.

"Oh," Challenger said.

"Challenger?"

"Nothing. I believe you." Challenger said, barely able to breathe. He had been so frightened that he was sure his hair was pure white now.

He fell onto his behind like a small child and tried to catch his breath.

"Challenger?"

"I'm…here," Challenger said finally between gasps.

Conan hissed. "Watch out for the walls."

"I know," Challenger said his voice barely audible.

Then a huge rumbling sound came, and the floor began to vibrate as if something quite large were moving outside.

"What in heaven's name is that?" Challenger cried out, jumping to his feet, and reaching for his pistol. But it was gone.

"Whatever happens next, don't fight back!" Conan warned.

Challenger heard a grinding sound and the tiny crevice filled up. He turned his head towards the door as it rumbled open to reveal this huge Troll, with double tusks hanging from either side of its mouth, which was drooling spittle. It had hair on its nose so long it made a tiny beard and the creature had festooned it with tiny ornaments made of a glittering metal of some kind.

Its ears hung down almost to the floor and were pierced multiple times by tiny daggers that were bent around to close off their loops. Its hands were covered with warts that had tiny faces on them. Each face grimaced as if in pain and they appeared to dislike each other as they tried to pull in any direction but their neighbors.

The Troll boxed his warts. "Cuts it yous, yous guys!" He bellowed.

Challenger almost fell to the floor. The Troll's breath was nauseating. It stunk of sewage and rotten vegetables. Tiny worms clung to and wriggled between their wide teeth, writhing as if to warn anyone off.

It wore no shoes. It didn't need them. Its feet were half the size of a grown man, and its toenails were deadly weapons with claw shapes chiseled to fine points. Anyone kicked by this creature would sure die almost instantly from the impact, if not for the actual stabbings themselves.

Its legs were bare to its midsection which was covered by a thick, leather jerkin woven from some kind of reptilian creature because the leather had scales on it.

The legs were thick as wine barrels and had multiple wars along their sides, like the lines of a soldier's pants, and were bloody red.

Its skin was a deep vermillion with streaks of olive green.

Its eyes were the color of honey but with strange flecks that seemed to always move about, as if alive on their own.

Its hair grew only from the back of its head and then formed a large knot of bone and skin that fell down its back to the ground and trailed behind it.

It watched Challenger's observations patiently for a moment, then scratched its huge bulbous nose with a scaled fingernail, and then its eyes, huge as large silver platters, looked down at Challenger. "You."

"Me?" Challenger replied like a dumb school child.

"Come!"

The Troll grinned next. "Or eats you!"

Challenger scrambled to get out the door, which wasn't easy as the Troll filled up most of the doorway. He managed somehow and squeezed out into the corridor, which was long, dark, and foreboding. Torches burned about every dozen yards. As the Troll gestured that way Challenger went in that direction only to find out that the torches were not made of wood, but human skulls with oil pooled on their insides. The eyes, however, still existed and they all looked at him pleadingly as he passed.

"What a dark place!" Challenger commented.

The Troll said. "A lovely place for a walk."

Challenger shuddered then because he knew he had fallen into hell itself, if not Fairie.

Lord Graystone

Lord Graystone found no problem with the food of the bazaar as they hiked along its wide passage where numerous Egyptian peddlers sold everything from chocolate roaches to the rarest of mummy soup. An item that made Harry nauseous when he realized what it was. He was about to sample it from the vendor, it smelled so good when Graystone's bronzed fist clasped his hand. "Don't."

Harry looked at him.

Graystone eyed the vendor. "Which tomb did you steal this from?"

The Vendor pretended he didn't hear.

Graystone rose to his full height over the smaller man and showed his canines. "I don't like repeating myself."

The Vendor let out a shriek and ran off, knocking over his vat of mummy stew.

That was when Harry saw the mummy wrapped at the bottom of the pot.

He had turned pale, and then almost vomited on the spot if Watson hadn't quickly put a fragrance in front of his nose. He inhaled it deeply, and then pulled away.

"Thanks!"

Watson smiled. "I did the same thing the first time I was here. Mummy stew is not for the weak of heart."

"Or for the strong," Graystone said fiercely. "It's a form of cannibalism. If this were my land, I would have him hauled off to jail, instead of letting him run off to sell the drudge again somewhere else on another day."

Holmes eyed Graystone. "I've never seen you so adamant about something being wrong."

Graystone shrugged. He was wearing only his loincloth now and his great bronzed shoulders and chest muscles moved like waves across his body as they flexed and rippled. "People do not eat people." He said with a tone of finality that caused Holmes to turn to Watson,

"You and Harry see if you can find the supplies, I spoke to you about earlier."

Harry nodded and he and Watson went in a different direction through the Bazaar, while Holmes and Graystone remained where they were. Holmes looked at Graystone.

"You are worried about Lady Shareen?"

"How did you know that?" Graystone asked.

"First, you are not wearing the proper clothing and

second you never get mad at Watson. Third, it's been three days since you've heard from your wife."

Holmes raised a hand before Graystone could comment further. "And I know the last because I have not heard from Madame Curie either and they were together."

Graystone's eyes lit up. "You think this is all part of the same abduction!"

Holmes said nothing. "What I think isn't important. What is important is the truth and that we must ascertain as quickly as possible and I suspect you are capable of that, are you not, which is why you shed your clothing."

Graystone nodded and in front of about ten shoppers and seven merchants he ran several steps, then leaped to the top of the nearest roof, which was a good twenty feet up. He looked back and waved at Holmes, then ran, leaping from rooftop to rooftop. Even as he did the skies overhead began to change color and boil with clouds that swirled in and out of each other.

Lord Graystone made a huge leap at the same time as something large and scary flew from the clouds and swept beneath him. Graystone clutched at the neck of the King of Dragons who had come for him and flew off to the North.

When Holmes looked down again, he saw shoppers and merchants all on the ground praying to Allah to protect them. He smiled and then continued down the Bazaar as if nothing unusual at all had happened.

Professor Moriarty

"Sits." The Troll drooled to Challenger as he stepped into a rather large chamber with an exceptionally low ceiling. Corrupt moss, which gave off a hideous odor, hung from the ceiling and grew from the walls. A huge iron-grated window looked outside into a very dark sky, devoid of any color or significance.

He watched the Troll nearly bang its head on the ceiling as it backed out of the chamber. He almost laughed at the ridiculousness of it, but as its eyes never left his own, he kept his face straight. No one wants a Troll angry with them.

"You're smarter than I gave you credit for, Professor Challenger."

Challenger turned around and a tall man with familiar features stepped from the shadows. He held an umbrella in his left hand and a cane in the right.

"James is that you!"

The tall man broke into laughter and opened his arms. "Come give me a hug!"

Challenger felt a cold chill rush up and down his spine. This man was not James, and his hug would be anything but a happy one.

"I think I shall not, if you don't mind, Moriarty," Challenger said with a growing sense of anger that he could barely contain. *"What did it take to kill this man forever? To rid the universe of his despicable accursed presence?"* He thought to himself.

Moriarty stepped further out and as he did torches, or rather skulls that looked like torches, lit up the chamber. Moriarty stepped to the center and stomped a foot on a five-pointed star. The floor began to shake, and a stone throne rose from the floor, forming as it rose into a throne shaped like a pentacle with five stars at each point.

Moriarty stepped painfully towards the throne, his face trying to hide the pain, but failing. "As you can see, Professor, I am but half the man I used to be, thanks to your friend.... James!"

Challenger said nothing. He didn't think he was truly expected to comment, and any comment he made could just usher in more pain for him and his good friend, Conan. So, he remained silent and watched the sinister man sit down, adjusting his body as if his bones were about to break if not careful.

Moriarty completed his adjustments and then eyed Challenger thoughtfully for a long time.

To Challenger, it felt like the room temperature dropped about twenty degrees at that moment and he could swear his breath became visible. Magic! He thought. Dark magic! Very dark magic!

Moriarty smiled. "I see you, unlike your scholarly friend; recognize the boundaries of your environment."

Challenger still said nothing.

Moriarty leaned forward on his cane and surveyed Challenger closely as if looking for a weak spot he might penetrate. Finally, he sat back on his throne and relaxed.

"We did not kill your friend, you know." Moriarty finally spoke.

"We know that," Challenger answered. "But not because you didn't try!" He accused. He immediately regretted saying those words, as that was the challenge Moriarty had been seeking in the first place.

"Perhaps we shall have to try harder next time."

Challenger's eyes narrowed. "You know where he is?"

Moriarty ignored the question. "I need help."

Challenger stood there in shock. Help? From him?

Moriarty smiled. "Oh, the good Professor is shocked that the lowly scoundrel should seek his advice."

Challenger wanted to explode at that moment but bit his tongue instead.

Moriarty began clapping. "Very good, Professor. Your composure does you well."

Challenger remained silent.

Moriarty leaned forward so that he was within several inches of Challenger's reach. He seriously considered going for the man's throat, but the grunt of the Troll behind him reminded him of his captivity once more and the consequences of overt action.

"You want to kill me." Moriarty smiled. "Once again, I commend you on your composure, but the eyes never lie. They are the windows to the soul. I'm sure you've heard that euphemism before."

"What...do...you...want?" Challenger said between clenched teeth.

"For a man famous for his vile temper, I'm surprised at your alacrity this morning." Moriarty decreed happily, looking ready to clap again, but deciding against it, instead gestured to the Troll.

"Bring the prisoner."

The Troll exited the room.

"Oh, and less you determine that I'm safe game now."

Moriarty clapped his hands in a cadence of ones and twos. Immediately slots opened in all the walls and arrows stuck from them.

"I don't suppose I have to point out the gravity of your situation." He laughed.

Challenger shook his head, even though his body was trembling with even greater anger now. This man was insufferable and a scoundrel...and unfortunately...quite mad!

Moriarty leaned forward again. "I have found a map. It was not in particularly decent shape, so I had to inscribe it on the most unlikely of places to secure its memory."

"And?"

"And I wish you to decipher it for me."

"What is it a map of?"

"The location of Excalibur."

Challenger was shocked for the second time that morning. "But we've...."

"Already found the pieces?"

Challenger nodded, unable to speak.

"What you found were the remains of the first sword."

"First?"

Moriarty shook his head. "And I thought you were always one to do his due diligence before galloping off over the horizon. "

Moriarty waited for the impact of his words to settle within Challenger and then continued. "There are three swords."

Challenger was shocked yet again. "Three! Oh, dear, God!"

"God has nothing to do with it."

"But three..."

Moriarty smiled triumphantly. "Do I have your attention now?"

"Undivided," Challenger admitted reluctantly.

"Good. Ah, here comes the map now." Moriarty commented.

Challenger turned around to see one of the most beautiful women he had ever seen walk into the room just ahead of the Troll.

"The map?" Challenger asked.

Moriarty motioned to the troll, and it spun the woman around, revealing an unbelievably detailed map on her back.

Challenger exploded! "This is monstrous! I refuse to help you in any way!"

Moriarty smiled in a gentlemanly way. "You sure I can't persuade you otherwise?"

"Bloody hell, you can't!" Challenger swore.

Moriarty spoke to the Troll. "You can tear off her right arm. I don't need her arm to read the map." He smiled at Challenger. "Not much of her I need for anything. So, we'll start with the basics, and work our way from there, shall we?"

The woman broke free and flung herself at Challenger's feet. "Help him! I beg you!"

Challenger felt this was a trap and said nothing. He had no intentions of harming this beautiful woman.

The Troll grabbed her arm with one large, gnarled hand and then the other.

He began pulling.

The woman screamed in pain.

Challenger went white as a ghost. "I'll do it, Damnit!"

The Troll kept pulling. The woman screamed louder.

"Moriarty! You stop it now, or you'll never get my help!"

Moriarty nodded to the Troll, and it let go.

The woman fell into Challenger's arms, and he almost plunged to the stone floor but caught his balance and hefted her up into his arms. Her eyes were still wide with terror and pain. She lost consciousness.

He looked over at Moriarty.

"I expect results."

"I expect food," Challenger responded, his face set. He wouldn't budge on this point.

Moriarty rose from his throne, and it descended back to the floor, leaving no trace of where it had been before.

He wagged a long, crooked nail at Challenger. "I will return in an hour."

Challenger almost exploded again, but when he looked into Moriarty's eyes, he saw nothing but death chilling there. He nodded, not trusting himself to speak.

Moriarty turned to the Troll. "Bring food and drink for both of them."

He went to the door, looked back. "You two make a charming couple."

He laughed and then exited with the Troll following.

The door to the chamber was slammed shut and locked.

Challenger lay the woman down on the floor, then took off his jacket and spread it, and scooted her on top of it. He gently stroked her face, striving to revive her. He wasn't going to do anything without her consent, even looking at her back. Moriarty is damned! He thought.

The woman moaned softly, and a thrill ran through his body. Her voice was like that of a gentle canary. Soft and sweet. Her eyelashes fluttered several times, and then she slowly opened her eyes.

She started to panic again. He put a finger to her lips. "You're safe."

He took his finger away and she sat up. The first thing she noticed was his jacket beneath her. She gave him a second look, and this time more searching, as if she were seeing him for the first time.

"You're a gentleman."

He didn't say anything.

"My name is Belenus."

She lifted her right hand, and he took it, and then lightly kissed it. "I'm charmed, to say the least."

She almost giggled, and then caught herself. She swiped a hand across her forehead, and then pressed it to her arm where it had been stretched rather painfully. "You saved my life."

"It's what a gentleman does."

"He will kill you once he has what he wants."

Challenger smiled broadly. "That's assuming I give him everything he wants."

She gave him a third appraisal, this time noticing that his mind was also quite sharp, as well as his courtly manners. "I've been here for three years."

He almost choked. "How monstrous!"

She looked down into her lap. "I don't even know if my family is still alive or not."

"How did this happen to you?" He asked, both curious and desiring to have as much information as possible to understand his situation.

The door to the chamber banged open noisily and the Troll entered with a rough tray made of stone. On top, it was one bowl of water and another bowl with some apples.

"Eats!" It ordered.

The Troll waited until they began to eat, before it stomped around, scratched its behind, blasted them with some noxious gases, and then exited, slamming the door shut again.

"Absolutely repulsive manners." Challenger finally said, striving to break the silence that had descended between the two.

She put down the apple she had been nibbling at, and then looked him straight in the face. “If you survive, and I do not, I want you to bring a message to my father.”

Challenger made a gesture dismissing the notion.

She remained adamant. “I must know you will do this!”

Challenger realized she wouldn’t budge and slowly nodded, a sense of dread suffusing his stomach like he was about to die or throw up. “I promise.”

She touched his right hand on the backside, where the hair was the thickest. “Close your eyes!”

Challenger gave her a wary look.

“Please!” She pleaded.

He closed his eyes, a touch of uncertainty coloring his expression as he did so.

He felt a hand slide inside his shirt, then a burning sensation. He cried out in alarm, and then shoved her hand away. It looked normal. Then he opened his shirt. A script was there and a map of sorts. It glowed bright blue, but even as he watched, the light began to diminish, and the script and map began to blend in with the rest of his chest and hairs so that it would not be easily seen or noticed.

He looked across at her. “What have you done?

"You promised!" She reminded him.

He sighed. "Very well, I'll play this little game with you. But how shall I know who to deliver it to?"

"Don't worry, he'll find you. That I also promise!" She told him, her words giving him again that sense of dread and discomfort he had felt earlier.

"Now look at my back while time remains." She commanded him and then turned to reveal her back.

He sighed once more. This whole affair was so ungentlemanly, and so much in discord with his Victorian upbringing, but he wanted dearly to save her life and his own. He began examining the map in detail. As he did, he began to see links and possibilities. The more he looked, the more immersed he became.

He shook his head to clear it. He could have sworn that the map was beginning to float off her back and turn into detailed reality. It vanished for a moment, but when he looked closer again, it came back stronger than before. Then he felt as if he were being pulled by his belly button somehow into the rising details and everything of this world became that of another, far more real at that moment and imminent!'

Egyptian Bazaar

Harry and Holmes stood juxtaposed to each other, with Watson standing guard from a high-rise roof, where various colorful quilts and blankets were hung up to dry. He kept batting them out of his face and eyes, sneezing at times.

"Dratted cloth. I must be allergic to the dyes." He muttered, meanwhile keeping his eyes on the bazaar below.

Harry very carefully raised a handful of his magical powder in his right palm, and then softly blew upon it. After having done so, he smiled as the power, a soft blue color, began to disperse, but formed a kind of living snake in the air, about five feet above the heads of the nearest villagers.

One merchant, in his shop on the second floor, saw the form and abruptly slammed the shutters to his room, begging Allan to protect him as he did.

Harry smiled and then began following the form, trying to do so in an unobtrusive manner so as not to rile any suspicions of the pedestrians around him. Holmes tracked him with his eyes until he was about fifteen paces away, and then carefully, checking out vendor wares as he did so, followed at a discrete distance, never losing sight of his friend.

Watson finally had enough of the blankets and quilts and ripped them down and tossed them to the rooftop. As he finished, he looked up and saw an older woman giving him a hard glance. He held his hands up. "It's not what you think."

His face flushed red, then he tossed some bills at her and ran to the rooftop's edge, and leaped to the next roof, striving to keep his eye on the form below as he now raced across the rooftops.

Holmes followed discreetly, gazing abruptly at a snake charmer who played the flute to a Cobra and a mystic who was busy climbing a rope into the sky, until one of his clients noticed the rope was fake and then deflated it, sending him tumbling to the ground to the roar of laughter.

Finally, the blue form dissolved in front of an older vendor's stall. The man had one missing eye and a bad right leg. He leaned on a homemade crutch made of rough wood and pieces of scrap iron. He looked weathered and beaten by life, but his one eye was as sharp as a hawk's. He had seen the blue form. He immediately went to the door behind him and knocked upon it, then he returned to his stall as Holmes arrived there, smiling.

"Is this for sale?" Holmes asked, pointing to an exotic fruit that had some blemishes on it.

"Yes." The Vendor said in broken English.

"Good," Holmes answered. "I'll take ten of them." He began pulling out a wad of bills, and if you have more inside, I'll give you an extra fifty besides the cost. I'm throwing a party for my friends at our hotel, and this is exactly what the doctor ordered."

The Vendor gave Holmes a blank look.

"What the cook wanted." Holmes clarified.

The Vendor smiled, revealing crooked teeth, black and rotting. "Many more inside. Wait here!"

The Vendor went to the door and then rapped three times. The door opened and he went inside. Holmes turned to his left, where Harry had been watching. Harry nodded, then slipped between the narrow spaces between that building and the next and vanished.

Holmes looked up and Watson held a thumbs up and vanished from view.

Holmes put on a smile again and began counting off bills as the Vendor reappeared with half of what Holmes had asked for, not the entire order. He gave Holmes an apologetic look. "All!"

Holmes made a show of it, shifting from foot to foot, eyeing the stack of exotic fruit the Vendor placed on the counter. He shifted them about, examining them for flaws, making sad sounds when he did. The Vendor began to get anxious.

After several minutes of this and the Vendor was starting to pull his hair out, and he didn't have that much, to begin with, and cursing in Arabic that Holmes was driving him crazy.

Holmes finally pulled out a note, then paid for what was there, and spoke. "Would you be so kind as to wrap them?"

The Vendor got out a dirty piece of paper to place the fruit within and Holmes touched him lightly with his umbrella. "Each one singly, please."

The Vendor looked like he was going to go crazy, then Holmes noted that Watson was on the roof waving a hand and Harry came out of the alley. Both men signaled Holmes. He nodded, and then pushed the fruit back at the Vendor. "Never mind. I've decided not to take them."

The Vendor refused to give the money back.

Holmes ignored his profanities and walked casually away. As he walked down the path, he heard the Vendor go back inside his building. As Holmes took a turn in the market, Watson and Harry joined him. They were both grinning like Cheshire Cats.

"Right about…now!" Holmes stated.

The sound of the Vendor's howl of anger and frustration filled the streets.

"Maybe we should hurry back," Harry suggested.

"Indeed," Holmes replied, and they all hurried as quickly as they could through the side marketplaces, distancing themselves as much as possible from the break-in.

Moments later an Egyptian Wagon with a burly driver and two huge police officers hanging on its sides rushed past, they were ignored as the police officers hurried to the scene of the crime.

Harry grinned. "That was fun."

"Speak for yourself," Watson said. "I'm sweating from the top of my head to the bottom of my soles. I can't wait to take a shower."

Holmes glanced at him. "They don't have showers here. Communal baths."

"As in naked in the same tub with other men?"

Watson demanded.

Holmes didn't answer.

Watson swore under his breath. "Ms. Hudson is going to hate me when she sees me next. I'm going to smell like a skunk."

Harry slapped him on the back. "Better than looking like one too, old man."

Watson scowled at him, and Harry barked with laughter.

We're not alone.

Arthur jolted back to awareness of the story he had seen unfold in his mind. But it was so real. It couldn't have possibly been a story.

And the man, Professor Challenger, he had looked at Arthur just the way the invisible man here had done so.

He looked about.

The invisible man was nowhere to be seen again.

"Don't worry, Arthur, you're not going mad," the invisible man told him.

This time he didn't jump.

"Who are you?"

"You know full well who I am."

"What's going on?" What's happening to me?"

"You're being prepared. It's not easy to die to one world and go to the next."

"And Excalibur…it really, really exists?" Arthur stammered.

"Yes. And one day you will help me to discover it."

"But I've seen us already doing so."

He felt that warm smile again.

"See…dying isn't so bad after all, is it?"

Arthur stood perfectly still. "I'm going mad."

The invisible man blasted into his right ear. "Stop that!"

Arthur jumped.

People stared at him.

He quickly replaced the necklace into its box, sweat suddenly profusely wetting his forehead. He had just carried on one of the most insane conversations possible with an invisible man no less. Maybe he wasn't dying. Maybe he was just going insane.

But then he felt pressure on his right shoulder. A familiar and warm one. He remembered it from his waking dream.

"You're not."

He didn't see the smile. But he felt it as surely as he felt the hand on his shoulder a moment ago.

He shrugged off the impossible. As in his stories, Holmes would always say, "When we have removed what is impossible; then we are left with what is probable."

The invisible voice added. "Watson, the game's afoot!"

"I'm not Watson!" Arthur stammered, getting angry.

"No, but you created him."

A long and poignant pause. "Only here, Arthur."

"What do you mean?"

"You'll see."

It was impossible! How can a man stand there, invisible to everyone but him? Therefore, it had to be a leftover from his moment of faintness. Because even though he could see nothing, he was speaking as if someone were right next to him. And there was no one!

He frowned. As a doctor that made no sense.

A mystery was unfolding before his senses, and it made no sense. What would Sherlock Holmes have done in his situation?"

"You've eliminated the possible, Watson; now we must inspect the impossible," Holmes's voice replied in Arthur's mind.

He was lost for a moment in thought. He wrote the words and yet here he was facing the impossible in a reality that was all too cruelly real.

As a doctor, it frightened him.

But as a man who evinced the great mind of Sherlock Holmes, he had to puzzle it through to a logical conclusion.

Only there was none.

Then the more practical side of him reared its ugly head and brought him back to reality. The necklace. So expensive. He cringed at the idea of spending so much on flashy things like this. He never had been one to flaunt what wealth he had and didn't intend to do so now, but his wife deserved some lasting respect from him. Something she would be able to remember him by, besides his words.

Even a delightful book, eventually is forgotten, but jewelry? He reminded himself.

Once more he was reminded of the latest Challenger novel he was finishing. He hadn't completed it. Didn't know if he ever would. After cracking open the earth like an egg on The Day When the World Screamed, he wondered if another adventure were even possible. But then, having read The Time Machine by H.G. Wells, he knew he might reconsider it if push came to shove. It had been clear in his mind to have the Professor chase after a mysterious veiled woman who possessed jewelry of great power that could raise the dead, but with the consequences of unleashing monsters in the process who should never have walked the earth.

He wasn't sure how proper Brits would respond to undead humans rising to life again, but it was a possibility.

They had responded to Bram Stoker's Dracula well enough, so maybe his undead would work with them.

Maybe he could take his own experience of an invisible man and with Wells' permission add it to his last Challenger story? The man he recognized now as the voice of the invisible man who had been annoying him now for hours.

He loved his Challenger story. He wanted to write many more. But time...

"There will be time," the invisible voice chided him. "You are the one, after all, who has scolded many because of their disbelief in an afterlife. Why now so critical of the truth of your life?"

"Because I'm scared," Arthur admitted. "I face it myself now."

"Yes, but you're not alone. No one ever is. It's only their silly beliefs that make them think that. Someone is always watching over us. We just don't fancy that idea."

Arthur nodded, and then realized people were beginning to point at him and talk worriedly.

He smiled and waved at them.

Several waved back with a nod or smile, but many others looked quickly away, embarrassed at having been caught watching him.

"I want to write about you."

"I know and you will. Just not now."

But it was just one of several stories he was fumbling with in his spare time. Surely, the walking dead would be a clever way to end the Professor's adventures. *Maybe even have him fall in love with one of them?*

How would or could he fit an invisible person into the story?

"It's quite beautiful, isn't it?" Roared that loud voice again from behind him.

"Even now you can't imagine anything more wonderful than writing yet another story. And about me!"

The invisible man's voice broke into a peal of loud laughter.

Professor Challenger Indeed

Arthur was so close to exploding. To hollering at the man who was intruding on his life that he almost did. But if the man continued to remain invisible to everyone but Arthur, then surely, he would be dragged off to a mental institution or hospital. He would ruin this beautiful purchase. Might even lose the chance to buy it later. He didn't think anything this beautiful would remain unbought for long.

Which for Arthur was a juxtaposition he could never have imagined. That he would be more worried about purchasing this valuable item for his wife than his reputation or life. His mind flashed back to Madame Blavatsky for a moment. She commented that one day he would realize that you cannot put a price on truth or...love.

At the time that statement had mystified him, even confused him. As most of her profound philosophies had for the most part, but this time it nailed home perfectly his present condition. His present need to put value where it truly belonged...not on how he looked, but on what he needed to do for his wife.

It irritated him to hold back, but he did. He felt like he should respond; maybe he knew who the voice belonged. Not maybe. He did, but how could he tell those about him that Professor Challenger was real but invisible?

Again, he asked himself. *Am I losing my mind?*

"You're not, Conan!" Professor Challenger said to him, his voice rich with sympathy. And with another indelible element, Arthur hadn't felt from another man before, except in his writing when Holmes and Watson said their farewells.

Genuine love.

Not loud this time as previously, but not more thoughtful, less arrogant, less everything that had annoyed Arthur. He was almost beginning to feel as if the two men were intimately connected somehow, although that was impossible. How can a story character and a real person ever be in the same reality? Close friends. Or brothers even?

"But we are. Or I should say, we will be. You must believe in yourself, Conan. I believe in you."

Once again, Arthur ignored the voice speaking to him. *How rude! One doesn't speak to strangers in such a familiar way.*

As soon as the thought emerged, he felt embarrassed.

Why?

Because he recognized the voice. It was a man he had written quite well; knew every thought of, because he had written them.

Yet, impossibly, he stood in a jewelry store in downtown London with that very same man…Professor Challenger…who sounded just as big in this world, as he had in Arthur's imagination.

He was breaking every common courtesy and decency by ignoring the man and that was not only embarrassing but showed him to be a cad for not acknowledging the man who had spoken. But his pride and stubbornness stepped on the toes of his civility at that moment, and he remained mute. For he had more to lose than just his civility if he were to explode and no one was there to receive his admonishments.

So again, he patiently stepped aside from his emotional state and waited. For the sale to continue or for the man to reveal himself once more. But the ensuing silence of the man who had been behind him grew louder. Perhaps the man had stepped away, perhaps in anger, perhaps in disappointment. But Arthur kept feeling as if someone were directly behind him, hovering over him, staring at the top of his head, like a farmer examining his prize pig before the slaughter.

Arthur jumped when a hand touched his arm.

The Prize Secured

"We will need to verify your notes, of course," Ms. Hudson told him as he turned to look at whose hand touched him.

She smiled. "Sorry."

He smiled back, then sighed. "It's been a most extraordinary day, but your kindness has lightened it. I apologize for my extreme behavior. It is not like me."

She nodded. "Your books certainly speak of a mind which is well balanced and in accord with itself."

Arthur sighed with relief. Once again, she was sparing him the demand for self-inspection at a moment when his life was becoming most distressing indeed. She had taken longer than he thought to speak with her husband, but for all, he knew other sales could have been in progress as well.

He nodded back. He reached into his jacket and took out his wallet. He carefully pulled five one-hundred-pound notes out and spread them on the counter.

He heard some gasps and looked about. About six other patrons were looking at the hard cash and the jewelry, muttering such nonsense as "How beautiful, he must love her very much!"

"I wonder what he's getting in return."

"Probably counterfeit notes."

"He seems rather old to be buying jewelry."

"How come you never do anything like that for me?"

"What a sweetheart!"

"Mister Conan?"

Arthur shook off all the voices and comments he had been listening to. He hadn't dared look to see who said what. He was too embarrassed as it was. But in the manner of a man whose dignity is exceeded by his graciousness, he excused the comments and those who made them. After all, it was quite early, and without proper nutrition and a cup of tea any man, even himself, might be lured into uncommonly churlish comments and behaviors.

The shopkeeper came over and took out eyeglasses. He peered at each note on both sides, then laid down a crisp inventory book, opened it, and began writing down the purchase. "Ms. Hudson, could you please do this gentleman the honor of dressing his present as nicely as possible."

"My pleasure, sir," she told him. He gave her a warm smile, which Arthur noted immediately was flooded with a deep and abiding love as the man had eyes more for his wife than the cash before him at that moment.

She blushed when she realized Arthur was watching, then hurried off.

Arthur watched Ms. Hudson hurry into the back with the jewelry to make it presentable.

Her husband followed her with his eyes, a smile on his lips, which confirmed yet once more to Arthur how much this man adored the woman of his life; even as he cherished and adored his beloved Jane. The man was so happy with her that Arthur could swear the man's thick mustache was dancing on his upper lip as if it were some kind of caterpillar that had miraculously learned to bob and weave like a remarkable dancer.

He smiled at the image, then sighed happily. He turned fully to the man. "I'd prefer it wrapped in the same color velvet as it was presented upon."

“I'll make sure it's done to please you, Mister Doyle. It's always a pleasure when you show up.”

Arthur nodded, a touch of embarrassment blushing his cheeks.

Sir Charles nodded, then hurried into the back to make it happen for Arthur. He fancied that the man was more in a hurry to steal a kiss or a hug than to make sure his presentation was done well. Though he would probably do that afterward, no doubt.

Arthur shook his head to clear his thoughts. Here he was acting like a young boy on his first date, instead of a decently married, grown man. He was glad to see someone who might live long enough to share their love. Which once more put him in the doldrums as he considered the state of his own heart, which he knew for certain now was failing him.

He could have, maybe should have gone to a doctor. But he was well versed in the ways of the heart. He wasn't just having mild symptoms. These were the symptoms of a failing heart. No known cure existed. He would be fooling himself to think otherwise. At best, he had a matter of a few days at the most. If even that.

"Your wife must be a wonderful woman," roared the man's voice behind him.

Arthur was so startled, he gasped in fear and clutched at his heart. He had completely forgotten about the man he couldn't see or place.

"So sorry, old chap!" The man apologized.

Arthur turned about so quickly he felt dizzy for a moment, and then he gasped. He could see the invisible man as clearly as his hand, which at that moment was clutching at his heart, which was hurting once more, horribly.

He gasped, thinking his time had arrived.

The invisible man, now visible, smiled and put a hand on Arthur's chest. "It's not your time yet, my good man."

He leaned closer, but there's something I want you to see."

He tapped Arthur on his forehead.

The world exploded before him.

Gingerbread Man

Conan struggled to orientate himself.

The explosion had left him stunned and off-balance, but now he felt better. He hadn't died, but he had gone somewhere quite strange.

He looked up at the sound of something loud in the sky, then almost fainted.

It was some kind of huge flying machine. Three elongated balloons tied together somehow with large props swirling the air and pushing it forward just beneath the cloudy skies of London.

A honk alerted him to where he stood.

He looked down.

Smelled something he enjoyed immensely.

Then his sense of reality went awry again, and he was no longer himself, but a witness to an unfolding story.

A man passed through him as if he were a ghost, but Arthur felt nothing. Then his consciousness was swept away, and he witnessed something no living author ever had the pleasure of…his creations coming to life.

Market Way

Ginger.

His favorite spice.

The darker the ginger the better.

He always went to the Market Way on Spencer Street at least once a week just to traipse through the ginger spice booths, looking for the ones with the reddest flowers.

He loved red. It reminded him of more pleasant things. Of love. Of hope.

And Ginger. Well, it just smelled so good and tasted even better.

His mouth began to water as he wandered the aisles. He passed a display of Rosemary, Thyme, huge white garlic, and small red ones, onions in various shapes, sizes, and colors, and rose blossoms pounded fine into a powder for use in teas and drinks. It was endless, the combinations, flavor, and scents. He felt almost as if he might fly away from the intensity of it all.

But red and Ginger hogged his attention the most. His eyes would sweep in the aisles of colorful items, but only note the ones of red and Ginger.

Ginger Bath

He sighed with pleasure as he watched the ginger fluids swirl about his knees, coloring them and bathing him with a sensation like an orgasm.

The sight filled his brain with satisfaction that he only felt when he was immersed in ginger. He dipped his hands into the liquid and began bathing himself with it.

He never used soap.

And he never wondered why people would always give him a curious look after they passed, having smelled the beautiful aroma so strongly on his clothing and body.

He washed everything in his flat with ginger, including his clothing. Even the polish on his shoes had some essence of ginger within it.

Now, though, he was luxuriating in the fluid, starting with his hands, making sure they were thoroughly cleaned in ginger, then his wrists and forearms. From there he would work his way up to his upper arm, and then down into his chest cavity, where he would close his eyes and savor the smell and the taste of ginger as he washed his chest with one hand, and sipped ginger tea with the other.

Some might have made a face at that, not realizing that ginger was perfect by itself. It needed nothing more to make it perfect. It was perfection incarnate.

It had been a good day for him. An incredibly good day. More ginger than a good soul had the right to. He began working the ginger into his loins, then his legs, ankles, and feet. Satisfied he was now thoroughly cleaned in ginger, he climbed reluctantly from his tub, then began to gently rub himself down with a satin red towel. Finished drying off, he stepped back into his pin striped pants, his starched white shirt, and cummerbund, as well as his Oxford shoes, which he made sure, were always polished to perfection.

“Ah!” He sighed, the sweet and pungent scent of Ginger scenting his body and the air about him. If he were not dead, this was surely the closest to heaven a man could ever reach without dying.

Complete. He looked down at the husk of a woman who lay there, arms spread out in a Christ-like position, her right side gutted open neatly and cleanly, just drops of blood oozing out now. "You have been a splendid cook, dear lady!"

He tipped his top hat to her. "Hats off for your courtesy."

He took a slip of paper and let it drift from his hand to the top of the body, where eyes stared into infinity, the horror and pain in them frozen forever in time. He stooped down and gently kissed her lips. "Parting is such sweet sorrow. But I will be seeking another Ginger for tomorrow."

With those parting words, he let himself out the front door he had been asked to enter some hours before by a woman expecting much more than he could ever give her.

But he did give her the only gift he could.

Death.

And with that simple gift, he gained hours of intense pleasure.

Hours and hours.

Crime Scene

The Inspector stared at the corpse of the fallen woman, his face set in stone, while Constable Evans, not one to get acclimated to death so easily, threw up in his hands and ran for the door. "This murderer has got to be stopped! He has the whole of London in fear."

Watson finished a preliminary and quite limited examination of the body, got off the tarp he had lain over the blood, and brushed off his knees. His face was also set in stone, but his right eyebrow twitched. He had known Dame Edith. She had been a family friend since he was a child. What kind of monster would prey on old women like this?

He sneezed hard. Once. Twice, then again. He put the hanky back to his nose where it had been as he examined Dame Edith. Something was triggering his allergies.

Holmes came from the bedroom, handed over several stoppered vials to Watson, who tucked them into the black bag he always carried with him. The two were inseparable at a crime scene, working like perfect parts of a machine. One doing the close examination of the body, while the other searched for clues...of any sort!

"I imagine the monster who did this found immense pleasure in both her death and her life," Holmes commented, though not with pleasure. He was as disturbed as the others but was able to restrain his emotions better.

Constable Evans stumbled back into the room, a hanky over his nose, and a slip of paper in his right hand. "I found this in the hallway."

"Ah!" Holmes said, grabbing the paper from the Constable's hands before he could release it to the Inspector.

Holmes looked grim as he read the missive several times, then sighed and gave it to the Inspector, who eagerly took it and then read it as well.

His face became grimmer as he crumpled it up in his hand and tossed it to the floor.

“Blast that man to hell and back!” He cursed.

Watson eyed the two. “The Gingerbread Man, of course.”

“Yes, triple damn his soul to hell and back!"

Watson looked at Holmes, who gave a slight shake of his head. This was not a time for discussion.

Holmes removed his surgical gloves, placed them into a bag that Watson offered, who then placed those also into his black bag. "I believe we are through here, Inspector."

"Then you have nothing?"

"What I have, Inspector, I cannot discuss at this time."

The Inspector was about to explode, but when he saw the hard look in Holmes's eyes, he relented and just nodded. "We'll be over once we clean up the scene."

"Very good, Inspector."

Holmes turned on his heels and exited the room and the home, with Watson following close behind.

The Inspector turned to Constable Evans. "See that she is brought out to the Wagon respectfully. I don't want the citizens to get wind of this being another Gingerbread Man murder."

"Yes. Father...I mean Inspector." He added on the eyebrow raise of his father.

They had a good relationship as father and son but when in a case the Inspector insisted on sticking to the book in the way they addressed each other.

The Inspector left leaving Constable Evans alone with the body, as several Constable Medics entered the room with a stretcher. "Father, for once I agree with you. Damn the Gingerbread Man to hell and back!"

The Medics were a bit rough with the body. "Here, here, she's dead, but we still owe her some modicum of respect, gentlemen. After all, she could have been your mother. Still could be."

Both Medics turned pale as ghosts at that comment, but instead of commenting, they lifted her body more gently and laid it on the stretcher, as Constable Evans muttered a prayer in his thoughts for her poor soul.

221 B Baker Street

Holmes paced back and forth in front of the fireplace as Watson sipped tea. Ms. Hudson sat next to him, knitting a table piece in shades of red, green, and yellow. Both were enjoying each other's presence. Plainly. No words were needed. Just being close was enough. Ms. Hudson had been gone so long to France that Watson began to go up the chimney every time something irritated him, which was often.

Now he was like a purring kitten with her by his side. *Mister Grumbly Bear* as she teased him had retired to be replaced by sweet honey John.

Holmes smiled at the thought, then went back to pacing. Something was bothering him. On the edge of his mind. Not quite clear yet. Pacing helped him to think better.

The sound of a constable's wagon blaring its sirens as it passed came from the open window. It was dark outside. The Inspector had come and gone with no plan of action yet from Holmes, which caused the Inspector to go crazy, but soon passed when he realized he was only tired.

"I'm sorry." He had apologized.

Holmes offered his hand. "I swear to you, Inspector, that I am putting all my powers of deduction upon this case."

"If it weren't for all that Dark Druid stuff going on, we would have had this case solved months ago, and look at us now, five victims. All older women. All dead." He growled. "Raped and robbed of their blood by some serial killer named the Gingerbread Man. Whoever wrote that awful children's story should have their head chopped off!" He cursed, then exited the flat.

"Watson."

"Yes, Holmes?"

"I want you to get ready."

Ms. Hudson rose. "But it's so late outside!"

Holmes turned to her. "Death waits on no man or a specific time. The clock is ticking, and death is searching for its next victim. Make haste, Watson!"

Holmes threw on his cape and cap, made sure his weapon was loaded, then stepped from the sitting room and exited down the stairs.

Watson turned to Ms. Hudson, who looked pale as a ghost. "I don't like being here alone with that monster loose in London."

"Don't worry, my dear, his victims are all much older than you. Besides..." He went to the window and pointed. She went to the window and looked.

Constable Evans sat in his police wagon, the window rolled down, his eyes on their flat. She waved and he nodded back at her.

She turned to Watson. “Constable Evans. Poor dear, he'll catch his death of cold out there. You send that child up here right away, John, or I'll have your hide for leaving him out there!" She ordered.

Watson gave her a peck. "I didn’t leave him there. He insisted…”

She glared at him.

He sighed, shook his head, then surrendered, “Anything for my sugar cake."

She giggled and gave him a peck on his cheek. "That's for being my honey bun, not Mister Grumbly Bear.”

He almost complained about that last name, then bit his tongue and smiled instead, which was rewarded with another kiss.

“You know me all too well,” he told her as he pulled away.

“Do I now?” She teased.

He laughed, grabbed his black bag and cloak, and

exited down the stairs. The door never slammed. Constable Evans came up the stairs a few minutes later. Ms. Hudson greeted him with a smile, then nodded to the chair opposite her. "I can use a little help here."

She sat down knitting. "Raise your hands, constable."

He raised his hands and she wound thread across them. Smiling, she said. "Now. Don't move!"

He gave her a look that indicated it was exactly what he would like to do but said nothing. He, also, like Watson, knew when a battle could be won or lost by a protest with this woman.

The Spice Shop

Holmes kept a brisk pace, with Watson huffing and puffing to keep up. "You really do need to cut down on those scones, Watson."

"Not on your life!" Watson swore. Though at that moment he was wishing he had already.

Holmes smiled and then turned to the side street facing him. "I believe we need to go in that direction."

Watson followed Holmes as they wound their way from one street to the next, executing shortcuts through certain alleys, avoiding drunken sailors and Midnight Angels as they did so, who hung out in the darker alleys plying the trade.

Finally, Holmes stopped before a posh-looking shop. A single light remained on within it. A new Tesla light powered by a battery that took ten years to expire. "Here we are."

"Spice shop?"

"Sugar and spice and everything nice," Holmes answered with the hint of a smile.

He rapped on the door. Nothing. He rapped again. Nothing. He rapped much louder. Nothing.

"Watson."

Watson sat down his bag and went to the door. He peered at its lock mechanism, then pulled out a twist of wires from his coat. He took one thicker than most and inserted it into the lock. He twisted several times, then the lock made a loud clicking sound. He opened the door, stepping out of Holmes's way so he could enter.

"Excellent work, Watson."

Watson nodded, glanced to see if anyone was approaching, then entered, closing the door behind him. He immediately regretted entering. He began sneezing. At first softly, then increasingly violently. "Drats!" He cursed. "Reminds me of the Chinas again! All those horrid spices always made me nauseous and coughed my brains out!"

"I hardly think that's possible, Watson."

"Easy for you to say," Watson grumbled, putting a hanky to his nose to stifle the fragrances. "You've got more of them."

Holmes turned to his friend. "A joke?"

Watson smiled, then sneezed again. After he wiped his nose, he asked "What are we here for?"

"Sugar and spice, Watson. Sugar and spice."

Holmes went from one aisle of spice booths to the next, then stopped at the section where ginger spices were laid out for viewing, along with bottles of pounded spices that were in various densities for consumption and cooking. "Ah, here we are."

"Watson," Holmes said, reaching his hand back. "Give me the red vial."

"How did you know I still had that in my bag?"

"Elementary, dear Watson. You are a creature of habit. You never take anything out I give to you until I ask for it. May I?"

Watson took the vial out and handed it over.

Holmes unstoppered it, then placed the vial beneath his nose. His eyebrows rose, then he went to Watson and placed the vial beneath his nose. Watson pulled his head back, making a face, then he sneezed. Once, twice, and then again.

"Now, Watson. I wish you to go along this aisle. Please take that hanky from your nose and allow the full bouquet of these spices to caress your olfactory senses."

"Caress, tosh! You mean batter them. You don't expect me to breathe in here?" Watson blasted.

"No, I expect you to sneeze," Holmes said.

Watson went down the aisle, then grabbed his mouth and nose and let out a huge sneeze. First lightly, then more strongly, and finally when he reached the last booth he sneezed so violently, that he was almost thrown from his feet by the force of it.

Holmes came forth and offered his hanky. Watson covered his nose immediately.

"I've seen enough. Let us return home to rest."

Watson knew better than to ask a question. He was just grateful to escape the blasted place without sneezing his brains out.

As they exited and Watson relocked the door, Holmes paused. "Please. Return to see that Ms. Hudson is safe."

"Where are you going?"

"A stroll."

"This time of night?"

Holmes smiled, then walked off, his hands behind his back. He began to whistle a piece of Mozart's Blue Danube.

The Gingerbread Man

He woke up fresh and feeling better than ever, but he missed the sweet smell of ginger. It has been a week now. He was finding his desire for ginger to come more frequently of late, so he had come prepared with what he needed for his task. He took out his message book, dove through it to find a name with which he was familiar. "Ah, Ms. Hendricks. I remember her well!"

He hurriedly dressed. He didn't bother to make his usual tea or coffee, but headed for the door immediately, his bag in hand. He carried everything he needed within. He was whistling happily as he opened the door to exit, then turned around to lock his door. He heard a sound behind him and turned.

Holmes stood there, alongside the Inspector and Constable Evans.

"Is something wrong, gentlemen?"

The Inspector nodded to his son. Constable Evans pulled out handcuffs.

He gave them a startled look. "I'm sure you must be mistaken. I have done nothing wrong. I am a simple spice man on his way to work."

Constable Evans took the bag from his hands and tossed it to the Inspector, and then handcuffed the man.

Holmes nodded to the Inspector, who opened the bag to reveal a surgical knife. chloroform and cloth, as well as several containers of ginger spices, all red.

"Satisfied?"

The Inspector eyed the man standing before him. "Mister Jerold Market Way you will no longer be needed at your store. I have much better employment for your skills."

Jerold brightened. "Oh, am I to be awarded a job of merit then? But why the handcuffs?"

"To make sure that in your zeal you do not harm yourself unnecessarily."

The Inspector nodded to Constable Evans, who herded Jerold to the back of their Constable Wagon parked down the street. Holmes watched, then took the bag. "I shall have Watson do all the necessary preliminaries if that will do?"

"However, in the world did you figure out it was him and that he was mad?"

"Elementary, Inspector. First, he called himself the Gingerbread Man. One needs ginger to make a gingerbread man. His use of ginger during his orchestrations of murder was the second clue. The final clue was Watson."

"How so?"

"Watson is allergic to ginger. Violently so. And only one brand of ginger. The one that this man has in this bag and sells at his shop. This is the only shop that carries it and..."

"And?"

"And he is the same person who imports it from the Chinas and sells it. The only one."

"But how did you know it was him doing the murders instead of some other Ginger-loving crook?"

Because the amount of Red Ginger used in the murders could never be purchased by a person from a retailer alone. He is the only one with that connection. I had Jules and Wells check with the Chinese suppliers and his name was the only one that came up."

"With all of them?"

"Every single one."

"Surely that wasn't enough. He could be working for someone else."

"Actually, no. You see, the bodies of the victims all had significant amounts of missing blood. Hence, the suspicion of a vampire doing the crime."

"But vampires don't eat humans anymore."

"I realize that and went one step further and contacted our dear friend, Count Dracula."

"And?"

"When I mentioned this man's name to him, he almost threw me out of his castle."

"Why?"

"Because the Count hates vampires that eat humans and this man has a history of it. He would have been tried in the Vampire Courts a long time ago, but he fled and assumed a new name."

Holmes smiled. "So, you see, dear Inspector, the man Constable Evans has taken away is not only a murderer but a vampire."

"Oh my God! My son's in danger!"

Holmes laughed. "Hardly. I had him use silver to handcuff the man. If he tries to break free, he'll burn his hands off."

"He'll still have teeth."

"Dear Inspector, a vampire that needs to use subterfuge to drain their victim's blood has a condition that is rare, but fatal."

"Which is?"

"He's missing his fangs!"

"Oh!"

He didn't bother to ask why the man's fangs were missing. He didn't want to know. He was only glad the case was solved, and the murders would stop.

Holmes folded his hands behind his back and began walking away.

"Don't you want a ride home?"

Holmes shook his head, took a deep breath of the morning air, the gentle fog of the morning mist moving about him. "Not at all. This is the perfect time to work off breakfast."

"But you haven't eaten yet?"

Holmes smiled and continued walking.

The Inspector shook his head in puzzlement. "I'll never understand the way that man's mind works." He shook his head again, then walked across the street to join his son in the police wagon.

Inside, the Gingerbread Man was howling in pain. He snarled at the Inspector, "I'll eat you when I get out of them."

"You'll have no hands."

"I'll suck your blood!"

"With what?"

Constable Evans grinned at his father. "Holmes told you."

"Aye, that he did."

Constable Evans snickered. "The man can't seem to get the idea out of his head that he can't break free of silver."

The Gingerbread Man gave them both an evil glare. "If you were old women, I'd eat you!"

They both laughed. "Not even if," the Inspector replied.

"Son let's get this rubbish into a cell as fast as we can. I can't stand his stench."

Constable Evans drove away.

The Gingerbread Man tried to bite the Inspector's neck, but when he did, his face smashed into a fine plate of glass.

He snarled and fell back.

The glass was blessed with Holy Water and laced with fine threads of silver, as were the doors and side windows in the back.

"Even if you had teeth, sir, you couldn't bite through Holy Water armored plate glass."

The Gingerbread Man snarled and sat back on his seat, his eyes blazing with anger.

Inspector Bloodstone opened a small box in front. An odor laced the air immediately.

"Son, where did you get these?"

"From Ms. Hudson."

The Gingerbread Man sat up straight, sniffing the air.

The Inspector smiled. "Well, bless her heart, son, gingerbread cookies. Tell her thanks!"

He took a bite.

Behind them, the Gingerbread Man went wild as Inspector Bloodstone continued to eat. The glass separating them from the back allowed odor through.

The Gingerbread Man, unable to get to the cookies, howled in frustration as the Inspector continued to eat gingerbread cookie after another in front of the vampire's face.

221 B Baker Street

Watson was reading the morning paper, a special edition, announcing the capture of the Gingerbread Man, when Holmes marched up the stairs into the sitting room and placed his cloak and cap on the rack for them. "Good morning, Watson. I trust you had a good rest."

Watson was about to answer when he sneezed instead.

Holmes looked alarmed. "Oh, my apologies." He took his cape and tossed it down the stairs.

Watson stopped sneezing.

Holmes smiled at him. "I must have brushed some of the ginger onto my cape as we passed it on the way out."

"Believe me, Holmes, I am more relieved than you to know that it wasn't something I was eating. That would have embarrassed my beloved Ms. Hudson to no end."

They both laughed.

"You know what a devil she can be at moments like that," he chuckled.

Ms. Hudson stepped into the room. "Devil about what?"

Holmes and Watson burst into more laughter.

Watson glanced at her, and she appeared to be quite odd-looking, almost as if...

"Ms. Hudson, why do you suddenly look so manly?"

She stroked a thick red beard that was now growing from her chin and jaw.

She laughed.

Not like her usual sweet laugh. Instead, it was deep and throaty, growly like Professor Challenger's.

The Invisible Man

Arthur shook his head to free the vision still clinging to him. Professor Challenger, the invisible man for so long to him, was leaning over him. He had the palm of his hands over Arthur's chest.

"What have you done to me?"

"You mean besides keeping you from running off too soon?"

Arthur glared at him.

Challenger shook his head. "Dear, dear Conan, I shall always respect you for your tenacity, when it comes to following through with your objectives...but this stubborn side of you does not suit you.

"What...did...you...do?"

"Opened your mind. And your heart!"

Challenger stepped back and grinned devilishly." How did you enjoy your little adventure with Holmes?"

"I don't know what you're talking about. I can't possibly be here and somewhere else at the same time unless I were hallucinating!"

Challenger laughed.

"Now give me a hand up. I don't fancy being on the floor with everyone watching."

Challenger gave him a hand up, but to Arthur's surprise, no one was watching. It was as if he were still in a state of dream.

Challenger laughed. "Harry told me you would be difficult to convince. Even with a miracle or two."

"Harry who?"

"Why Houdini, of course. Another of your friends waiting for you."

Arthur scowled at him. "I am dying, you blaggart, don't treat me like a fool. Harry Houdini and I have never met!"

"Not in this world."

"On any world!" Arthur insisted.

Challenger laughed again, "But you have, my dear Arthur. Just not yet. I'm almost done preparing you for our little adventure. I'm quite sure you'll find it exciting, but not nearly as much as the larger adventures with Holmes of course."

"If it's anything like what I've been witnessing..."

"Oh, it's so much more than that."

Arthur groaned. His anger was causing his heart to act up again. But he didn't want this man to pity him, even if he didn't like him much. So, he bit back his cry of pain, not wanting to give the man a further reason to touch him.

"I beg your pardon!" Arthur almost shouted, his face reddening with a flush of anger he rarely felt these days, except at the charlatans. Misbegotten souls who insisted they spoke with the dead just so they could scrounge money from the weak and defenseless who only wanted to feel that all wasn't lost when their loved ones crossed into the light to be with God. They just wanted to spend just one more moment with the love of their lives. *God have mercy on their souls.*

Arthur almost froze. He was trying to grasp who was standing before him. Who was this stranger? What was he doing in his bedroom?

“Do I know you?”

Challenger gave Arthur a worried look, then smiled.

“I should hope so. We’ve been having a rather nice chat now for some time.”

“Really?” I don’t remember any chat.”

Arthur strained to think. Why was his mind so murky? So, clouded. As a doctor, he should have recognized what was happening. He had just had several strokes, side effects of his weakening heart.

But as he pushed at his memories, he thought he finally recognized this man standing before him. But how? He can't remember anywhere he could have met this man. He was so unique he would stand out anywhere, but to Arthur, he was not unique, but impossible. Who was he?

A very tall man. He, himself, just breasted six American feet and this one surely topped out a good half a foot more. The man was stocky and very well-muscled. He had a thick mustache and beard that made him appear professorial, but at the same time, somehow fierce and powerful. Almost as rascally looking like that odd mystic fellow from Russia, Rasputin.

This was a man to be reckoned with for sure. A man much like someone else he knew. But for some God-forsaken reason, he couldn't bring to his mind who that was.

But this man.

He had such a thick beard and mustache so fierce and determined as if they were accents on the man's personality, rather than part of the edifice of his face, should have been the decisive factor for him, but he was suddenly too tired and weak to put his thoughts together in an orderly manner.

It was like he was looking at some kind of drawing of a character he had created.

The name flashed before his mind but didn't stick.

He rubbed his brow, hoping to get it back.

It refused to come.

Somehow, he knew the man. Recently. But now he could not. That frightened him. Was death taking away his memories as well as his life?

He put a hand over his heart, feeling a pinch again. The man's eyes widened a bit in alarm, but he didn't speak.

"Have we met before?" Arthur asked, his voice etched with pain and yet, a touch of curiosity tweaking him for a moment, even with the pain he was experiencing. Some of his better manners were returning now that he saw the genuine concern on the man's face and in his eyes.

Such eyes they were too.

Fierce, proud, dominating, and powerful. Just like a man's body.

He suspected this man would be equally as difficult to face in combat as on a political platform.

The man gave Arthur a very warm smile and reached out one of his large hands. "I am known to many where I come from and not so many here, but someday soon, you will have done so for me here as well as I have been done elsewhere."

"That sounds so...so mysterious." Arthur shot back, a bit short-tempered at the man's comment, thinking it seemed somewhat condescending and arrogant. And for a moment, a flash of this man's image surged across his mind again. But this time he saw him, not in a suit as now, but in a jungle wearing a pith helmet.

He was certain he had to have met him before. Everything about him was so...so...so dratted familiar. *Why couldn't he place him?*

"Oh, I'm so sorry." The man said, recognizing the anger in Arthur's eyes. "I have offended you and that was not my intent whatsoever, my good man. Far, far from it."

Sometimes Arthur wondered if that was also why he had been spending so much time going after those charlatans who robbed the innocent and the helpless with their fake séances and claims of speaking to the dead. He had spent a good part of his last years trying to dissuade the horrible practices but to no avail. It wasn't the charlatans at fault, but the poor, uneducated souls who trusted them to offer a path to reality, that they refused to acknowledge and cultivate through genuine efforts of their own: That death separated us all. And no one returned to speak of the other side.

At least none he had sought or found.

He still believed it was possible; he just hadn't seen anyone who had that skill or blessing.

For whatever the reasons, the Creator kept that door between worlds shut firmly. Perhaps because he didn't want to frighten anyone, or perhaps because he did. Though in his heart of hearts, he believed God to be more like a teacher and a father, than a horrendous judge and punisher as some of the religions about the world claimed.

He hoped fervently that they were wrong, and he was right, even if off somewhat, because the concept of hell was not only frightening but inhumane in every sense of the world. Hasn't man beat himself up enough by the time he crosses over? Why should he have torture and pain added to that in the end? He just couldn't believe in a Creator that was that cruel. He would not judge others for their beliefs, but neither would he accept beliefs that defied common sense and human decency. Any God worthy of that stature would not stoop to punish; he would be a teacher like a good father should be.

“Speaking to the dead indeed!" He muttered angrily to himself.

"I'm sorry. What did you say?"

The man smiled broadly, his beard whipping upwards from the movement. “I am not dead at all.”

“I didn’t mean you,” Arthur responded with embarrassment.

The man studied Arthur’s face a long time, then nodded. “I knew this was going to be hard for you; I had no idea how hard it was until this moment. For that, I ask your forgiveness.”

Arthur shook his head. *Why had he said that?*

“Sir, I have no idea who you are, let alone why you should ask for my forgiveness for something that my heart tells me comes from a deep and profound sense of humanity, rather than the seeking of contact with one more famous."

"That’s because I know you so well. As if we were...uh...close family," the man assured Arthur.

Before Arthur could respond, Ms. Hudson returned with his gift, fitted into a beautiful red velvet box with a pretty blood-red, velvet bow topping it off. She presented it to Arthur. “I suspect you’re going to have one happy night.”

Arthur blushed.

Her husband, Sir Charles, returned, saw the box, and nodded with pleasure. "I suspect you will be a hero in your home for quite some time after you present this marvelous gift. Even the Queen of Sheba, the great Cleopatra, would have been awed by it."

Arthur forgot about the stranger again. He felt this unreasonable anger surge within him because of the comment and snapped, "I should hope so! I certainly paid enough for it!"

Regret and Pain

The two kind souls gave Arthur a look he would never forget. But he was so angry with himself at that moment, he couldn't relent. As the stranger, Challenger, or whoever he was, had said, *he could be stubborn!*

Instead, he gave them both a nod. stepped past the stranger who was, but could not be Professor Challenger, ignoring the look the man gave him...something like pity mixed with humor...and stepped back onto the street where his carriage was waiting for him.

"Where to?" His driver asked.

"Home. I am tired." He climbed into the open door. The driver shut it and hopped back to his position. He made a shushing sound with his mouth and the horses began pulling the carriage away.

Inside, Arthur could finally let go of his shame and regret. He had just acted like a boor and a cad. That thought jolted his sense of dignity as the coach jolted him as it took a hard turn for home.

He sighed. "Blast me all!"

He, at once, swore an appointment in his mind with himself, as soon as he was home, he would send Ms. Hudson and her fine husband an apology with his driver and a small token of his esteem...perhaps another hundred-pound note...to make up for his unforgivable behavior.

But it was done. No way to take it back. And he was not the kind of man to rush back and personally admit such a horrendous mistake.

One thing was certain though. He knew why he had been driven so suddenly to anger. *The idea that he only had so much time left.* And no idea of how much time was left was eating him up inside...was too painful to consider.

As the drive home continued, his remorse, self-pity, as well as anger began to diminish. With each block they passed he thought less of his mistakes and more of how he could imagine the look on Jane's face when she received the gift. It would have made all this worthwhile, even his injurious behavior to see that precious moment when it blossomed.

So, from that point on, as he was driven home, he had only one thought on his mind: The gift and the magnificent smile he would see on the only woman he had ever loved. But then now and again he would remember that smirking smile of the stranger. He would feel the heat growing in his heart, then let go and think of his dear Jane once more and relax.

"What in God's name am I doing to myself?" He cursed angrily. "Killing myself over nothing. He was just some bollocks of a fool out to pray on an innocent man's mind. That's all! And if I knew him and he knew me, then why did he play me for a fool and not introduce himself properly. What was he hiding? What was he afraid of? What manner of a cruel game was he playing with my feelings?"

Having uttered those words, he felt a weightlift, but as he came closer to home, he felt a stronger pinch in his heart. "No, no!" He cried out in alarm as the pain increased.

"We're here, Mister Doyle." The driver called to him, as he pulled the carriage to a stop in front of Arthur's home, then hopped down to open the door for him.

Arthur got out and without thinking, brought his wallet out and pulled out two one hundred-pound notes.

"I want you to give one to Mister Charles at the jewelry store I was just at. Tell him that Mister Doyle acted like a cad and begs for his and Ms. Hudson's forgiveness."

"Sir."

“And...” He eyed the man with a warm smile. “After all these years, I feel like I should do so much more for you, but will you please accept the other hundred as a token of my respect for your glad and kind service?”

“Sir! That’s more than I make in a year!”

Arthur shrugged it off with a smile. "I suggest you make the most of it then. You have four children, do you not?"

The Driver smiled. "Five now that the missus has given birth finally."

Arthur pulled out another two-hundred-pound notes. “And this is to make sure that your fine family can all go to a proper school as well.”

“But sir!”

Arthur shook his head. “You can’t spend it when you’re dead, good fellow.”

The man gave him a startled look.

Arthur ignored it. He felt as if he had just had an epiphany of sorts and didn’t want to waste that newfound emotion on embarrassment or explanations.

Arthur clapped the man on his right shoulder. "May your new child..."

"A boy, sir."

"The young lad," Arthur continued. "Live long and prosper. For I certainly shan't!"

The man looked as if struck by a board across his chest. "Sir!"

"Now, now, I didn't mean anything by it."

The man knew then that Arthur was lying. He was quite sure that despite his jovial words, the underlying sadness he felt was exuding forth brightly.

He shook it off.

The man sensed it and smiled. "However, you will do or go, sir, I appreciate this with all my heart. My family and I shall honor your name for generations."

Arthur smiled. "How about you just deliver my message for now?"

The man's face lit up again. "Sir, I will deliver your message promptly and I thank you from the bottom of my heart for your generosity again."

"That's better now," Arthur assured him. "I only meant that when the Good Lord calls, we all have to let go of this world now, don't we?"

"Pardon me for asking, Mister Doyle, but it would be a great loss to this world to have you leave it just now. Your stories are sometimes all that keep me going when things get rough. Especially your ones about Sherlock Holmes."

Arthur felt another kind of pinch then. His last story lay in the form of an incomplete manuscript. It might never be completed, he thought as a renewed sense of pain blossomed in his chest and began reaching for his arms as well. But then he remembered his vision and his ideas began to flow again.

It would be finished!

He struggled to keep it together, fighting back the pain so it didn't show on his face. He put a hand on the driver's shoulder. "Love your family. Cherish them. For you will be bringing nothing else with you when it comes to your time. Stories are stuff and nonsense compared to the wealth of love that a family provides."

Leaving the man even more confused than before, the pain in his heart growing worse, his arms aching so badly they wanted to ignite into flames, he managed to climb the steps to his home, but barely. He knew then that his time was near if not come. He fought against the rising darkness filling his vision.

He managed to open the front door. As he did, Jane saw him as she came down the stairs.

"Arthur!" She called to him happily.

"My love," he said, "I…I…" He opened his mouth to speak, and then darkness consumed him, even eclipsing the brilliance of the warmth of her smile.

His gift for her tumbled to the floor next to him.

A Flickering Flame

"You are avoiding the truth!" Watson accused his friend and partner.

Holmes merely smiled and spoke. "I avoid dishonesty, but never the truth, dear Watson. For the truth is the bread and butter of our lives."

"Maybe for you, Holmes, but myself, I prefer toast with a pinch of honey and marmalade on it."

Holmes laughed.

-- From the Journals of Doctor Watson

The invisible man from the jewelry shop was, in actuality, Professor Challenger and not from this world at all, looked at the piece of paper in his hand, then at the address on the building before him, and nodded.

"So, this is Crow Borough, East Sussex, and the home of my father." He said in a tone that would have been mystifying to any who knew the man who lived in the home he faced: Sir Arthur Conan Doyle.

He watched as a young doctor climbed forth from a horse and buggy and hurried into the home, greeted by a lovely older woman, who invited him inside, her face filled with worry and fear, but still with enough kindness not to be rude.

"Ah, my dear Missus Doyle." The Stranger proclaimed as he stepped into view.

She looked out at him, surprised. Then grew fearful and was about to shut the door. After all, he was quite a large man and extremely frightening to a small woman such as she was.

“Please,” he greeted her now with a smile. “Don’t shut me out, if you knew what I know, your fears would not be so great."

I am a good man.”

She clutched the door, halfway between slamming it shut and half between opening it up.

He didn’t move further.

Her choice was as important now as her husband’s choice would be later. He could not change free will, nor did he want to play God and try to. Let fools try that, but not he. He was here to offer a longtime friend a chance to do right by himself at a crucial moment.

He looked up towards the second story of the building, where Doctor Tatsand’s body was seen briefly through a window, and then he pulled out a pocket watch, made of hammered gold and diamonds set in rusted metal. He flipped it open and examined its face intently, watching as the second hand caught up with the minute hand and passed it.

He shook his head. He felt like this moment should have fireworks, dancing, and people laughing with joy. But it had none of those. He knew that what was to come would bring joy, but also pain.

Great pain.

"Ms. Doyle, please..." he pleaded.

She finally sighed, letting her fear subside. She nodded with a smile.

He put his pocket watch away.

"I thank you sincerely. Conan, I will always be grateful for this moment."

"Conan? No one calls him that anymore."

Professor Challenger pulled on his beard and grinned mischievously. "Oh, I've called him a great deal more things than that."

"And soon I will be again," he said, causing her face to cloud in confusion.

This time she merely nodded.

A cry came from inside and she ran from view.

Professor Challenger stood there, pulled out his watch again, looked at the time, and frowned for a moment, then as the minute hand rose to the vertical, he said, “Soon!”

Madame Blavatsky

Doctor Tatsand was a younger doctor with a great mind. He had often attended spiritualist sessions with Arthur when he held them. He had been accumulating increased interest in the author's speeches and his presentations. He was the son of an even better and more famous doctor. His father had a brilliant mind. He could discover the truth of any disease with just a few clues.

Doctor William Salk was not a man to be forgotten or ignored in the annals of medical science.

He adopted Doctor Tatsand on a trip to the Indias to study diseases and to help cure the ailing people there as much as he humanly could.

A trait which his son had followed closely in and now was here, hoping to make a difference for Arthur, even though medically that just didn't seem possible. Even a doctor can pray for a miracle.

He just wasn't prepared for the kind of miracle that was about to happen.

Arthur honored him in his stories about Sherlock Holmes and Watson, changing Doctor Tatsand's real name to Watson to protect his friend's identity. His Doctor Watson, after all, while perhaps not having as genius a mind as that of Holmes, must be perfected enough to be able to match wits with him, which he often did with admirable charm and verve.

The younger doctor had started attending Arthur's occult meetings after his father passed on, hopeful for something that would relieve the profound sense of loss he felt from his own father's death. Arthur never lied, otherwise he would never have descended to such a lowly state as to consult in a spiritualist raising of the dead that Arthur hosted.

But he trusted Arthur. If he knew something, he said it. His mission on earth, he felt, was to encourage the proper understanding of life and living, not to hamper it. That was why he hoped that Arthur might lead him to a spiritualist who could gentle the pain of his loss and the emptiness of his soul.

But that never happened. Arthur replaced fake occultists and spiritualists with pragmatic speeches and presentations about life on the other side, how this world was just a school and preparation for a much happier and more fulfilling life once one crossed over. He never pretended to understand how Arthur came about these revelations. He only knew they were comforting to his soul.

But that didn't mean he no longer prayed for someone to raise his father once more to love and to cherish, but he was resigned now at least, to holding the memories dear, if not longer to the person.

One time even the great Madame Blavatsky had come to listen to Sir Arthur Conan Doyle, nodding during his presentation and at the end remarking, "We are on the eve of a great discovery, dear Mister Doyle."

"And why is that?" He had asked, his spirit lifted by the nobleness of this woman, whom he knew to be beyond expectations of himself and many others. A spiritualist of the first magnitude! A true spiritualist, not a fraud artist cloaked in feathery robes and decked out with Tarot cards and fake crystal balls.

"Because soon the truth of God will be revealed," she told him and left.

Another reason is Doctor Tatsand had faith in Arthur. Any other spiritualist had said that he would have immediately called them a "fraud," and chased them from his house, instead of honoring and respecting them, as he knew Arthur did her.

Neither Arthur nor the Doctor knew why she had made such a statement of finality at the time. Which had been but a month ago, but her words had lost their import until this day, when Arthur lay upon his bed, wondering how much longer he had to live in this bright world of possibilities and the Doctor found himself doing something he hadn't in a long time. Praying for the soul of the man who had been like a second father to him. He had a tough time holding back his tears as Jane, the author's wife, held tight to her husband's hand as if that would stop his flight from this world of pain and sorrow, joy and laughter into a larger world of everlasting peace and joy.

As he lay on his bed, his wife seated next to him on his right and the Doctor holding a stethoscope to his chest from the left, all Arthur could think of was how the world had so much to offer that was just so much glitter and glow, but the hand of his wife held the promises of heavenly treasures no man would be foolish enough ever to abandon. Inside himself, he knew he was failing. His heart was stopping and there was nothing he could do to prevent it.

He had been working harder these last few months to spread his teachings and to let the world know about the higher truths, but now it would have to wait for another soul to take up the mantle he had carried. Time for another, stronger and braver soul to carry on his mission of enlightening the masses.

"Arthur." Doctor Tatsand spoke.

Arthur withdrew from his thoughts and eyed the man. "I know. You don't have to beggar the question by stating the obvious. I'm dying."

Doctor Tatsand didn't disagree with him. He didn't have to; his eyes were filled with remorse and sorrow. He had a great love for Arthur, having known him for most of his life. Once more he wiped his eyes to stop them from wetting Arthur's chest as he leaned over him to administer care.

Jane clutched at her own heart. Losing Arthur was like having one of her precious hands cut off, her heart torn from its throne in her chest. "Tell him the truth, Doctor. Don't lie to him!"

Arthur turned his eyes upon his beloved. The effort caused his chest to spasm in pain, but he persisted. "My darling, beloved wife, ever has he told me the truth and the lack of words need not poison its certainty any more than rain dilutes a pond or a river."

She flung herself across his chest and held him tight. "I won't let you go!"

"You must!"

“No,” she cried out, pulling back to look into his eyes. “I will come with you!”

He raised his hand. Painfully. He caressed her cheek gently. “My dear, when your time comes, I will be waiting for you. But now is not that time.”

“No, I won’t let you go!”

He felt tears surfacing, but he couldn't wipe the shameful things away. So, instead, he smiled and whispered. "No matter where I am taken, I shall always return for you. Never forget that!"

She pulled away and wiped tears in her eyes, and then pressed her handkerchief gently to the moisture on his face. She leaned forward and kissed the new ones away.

"You are the heart and soul of my life as my writing could never be," he whispered, his voice fading.

"I love you." She told him.

"And I, you!" He gasped.

He spasmed again, his eyes shutting against the pain that clutched his chest.

Doctor Tatsand immediately came over and administered a shot. "This won't stop..."

"I know. I know." Arthur told him and then sighed with relief as the pain washed away with the help of the soporific he had been given.

He felt himself falling away.

Beneath him, a huge tunnel of pure white light was opening.

He was falling towards it.

Then the tunnel began to rise, and he continued with it until he stood on a bright path of fresh dirt and green grass, with beautiful flowers on both sides of the path.

He began walking the path.

Professor Challenger

The Stranger eyed his pocket watch again and then smiled.

"Time," he said.

Whistling, he shoved the pocket watch into his vest, then mounted the steps into the home of Sir Arthur Conan Doyle. He didn't bother to knock.

The door was open.

God in his providence had given Jane the strength to leave it so.

He knew what his mission was now.

What he must do.

And nothing.

Nothing!

Nothing could stop him now.

You are Wonderful.

Arthur awoke.

Jane and the Doctor were both gone.

He was alone.

He managed to smile.

It doesn't matter. *One is never truly alone*, he thought, though it would have been nice to have some pleasant company.

He felt like a man clinging to a thread over a cliff's edge, barely hanging on. It would be so simple, so easy, so natural to just let go now, but for some reason, he couldn't. Or couldn't. He wasn't sure, just knew he had to cling, however tenaciously, to his mortal coil.

He lay on his bed, doing as many do at such times of great pain, considering the weight of this world and the possibilities that lie beyond it. No one wants to die. Not really. The uncertainties one faces at such moments are greater than the weight of the life we live, but for Arthur, it was not fear of death that weighed his heart or the sense of grief and loss he saw in the eyes of his loved ones.

No, it was the loss of the friendships he had made over the decades and the loves he had wrought so deeply.

As he contemplated these revelations of truth, it helped him to deal with the recurring pains in his heart. He felt a profound sense of contentment begin to well up within the domains of his spirit. He felt a lightness and he could swear for a moment that he saw a man he had only envisioned on paper smiling at him from the foot of his bed and another more aloof man with a beak nose and a deerstalker cap eyeing him from beside him on the other.

"The game will soon be afoot, dear Conan." The beak-nosed man said, his eyes glinting with good humor.

Behind these two men stood a dozen or more other men and women, some of whom he knew quite well as he had imagined them himself and others he knew of only by reputation from other authors' stories. Who were all the strangers?

As if reading his mind, one of the strangers moved to the forefront. He was wearing a show costume. He was muscular, dark-skinned with light-hearted energy about him, and a smile that could melt the winter. He also had a wand in his right hand, which glowed this soft blue color. Or was it the wand that glowed? They were so close together in Arthur's vision he couldn't be certain.

This man he recognized immediately from a recent poster for him at Piccadilly: Harry Houdini.

Harry smiled radiantly. He laughed. "Sorry about the silly old wand, but I felt it important to have something that would help trigger your memories. I also came because I care for you and I wanted to tell you, Conan, that the adventure is not over.

"It has yet to begin."

Another man stepped forward. He wore an outfit that could only be that of a wealthy Count. His face was pale, his hair pitch black and swept back. His eyes were magnetic just like Madame Blavatsky's were. His smile was warm, even though two very sharp-looking fangs protruded into view when he did.

He bowed to Arthur.

"Though you did not create me, gentle sir, I am obliged to thank you for your including me in your world of friends, without whom my personal life would be much less worthy."

"Count Dracula?"

The Count smiled and bowed again. "You do recognize me then?"

"Only because my dear friend, Bram Stoker, wrote you so well."

The Count bowed and stepped back into the crowd behind him.

Another man stepped forward. He was a bit heavy in the stomach, with a bristly mustache and thick hair. He wore a bowler hat and had a crisp bow tie across the lapels of his starch white shirt.

"Watson!" Arthur sighed with pleasure.

"Doctor to some," Doctor Watson admitted with a grin.

"And the kind man next to me is..."

"Sherlock Holmes!"

The beak-nosed man put an arm about Watson's shoulders. "We'd like to thank you for your conclusion to our journey on this world."

"This world?"

Holmes gave Arthur a wink. "Oh, dear fellow, if you could only see several of the worlds I've already lived upon, you would realize how great your imagination has been, how widely you have created."

"I'm not God, I'm merely a writer!"

Holmes smiled. "How can something so great not include us within its body? How can we not all be God in our ways?"

Arthur brightened. "You know Madame Blavatsky?"

Holmes grinned. "Oh, we speak to way many more souls than her, good man."

Watson came a step closer. He put a finger to Arthur's throat, then his hand over his heart. "Conan, just a little longer and the pain will be gone forever."

"No one calls me Conan," Arthur replied, his words barely audible.

"Oh, but your friends do," Holmes assured him.

Arthur felt his eyelids becoming so heavy he could barely keep them open. Finally, he could do so no more. He didn't want to let go of this feast of friends. These charming people he had created and others. He had become so deluded now by his imagination as he lay dying that he could even accept his hallucinations as real people. But as he did an image of Jane came into his mind.

"Farewell my love," he whispered.

Everyone vanished that had stood about his bed. They vanished, but the smiles and warmth that were their personalities remained in the room, lulling Arthur into a deeper and deeper sense of contentment.

His eyes opened again just as a tunnel of pure white light began to open before him.

He felt himself start to rise from his body. He was, at last, going to learn the secret of the Great Mystery.

The door to the room was flung open. Jane rushed inside. She was followed by Doctor Tatsand and

Professor Challenger, who immediately gave Arthur the brightest of smiles and a look that told him he knew what had just happened. And more!

The tunnel of white light vanished.

Arthur sighed unhappily. He just wanted to rest. To sleep now. He was so tired. The pain was so unbearable, and yet somehow, he could not once again. Something kept his eyes open.

Jane sat on the bed and held his hand between hers. "I've brought someone for you."

"I know."

He knew he was close to crossing over to the other side. His heart was failing him for once and all. Even his dear Jane would not be able to keep him from leaving now.

But she tried.

His dear wife held his right hand steadily, her eyes never leaving his, even when his own drifted to the visions before him which returned. Sherlock Holmes and all his wonderful friends stood in the room again, but they now stood in the tunnel of white light.

They smiled in anticipation.

His eyes focused on Jane again. She had been his pillar and anchor in this life, without which his stories would have come to naught nor would have even been enjoyed by himself as he wrote them.

Doctor Tatsand watched silently. The look on his face told Arthur that he knew.

Professor Challenger never lost his warm smile. His sympathetic look gave Arthur a sense of comfort and strength, he had felt was leaving him now. But even with that, he felt his body becoming lighter, even as the pressure on his heart increased.

No, he didn't fear death. Why should he? He had courted it countless times in his adventures on paper, and his myriad debunking of so-called spiritualists, those people who sucked on the emotions of those who had lost ones dear to them like some kind of fiendish vampire of ancient legends. He also knew there was life beyond life and that there were splendid and remarkable creatures of nature, invisible to most, which existed all about him. These revelations and adventures of the spirit gave him a deep sense of contentment as he faced the demise of his physical form in preparation for his emerging into a much wider more radiant world beyond.

He was the caterpillar about to morph into a butterfly!

He was pondering all those things when Professor Challenger entered the room.

Again!

Arthur blinked.

But the man had already entered.

The man was tall, heavily built, with a thick mustache that seemed to have a life of its own.

"You are the Invisible Man I met at the store," Arthur greeted him.

Professor Challenger grinned. "Not likely, but sometimes I wish I were. But I do know the man. His name is Professor Langston, and he is quite a brilliant chap. Nothing at all like those horrid stories written about him on this world."

Arthur cringed.

Challenger didn't realize it was his best friend, Herbert Wells, who had written the Invisible Man. But at this moment he didn't want to fight over details. Herbert had enough on his plate to not worry over the criticism of this man.

Arthur sighed inwardly. He was just too dratted tired. He just wanted it to all be over so he could rest for the last time.

Challenger seemed like a man used to having his

way, doing what he wanted, being the man in authority. His hair was almost a blood-red, blonde color as if the sun had melted into it. His eyes burned with the fires of an unknown sun that infused his face with sparkle and lightness at the same time it became almost fierce looking.

"You know him, Arthur?" Jane asked. "He insisted on coming into our home. I haven't the strength to say no to a man who claims your friendship."

Arthur had to think about that. Did he know the Invisible Man? Was this the same man who had so rudely interrupted him repeatedly at Sir Charles Jewelers?

His eyes began to droop again.

"Arthur!" Jane begged.

He patted her hand. "Not yet."

He opened his eyes. The Stranger seemed to be surrounded by a brilliant white light. Arthur now knew who was standing in his bedroom. His memory was coming back to him. But it was..."Impossible!"

"What?" Jane asked.

"This man is impossible. I recognize him."

Challenger had a hopeful look on his face but remained silent.

"I recognize you now! You're not just the man I met at the jewelers, are you?"

"I am not."

"Who is this man, Arthur?" Jane demanded, not knowing whether to send for the police or to demand he leave. She had taken a chance to admit him. He had said he and Arthur were close friends.

"Dear lady, I am the delight of your good Conan as I call him and Arthur as he is known to all else. I am that which all men wish for, and few men ever achieve. I am all those things and yet I am just a humble being like you."

Arthur closed his eyes a moment, struggling to deal with the pain he experienced, feeling it encompassing his consciousness increasingly, like a dark shroud being pulled over a bright light. Was this truly what dying felt like? "You can't be him!" He said in an almost accusatory manner to Challenger. "He's not real! He's a figment of my imagination. You're a figment of my imagination!"

"My good, Conan, you should know by now that nothing is impossible, despite your lifetime spent debunking it." He pointed out, tipping a thick hat, with decorations of an odd sort about its band. "Not all who claim to know the Greater are charlatans."

Ms. Doyle rose to face him. Her courage and strength had returned, as well as her protectiveness towards her dying husband. "Why did you tell me you knew my husband. It is obvious he does not know you?"

The tall stranger took her hand and pressed his lips lightly to her fingers.

Her first reaction was to pull away, but something about his eyes and his manner quelled her fears. She allowed him to kiss her fingers. But he did not let go. She felt this strange kind of warmth seeping into her body as if she were a child with her parent and being kept safe and warm.

He spoke. "Madam, I did not mean to horrify or frighten you. Perhaps Arthur is not as astute in his observations as I had thought when he wrote them down. But you, Ms. Doyle. You expected to know me to the last gray hair in my beard. I expected you to recognize me as whom I rightfully am!"

Ms. Doyle turned to look at Arthur, who seemed more alert than usual, despite being on his death bed. He gave her a slight nod of his head, hard as that was.

Arthur smiled weakly. "Don't you recognize him, my dear?" He asked, and then he began reciting words as if reading them from a book. "He was tall, burly, and browned from the sun. A perpetual caterpillar of a mustache twisted incessantly above his strong lips as if putting a question mark on who he was. A beard shrouded his chin and jaws, making him look like a modern-day Svengali. A scourge and a genius embodied in one personality. A man of strength, character, and mystery. A man who would put any modern scientist to shame. And did. Frequently, I might add."

"The dinosaurs!" Ms. Doyle uttered, suddenly recognizing him. "Dear God in heaven!" She stammered. "You're alive. But everyone thought you dead when you entered the land of the Smoky God." Confused for a moment, she shook her head. "I mean, in the stories Arthur wrote. Not our real world. But this is impossible. You're not alive. He invented you!"

"And what if he did? Does the Creator have so little regard for the children of his authors that he would just allow them to vanish once read?" The Stranger asked. "I think not. My adventures are not just my own, but your husband living through me. His spirit has become part of my own and the world he has created. The world and universe that all great authors have created together...even if unknowingly."

"I don't know how to relate to any of this," she said, feeling suddenly quite weak.

He steadied her.

"Come now, if you can imagine angels and believe in them, is it then so hard to imagine people like me living as well? We all have our purpose in God's works."

She sat down again as if a heavyweight had dropped on her shoulders. This event was taxing not only to her imagination but her heart as well. She was but a short run from death herself these days, staving off a recurring heart condition that left her weaker by the month as well. She had not told Arthur about it. He had enough to carry.

She suddenly felt this burst of fear. "You're death, come to take my love away! The last adventure we all must take."

"Exactly. But not in the way you mean. He need not die that way. He can live on as I have, in a new world. One he has helped to create. This is precisely where I intend to take this grouchy old man. For one last adventure, perhaps even a few more than that if he's willing to stick around, that is!" He winked, putting an exclamation mark to his words. He smiled broadly. "And better yet, dear Ms. Doyle, there is room yet in that story for you as well!"

"But Professor Challenger is only a story. He's not real. I mean...you're not real!" Jane insisted.

Challenger put his hat on and looked at Arthur. "Will you not come with me, Conan? It's the least I can do to thank you for the love you have created me with." He looked at Jane, who was terrified of her husband's life now. "I am that I am." He told her.

But Arthur couldn't answer. He saw the man standing before him. He wanted to believe more than anything what he was being told, but he was so tired. So very, very tired. He would just shut his eyes and think about it. He shut his eyes. "I will go if Jane will be there."

"Conan," his wife screamed.

His eyes jerked open. "You never call me Conan," he managed to croak, the hint of a smile on his lips.

She gave him a look that broke what remained of his heart, which he returned with a smile and uttered the last words his mortal body would speak in our world. "You are wonderful!"

Jane threw herself across his body, moaning in pain and loss.

"Arthur!" She wept.

Then she let go.

He was still smiling.

She turned around.

Professor Challenger was still there.

He was also smiling.

"He will always love you, Jane. Thank you for your love and help," Challenger said, then vanished.

Soul Journey

Arthur saw Jane cast herself across his body as he rose from it. He noticed that Challenger was not looking at her, but instead at him as he rose.

Challenger winked.

Arthur felt this tremendous weight lift from him as he continued to rise into the air and then drift through the ceiling of their home. He landed on his feet atop the roof and looked one last time over his beloved London. “Beautiful!” He sighed, then he looked in the other direction, where a tunnel of pure white light opened.

Standing at the entrance of the tunnel was Professor Challenger.

“My good man, surely you didn’t think I would abandon you at this moment?”

"Wait!" Arthur cried out.” How can you be in two places at once?”

Arthur floated there; his body lighter than he could ever remember it. He heard a chorus of angels singing in the purest and sweetest of melodies, their voices so high and hypnotic he wanted to race past Professor Challenger and greet them.

At last, he would know the final truth, the one he had sought all his living days. But he could not see them for Challenger was blocking his path, a determined look on his face.

"Would you abandon all the adventures you've yet to experience, friends to make, people to save?"

"You are just a very pleasant figment of my dying imagination," Arthur told him then tried to scoot around him.

But Challenger blocked his path yet again. "I say no you shall not pass until you have experienced all that the Creator has set out for you."

Arthur hesitated at those words. "But I have had more than my share of all that is right and good in the world. Why would my Creator want more for me?"

Challenger leaned closer and whispered, "If you pass into the Light now, you will never know, will you? Or will you? That is the mystery. But it's a mystery about which you need not worry. Come with me. Keep learning. Keep growing. Or do not. See what then happens next. God is kind and loving. He will not let you down no matter which path you choose."

With that Challenger turned his back to Arthur and began walking into a side tunnel that had appeared in the tunnel of white light.

Arthur's first and most direct impulse was to dash forward. Even as he did so he could see people he knew and loved and had passed on. They waited for him with bright smiles on their faces.

He wanted desperately to be with them, but as he passed the side tunnel he slowed, then turned to look.

For some insane reason that defied all logic, if any of it made any sense now, he felt compelled to do what he would never have thought to do. As if with new eyes and senses he saw a new world. One so extremely like that of Earth's and yet clasped like a pearl in a necklace brooch by the hands of a radiant being, whose eyes he could not even dare to investigate.

He knew he was at the crossroad that Challenger had educated him about.

The one that Madame Blavatsky had intimated.

"There is much, much more to reality than we can ever possibly imagine," her words came to him.

He felt like a butterfly attracted to a bright light; a moth to flames as he gazed at the heavenly view before him. It dazzled his eyes, his mind, and his heart.

"It is true!" He uttered. "All of it!" He finished.

He turned again to look forward into the tunnel of light where his friends and past family members were gathered. They still waited patiently, smiling even more than before. Their arms were opened to welcome and embrace him.

He smiled at them. A burst forth from his heart and soul like a morning glory raising its blossomed face to the new morning sun.

"Another day," he told them.

They didn't object. They smiled even more. That tunnel vanished and only the side one remained. He turned fully into it; his eyes once more dazzled by the heavenly view before him.

Later, he would remember little of this passage, but the smallest portions. The far greater part of the vision...the heavenly being, the gigantic universe he was seeing...all of that would become faint memories.

But he would never forget that death was only a new direction and never an end. That was now embedded in his very soul. Without further ado or farewell, he shot down the side tunnel towards a destiny that herewith shall be told.

Challenger had sought to retrieve his friend and done his job well.

The heaven you and I wait to rest in was not the one that Arthur chose. He chose the one that only a writer might. There was another heaven to visit now. A new place to stretch his wings and fly. To become more than he had ever been before: To dance with the angels of his imagination!

The Baker Street Universe.

Arthur's Revelation

And so, it was that I, Sir Arthur Conan Doyle, the creator of Sherlock Holmes and Doctor Watson, began the greatest adventures of my life, even after my death to your world, even as we all do, dear reader, travel on to higher worlds where we continue to learn and explore and become all that our Creator has in store for us. Even as we all do. But my adventure is not yours, just like yours will not be mine. No, my adventure was to be with one of my best-known and loved characters, Professor Challenger, along with a few other surprises I'm sure you'll find interesting, and I intend to enlighten you about.

As you know, dear readers, Professor Challenger's last adventure exposed him to an impossible truth. One that involved the end of all life as we know it. But that is just a writer's way of saying he is tired of writing any more about that character, or perhaps he wasn't making any money from putting his strength in that direction. Or maybe he was just bored with being a writer. Or had a new romance or a new fancy.

But for whatever practical or impractical purposes it may be at that time, I did not continue the stories further.

I failed to see any reason to proceed further. Or did I? What do I mean by this insinuation? Modern science has revealed the possibilities of infinite timelines, or alternate universes splitting off from each.

It is believed widely that every action we incline ourselves towards and accomplish or not creates a new timeline, a new and alternate reality.

The Almighty Creator's way of amusing himself, or perhaps an intellectual game far beyond anything a man can comprehend? Or perhaps a grand design that humankind plays out with the assistance of a Force beyond our comprehension?

Then it does not necessarily follow, if this is true, and for our purposes, we will assume it is. Does it not then follow that perhaps I was being a bit misleading, or circumspect in my tales of adventure? Was I truly dictating what I saw in my writer's eye, or what had happened, or more pointedly, was I discussing a greater metaphysical reality based on a more profound truth that the world was ready to handle the truth of?

You may well ask and probably should ask what is meant by Egg World. As you know, being the astute reader, you are, Professor Challenger found the Lost World, and that adventure led to fame, fortune, and greater adventures, until he found out that our world was an egg and about to hatch. Quite a ponderous ending to an exciting series of adventures. If it had been true, we would never have been able to enjoy all the splendid adventures of Professor Challenger's best friend, Holmes, and that good man's best friend, Watson, which I shall soon reveal to you.

Because it didn't happen the way you expect. No, what truly happened is what follows. I hope you will be patient with me as I disclose the nooks and crannies of this story, as I need to tell it in spurts. Just mark it up to the whims of an old man...a very, incredibly old, but young man, I point out with great humility and humor. As well as honor. For my friendships are a treasure worth more to me now than any gold or jewel could ever embody.

I shall not bore you further with the details of my death, as they are greatly misleading. Death to one world need not mean death to all worlds. So herewith, and herein I ask you to be patient with me as I describe what happened after my adventure with the old world of mine, which you have been reading about and has ended. Now we move on to my new life in this new world, which is so bright, so challenging, and so, very, very…how shall I say it…incredible!

We shall continue my new path, my ascension into new heaven or universe. You take your pick. We shall see it through the eyes of our friends, as well as ourselves.

Thus, you shall see why death is not our enemy at all but is also a wonderful friend when the time is right.

This means when your time here has become an open door to a new world elsewhere.

Welcome to my adventures…in all the worlds of my Baker Street Universe, which I can happily now report exists and is the crowning glory of my writing career as well as my personal life.

Awake to Me

I must admit that I was totally surprised when I awoke in my own home, no longer an insubstantial etheric body plummeting through a white tunnel of Light to a new world.

I was here.

And here was not at all what I had seen from the earlier view.

While my first view had made me think of heaven, my current view made me think I was repeating myself. Living my life all over again. But with a difference.

I sat up on my bed and put my hands before me. Astonished by what I saw, and without thinking it was impossible to do, I flung myself from my bed and scampered to my full-length mirror.

"Dear God!" I exclaimed.

Challenger came into the room and gave me a hearty smile and a cup of steaming tea. "I thought you might need this once you came to yourself."

I looked at the tea and made a face.

"Really, old fellow, I've...um..." He smiled broadly. "Uh, enhanced its recuperative powers somewhat."

I then sniffed the tea and made another face.

"Rum? You know I hate Rum!"

"Actually, I don't. I know what you like here because you lived here as my friend."

I sniffed the tea again suspiciously and then raised it to my lips. I took a sip, then another. I didn't stop until the cup was empty.

I felt a warm glow suffusing my body.

Challenger grinned.

"Did the trick, hey?"

"Indeed," I told him with reluctance.

I gazed into my mirror once more. "I am years younger!"

"By quite a few."

I turned to him. "Will I die the same way here?"

"That's quite up to you, Conan."

I started to protest my name, then realized it didn't matter at all. I was starting over. With a fresh body, by Jove, I had nothing at all to complain about...well, maybe the rum.

"I see." I didn't, but I had to keep him in his place, or the ruffian would badger me endlessly trying to get me to admit I was wrong.

That's one thing I write about his character. Stubbornness. I suppose you could call him a mirror of myself. As writers, we often mirror our habits. Of course, at the time I wrote to him, I had no idea I was mirroring my stubbornness.

But when I showed Jane the first draft of my Challenger character, she burst into laughter. After months of badgering her to explain her laughter, she had turned to me and with a sweet smile said, "Arthur, you are Professor Challenger!"

That took me totally by surprise.

She had left for lunch with some friends, leaving me quite alone with her revelation. I immediately dug out my Challenger stories for another look. And she was right.

I never admitted it to her, but she knew I knew and that was enough for her.

I eyed Challenger sternly. "Jane…"

"Out to lunch here as she would have been on yours."

"Am I going to feel the same when I see her?" I asked, fearing his answer.

He didn't.

Instead, he said, Holmes has a bit of an adventure to put us on to help you adapt to your new home.

"What's so new about it? Looks bloody well the same to me!" I admonished him.

He went to my windows and flung the curtains aside.

I almost died again.

I rushed to the windows to look, not believing my eyes.

A man was driving by on a steam-powered monocycle in one direction and a huge dirigible hovered in the sky made of three distinct parts tied together with bridging compartments. It sported huge cannon on the side I could see.

Then I saw something flying that shouldn't have been. People holding hands as they flew a small dirigible above their heads with steam-driven propellers.

"My god!" I gasped.

"And wait until you meet Harry and see some of his magic."

I turned to him, I'm sure wide-eyed and amazed. "Magic??

Challenger stepped alongside me and smiled. "Welcome to the world you created Conan."

Changing Boundaries

"Took a great fall and all the king's horses and all the king's men couldn't put Humpty Dumpty back together again."

--Mother Goose.

Don't be alarmed that I am no longer Conan speaking. His voyage across time and space to the Baker Street Universe he created has been completed. It's not time to let you see what he had gotten himself into...with a bit of help from yours truly of course.

I'm sure most of you thought his death would be the end of the story. Far from it. It continues to this day and beyond. I am going to just introduce you to a small portion of it that he and I have traveled since that momentous day he awoke in a brand new, much younger body, healthy and still alive!

Challenger's Tale

I woke up with a slam to my forehead. Most peculiar, I must say. It was a chilly August morning in downtown London. I was sure I had just before this moment been running down some kind of corridor and then...here I was. Or was I? My mind seemed to be flooded with conflicting images, my heart with conflicting emotions. I felt a profound sense of loss as if I had the door to heaven open for me and then slammed shut in my face.

Then I opened my eyes to cold, hard reality. I was lying on a darkened flat stone with soot all over it. I sensed, rather than felt something exceptionally large and hard above my head, which felt very sore and painful at that moment.

As I looked at the black soot all around me, I mused for a moment longer about the pain flooding behind my eyes in bursts of pure color. What a wondrous firework show! Splendid indeed, I thought to myself, before I remembered what I had been doing.

I pulled myself back from under the furnace pit and considered myself lucky that I would only have an egg on my forehead and not a split skull on the back of it as I felt at the tender spot between my eyes.

The great Professor Challenger was reduced to an idiotic sprain of his massively well-proportioned brain. What a nightmare that would be to explain. Henceforth I would wear my widest hat to bury the egg where it rightly belonged. Out of sight!

"I say, Conan, where are you when I need you?" I asked no one because that was all I was likely to have a response to. I was in a hellishly clever trap of a prison. For once my wits had outwitted themselves, been outfoxed by my cleverness.

"Yes, Dear Conan," I had told him, as he mused at me as he was wont to do. "I shall explore the basement and you shall help me in this by keeping the young lady's attention on you, and not on myself squiggling through her basement window like a fat porpoise proposing to squirm through a tight bed of coral."

Conan burst into laughter. I fumed for a moment and then relented. After all, it wasn't like I had not done the same with him...a few times before. I blushed. Perhaps a few dozen times or more, to be realistic. Neither of us was fat, just well-padded in some places. I, a bit more of late as I had not been exploring, as I was wont. Keeping my body as trim as it could be with exercise.

I pulled myself out and clutched the photo with the

frayed, burnt edges upon it. It was a miracle it had not perished in the heat of that furnace. Or I for that matter I thought with bemusement. Well, quite impossible as the furnace was off, but the igniter was hot enough.

My forehead was caked with sweat and soot. Not much cost compared to similar accidents of the past, where I had lost more than a few inches of the scalp.

Once I'd crawled back out the basement window Conan caught my attention from the window he stood near, and then came quickly to speak with me. I had found what we were looking for. But it had taken a lot of conniving. I rubbed my forehead, which reminded me that it took a bit of pain to achieve my goal.

At first, he was going to fight me for the honor of being the rat in the trap. He was not the sort to consort with single women, especially as he was a very happily married man. Even after he transitioned to our world, he has maintained a steady character, not lapsing into melancholy or regret, but taking advantage of his newfound youth, even renewing his relationship with Jane once more. Even though she was quite a different woman in my world versus the one he had left behind, still she was the one he loved in all worlds. What can I say? Love is blind.

And once she set her eyes on this newly born author, maybe God's Will, karma, whatever you like to call it, she couldn't stop calling on him. At first, as a doctor for illnesses she did not have, then social events she could now invite him to and eventually to meet her parents and cement a bond that he willingly and wholeheartedly jumped into with open arms and eyes.

I must admit, I expected him to do a grumbly sort of thing for a time having been drawn away from the traditional heaven to this world...but he soon got over many things, including himself.

And now, here we are, hacking away at crimes, banging our heads and our brains in the name of bringing law and order to this universe.

Back to the present, Conan, instead of prodding at me, instead, once I'd laid a photo, somewhat crumpled and worn from its drop into the morning sunshine rain of good old London, into his hands, he fell back to the more familiar personality I had known throughout the years of my future.

He eyed the woman's portrait and smiled. "I say, she is a looker, isn't she?"

"Yes. If you like women who can turn you into a frog if you sully their name," I reminded him.

"Oh!" He mumbled. "Forgot about that."

"You would!" I reminded him.

"We need to find that blasted wall before it gets too late," I reminded him yet again. "If we hadn't found this picture, we wouldn't have known it was so close."

He nodded. "True enough. Last time it moved at least four city blocks."

I snorted. Good Conan had no fear of his dear wife being jealous. He was so totally intertwined with her soul that not even an angel could have gotten between them. When I brought him to our world, I never dreamed that he would end up with the same woman again, just as loving and kind, just as madly in love with him.

It was as if God had given him a second chance, not just in his life, but in love as well. I suspect he would not waste either blessing.

I know I wouldn't. Both chances are so rare as to be never and should be accepted with the greatest of thanks and humility.

I suppose you're screaming for me to explain what I'm talking about in a bit more detail. Well, as you know my mission on your earth was to send Arthur, the duplicate of my Conan to mine. Simple as that.

To put it simply there are multiple Earths. Multiple versions of each of us...on most of them. Some good. Some bad. Some mediocre. But mostly just ourselves with some variation. I and my good friends at Baker Street had learned through the help of one Harry Houdini...yes, that ONE! We had learned ways of crossing over. We usually ignored such doorways. We had been warned there could be consequences for upsetting the natural balances created but like all hard-headed fools...I am being one of the worst...we assumed we could do it and get away with it.

And if not, we would be willing to pay the consequences if it meant helping or saving one soul. That's the kind of people we were. Wanted to be and had to be!

Harry had helped me with the mechanics of it. He's good at that sort of thing, as well as some other of my friends. Any more than that I can't reveal. Some things we just must take on faith, even as Conan had and been lifted from his world to this one...but not in his older, ailing body, but to a younger, healthy one. The transitions here are not always so welcome, nor so hardy, I might add. But he was a creator who had slammed no doors on his creation, let alone his ability to overcome any difficulty. Even facing one's death.

This brings up another fact. For some reason creators...artists, composers, and writers can create their universes and often have...the only thing bad about it, is that they are unaware of their creations. I would have to assume, and Harry assures me it is so, that the Creator doesn't want to give us big heads, nor to upset the careful balances that are created by such zestful energies.

Then you must ask, why can't some of those creations be so dark that you would fear for your life? To that question, I must reply, again, that because of the delicate balances there can be no pure evil. Evil exists solely because of poor choices, not because anyone is pure evil. Though with a bit of work they can surely appear that way...such as Moriarty!

I know that some enlightened men and women believe that the soul travels to a new world where it is reborn with a brand-new body of about twenty-five years of age. But what many of them don't know because they had never made that journey. Consciously at least...is that most that do so have their memories wiped. Conan had not. He was meant to remember. Meant to regain his past. To triumph over the adversity of his death. And he has so far. Graciously and with great humility.

The gates between our worlds are very closely guarded and hard to find, but those lucky enough to find them, can easily pass through for some reason I can't understand. That's more Harry Houdini and Conan's alley than mine. The mystical, spiritual mumbo jumbo. I'm more of an I can do it sort of person. Give me a mission to accomplish. Done! That's it!

But getting back to Conan's seeming disdain for other women, I could relate to that, even if I were happily married, which I am not, much to my regret. Finding women to love me is not hard but keeping them doing so is infinitely more difficult.

Perhaps someday I'll figure out why, but for now, I gain my joy in watching others at least build long-lasting and loving relationships.

And another and probably more important reason women inevitably tire of me is that I tire of them. I've only known one I might have stayed with. She is the Queen now, but as to the rest, they have been nothing but trouble to my soul. While I still had a few healthy years to look forward to, it's getting harder and harder to fit a feminine presence into that picture.

Had I only known then, what I know so well now, I might have ventured on a better path. But I did not.

I was brought from my musings when Conan snapped the picture against his side to shake some soot off, then stuck it in his trouser pocket before I could reclaim it.

He smiled at me in that kind of cunning way I suspect most authors do when they're appraising a worthy subject for their next story and then said, "Wouldn't want to tempt that crusty bachelorhood you've been cultivating over the years, Challenger." He spoke lightly, a twinkle in his eyes. "Maybe you'll get lucky in your next incarnation."

I could've popped his head like a rotten egg at that moment when I saw that look in his eyes, but instead, taking the higher ground, I merely stomped my right boot into the mud at his feet and splashed him with it.

He grinned. He'd won. I'd lost again. I fumed even more, and then stomped off for the back of the stately building, facing the steamy streets of London.

The Hunt for the Portal of Fairie

Baker Street was just a few blocks down, and I didn't want my good friend, Holmes, who lives there with my other friend, Doctor John Watson, to see my situation. I stormed around the corner of the old brick building, briefly admiring the efficacy of its mortar, which kept the storms and years of rain and sun out from the insides of the antique interior. I could see a grandfather clock on one wall as I passed a barely closed window curtain. It was of the old Barony, the ones made in Bavaria under Einstein, the genius from the past.

Not the new one, Sir Albert; he was that man's son and quite alive, thank you.

Legend says that his father came from another world. He had stumbled onto ours, white-haired, mustached young, and confused as he stepped into one hellishly wicked winter storm. Not that they aren't all a bit of that these days. Something to do with climate change, which I had warned the Aristocracy about, but who wouldn't listen, as it would mean cutting back on coal factories, and that new, idiotic contraption of the automobile.

Fortunately, Tesla and Edison have been building cars of a different nature. All electric. While not selling as fast as the steam and coal-driven ones, they were gaining popularity.

Popular thought for the most part, still maintains that a proper horse is the only way to properly carry a man from one point to another in safety and sanity. And the bonus is that they always left a hefty deposit of fertilizer for farmers to distribute safely to future crops. A solution where everyone benefits if ever there was one.

Many conflicting thoughts about the introduction of steam-driven automobiles were now fighting to stay alive with the introduction of the Tesla electric cars, which used no combustible fuels whatsoever to work.

And with Tesla paving the way with his friend Edison with his contraptions I felt caught between the hammer and an anvil by technology. Even though Tesla intended to remove the burden of coal from humanity as he called it, it was still a long road to travel to implement his goals across an entire planet.

I fear our world might not survive that long the way most other nations are clamoring for increased oil and coal. Worse yet, the moguls of wealth are digging in their heels and buying out anyone that threatens their hegemony of power and wealth.

I grunted angrily to myself. Technology should free a man's soul, not labor it.

"Good God in Heaven," I thundered at Conan. "Can't believe the state of affairs in these noble edifices. London is surely falling to pieces."

Conan stepped over a broken piece of chimney brick and glanced upwards to admire the leaning chimney barely attached to the building above. "I think, rather, that it's more likely that we are the ones falling apart. But then again, according to Einstein, there are worse things in store for London than stinking automobiles and disintegrating chimneys."

I glanced at him questioningly. I hadn't heard that. Must have been his father who told him that. Supposedly, in his old world, modern humans were using bombs that could wipe out entire cities with one blast.

I kicked the chimney piece aside and cleared my throat in a gruff manner. "There are always worse things in store with you writers. Can't you ever think of anything besides the end of the world, collapsing stars, and time travelers that travel to God-forsaken futures where cannibals delight themselves with dainty damsels in a sauce of rare meat?"

"Now, who's being negative?" Conan asked as he drew them both to a stop before a stretch of wall that had a peculiar essence to it. "Go ahead and touch it, Challenger."

"Nonsense. Won't bother. Just cleaned my nails this morning." He uttered with disdain and a total lack of conviction. He knew quite well his fingernails were dirty with soot from his earlier adventure, as were his clothes, which he gathered didn't make very many comfortable to view him, which explained so many pedestrians quickly adjusting their path to the opposite side of the street as he approached them.

But back to the wall, any idiot bystander would perceive that he was dying to do anything but touch it.

"It is morning, Challenger." Conan pointed out with a touch of irony to his voice. "Quite early as a matter of fact."

"Bloody damn well if I care, you oat-eating wisp of a man," I snorted.

Conan turned aside to hide his smile. He was hardly a wisp, with a waist of forty-five that made him more resemble a pork barrel, or a pickle barrel, than the handsome, shapely man I was with my daunting Apollonesque physique, even if my belly was putting on a touch of pear to its shape as well from my lack of exercise of late and too many scones at Baker Street.

"Right then, touch it I will if only to soothe that ghastly sense of humor you worship." I snorted again, my breath sending brief squirts of fog into the early, chilly morning London airs. "And don't go telling me there are fairies behind this nonsense of a structure, or I'll expose you for the fraud you are."

Conan grinned mischievously. "And I the fact that your dinosaur egg never hatched, and a mechanical dinosaur cleverly constructed by our good friends, Jules and Wells, was in fact what everyone saw!"

I barked with laughter for a moment and then realized Conan wasn't kidding. "You knew all this time and said nothing."

"Challenger, one thing about a writer you're bound to discover in one of your lifetimes, hopefully, this one, is that they have a broader perception of reality than the average person does. Not that you're common." Conan quickly threw in to keep me and, I'm sure, my red face from exploding. He touched my broad shoulders. "Please, continue."

I gently plied the wall with the palm of my right hand, a solemn look on my face, which soon thereafter turned into one of astonishment. I turned to look at my friend and good companion, Conan, with a look of surprise on my lips and in my eyes.

Conan nodded his head. "I told Watson about it last night."

"And?" I whispered, as if afraid to hear the answer.

"Nothing," Conan responded. His right eyebrow arched significantly. "I suspect our friend in the deer hat had something to do with that."

"Quite." I agreed. "Well then, we're done here." I pointed it out and turned to leave.

"Where now?" Conan asked.

"Why to fetch our dear friend from his labors!" I roared. "And just like I, the games are always afoot with that good man."

Conan sighed. He knew exactly where this footing would head for, and somewhat reluctantly had to admit, despite his trepidation about it, he was just as excited about it as I was, as it would go far to prove his theories about life and evolution.

"Fairies," I muttered as I pushed past Conan. "Drat them all. Drat them all to damnation!"

Conan fairly exploded with laughter.

Then he stopped when the weight of my words reached that brain of his. Fairies were real!

221B Baker Street

"Dear God, Watson, must you always be playing that violin. It drives shivers up and down my spine." Holmes told his companion, the good Doctor John Watson.

Watson laid his violin down and carefully began polishing it with a soft cloth made of velvet. Ignoring Holmes's rather emotional outburst, he instead said quietly. "It is illogical to stop something now that I have persisted in doing every morning, bar none."

"Surely, you torture me only because I have kept you awake many a night with my playing?"

Watson gave Holmes a sly look and then continued to polish his violin. "Now why would I condescend to such an idiotic level as to seek vengeance against my best friend?"

Holmes tapped his pipe into his palm and then dumped it unceremoniously into the outstretched palms of a miniature cupid seated on his highly veneered writing desk. "I see. Then you are instead telling me that you digress to such a low level of contemplation of the truth, you favor me with irritating bites of misinformation?"

"My dear Holmes, were I to do that, my dear beloved

Mary would rise from her grave and beat me to death with one of your smelly pipes. When will you get that horrible thing cleaned properly?" Watson asked, and then made a face as Holmes began to tamp it full of tobacco again.

"And you with that contraption you call a violin? Why the wood is not even of the finest Cherry as it should be." Holmes countered.

"Touché." Watson replied.

"Indeed," Holmes remarked agreeably after he puffed a few times on his pipe and blew several rather curious smoke rings which he pondered deeply a moment, before turning back to Watson, who was continuing to polish his violin.

"You really should try playing your violin again, Holmes. It would do wonders for your temperament." Watson declared.

Holmes shrugged off the jab. "The only problem with my temperament, dear Watson." Holmes proclaimed. "Is that it is about to become sorely abused in about five seconds."

Watson grunted. "I still don't know how you always know when someone is arriving." He rushed down the stairs to the front door and was about to reach for its knob when a loud, burly knock struck it.

Watson fell back a moment in shock, fearing it might be someone he'd best not allow in, but then he heard a snickering sound.

He growled angrily, "Challenger, you devil you!"

He threw open the door.

Front Porch

"Watson" I greeted him as I stepped inside the building. “Please don’t mind the tease, you’re so easy to scare.”

Now you may ask why I, Professor Challenger, would stoop to such a ploy. But of late Watson and I have been vying for the last scone that the ever-delightful Ms. Hudson bakers for us. I’m afraid Watson is exceptionally more jealous of losing his scones than his dear Ms. Hudson sometimes.

Watson ignored my greeting and burst into a complaint about Holmes, “That man is always playing me for a fool with his parlor tricks."

"What parlor tricks?" I inquired.

"As if you didn't know, Challenger, as you are his only equal in such," Watson pointed out in a resentful tone.

Conan passed me, took Watson’s hand, and pumped it. "So, kind of you to invite us in. It's rather miserable outside right now with the biting northern winds and all."

I watched Watson's face calm. He liked Conan a lot. He had been the doctor at Conan's side when he lay on his death bed here in this world.

And yes, the balances were in action even then. You cannot bring a duplicate to this world, without the other one leaving on purpose or dying.

Death or evacuation were the laws here.

Conan here had died of consumption. He was quite young and healthy otherwise.

Since Arthur, the new Conan had transferred with a bad heart and not consumption, he had not risen in a body ravaged by the dread disease. But instead, he had a young, healthy, and vibrant body.

A benefit of the transfer was that you did not take your diseases with you, nor assume the one you were troubled with here.

We climbed the stairs into the sitting room. Holmes rose from his chair, his face lit up with a bright smile.

"Ah-ha!" Holmes exclaimed. "Challenger, can you tell this friend of mine how offensive it is to tempt the gods with music fit only for the cock's crow at dawn? And the game's afoot, and with music like his, the game will soon be on our feet, instead of beneath it!"

I ignored him, knowing full well it was only part of the friendly banter between the two. I had no intention of stepping between them in any way whatsoever. "Holmes! So good to see you again." I greeted, ignoring his jibes at Watson, who was also ignoring them while rolling his eyes quite dramatically. Holmes took my hand, and I could feel the fineness of his bones through his grip. Strong, but delicate at the same time.

"And you look stout and strong as always, Challenger," Holmes replied, his sharp eyes losing nothing of detail.

Watson snorted. "You mean fat and sloppy, don't you? His weight is twenty pounds above normal, and he's wearing his jacket reversed to hide his expanding waist."

Holmes shook a finger at Watson. "There you go again, showing off your intellectual prowess, and hurting my friend's feelings."

Watson preened beneath the complaint. I merely shrugged. Watson couldn't help his nature. Nor I. He loved scones. I love healthy food in general. We were both quite comfortable insulting each other's weight gains. Neither of us held onto the weight for long, as our adventures were usually quite grueling physically and drained excess weight quite quickly.

Though, I must admit that Watson tends to eat a few sweeter things than I, which would explain why his stomach never quite reduced as much as mine.

Conan made his way around the room shaking

hands, and then settled on a nice Scots hard-back chair with the emblem of the Queen Mary of Scots blazoned on it. He shuffled a bit to get comfortable, then crossed one leg over the other as he watched his two famous friends continue their affectionate squabble.

I often wondered how the author viewed this world through his eyes, having come from one where none of us existed, except on paper.

Watson finished polishing his violin, gently put it away in a velvet-lined wooden case and shoved it carefully onto a shelf over a desk, as tidy as a spider's web. He brushed his oxford suit twice and then turned to reach a hand out to me.

"I am glad you could make it, Challenger."

"And I," I replied with a smile.

I took his hand and pumped it several times. I gave him a cocked eyebrow, indicating my curiosity was aroused, and said, "Remarkable, how you are always somehow able to guess my weight so easily."

Watson stepped back and smiled, stroking his thin mustache for a moment in thought. He glanced at Holmes to see if he was listening and then said. "Well, first you are wearing a Pennington, which everyone knows is the Big and Tall shirt found over in Piccadilly. And they start at over twenty pounds. There's a stretch to the shirt, and it fits tight around the collar, which only that size does."

Holmes sat down on his Elizabethan couch, folded his hands in his lap daintily, and pretended not to hear, but to prepare for the coup de grace that would top off this silly exchange between us. "What about those with fat heads?

Watson shook his head. "How utterly preposterous, Holmes, everyone knows a Pennington..."

Conan burst into laughter, as did everyone else.

Watson sat down a bit harder than he intended on the other end of the couch, then scowled at Holmes for a moment, then uncrossed his right leg over the left, and put his left over his right in protest. "I'm not amused."

Holmes shook his head and then turned to me. "Please forgive my dear friend, Watson. He's been out of sorts since Ms. Hudson has stopped making scones for him to help him lose weight."

"She did not!" Watson protested, his face turning a deep red.

"Watson," I told him. "He's just teasing you."

"I know it." Watson proclaimed, folding his arms stubbornly. "But his jokes are sometimes laced with truth."

"As all good jokes are, Watson," Holmes admitted. Finally, he went to Watson and offered his hand. "Please forgive my frivolity. It's just that I am eager to learn of what our friends have found and to be off."

"Off where?" Watson demanded, suspicion rising in the back of his mind as he looked at both me and Conan, who tried to appear busy with other things but failed.

Holmes saved us both when he said, "I assume it's about the Wall of the Fairy Kingdom you're here about?"

"Bloody right, he is." Watson pointed out.

I sat down on an antique King George chair with a throne back and plush red velvet lining. "Actually, it's more than that. I need your help."

I think I've never seen more surprised looks on my friends' faces than at that moment.

They both rose to go for their outdoor jackets.

Game Afoot

"The game is afoot!" Watson blurted out,

I held a hand up to stop him. "No, not the wall. That can wait! It's the Bollocks, weasel-faced fairies who have been invading my dear Margaret's favorite tomatoes. As you know the fairy tales all claim there are no tomatoes in Fairie, and so they steal them to offer to the monsters that live there to spare their miserable little lives."

"You don't really believe that Challenger?" Holmes asked. His eyes were veiled as he stared at me, hiding what he thought.

"No. What I believe is that if I don't stop those little tramps, I will not have enough to offer to our lovely Queen Mary of Scots. You know I am her supply source. I've traveled half the world to find tomato plants that will grow in my garden for her. The thought of them all being eaten up by a bunch of inky dinky fairies with no clothing and blank minds just isn't right!"

"Watson, is that true?" Holmes inquired as he sat back down, reaching for his pipe once more.

"First I've heard of such nonsense. He sat down on the other side of Holmes, and folded his hands in his lap, eyeing Challenger thoughtfully. "Oh, dear God in heaven,

Conan, will you please put your disposition down in your favorite chair before I toss it at you."

Conan was staring at a painting of the Royal M. Marymount, a heritage castle owned by Queen Mary of Scots.

Holmes and Watson gave each other side glances and then waited.

Finally, Conan sat down on the stark settee, with its embroidered, flowery patterns stretched from one rosewood corner to the other. He ran a hand across its patterns, a very childlike look on his face. "Had I been alive when she..."

I stopped fantasizing with a wave of my hand. "Conan!"

Conan stopped and looked up, a bit startled, and embarrassed at the same time.

"We have more precious items to discuss than some old Queen that everyone has already forgotten about a hundred times over!" I chided my old friend. "This is not about her great, great grandmother, but the sitting Queen!"

Conan bowed his head to the words, but Holmes could see that Conan was aggravated anyway. He crossed his hands over his lap in a gentlemanly fashion, and then looked up.

"I do believe Hyde is out and about again." I finally managed to build up enough courage to speak the dreaded word and spit it out as if my mouth were defiled in the act.

It was.

The creature was the deadliest monster we had encountered yet and may ever encounter.

Holmes and Watson both tensed. Watson reached into his desk to pull out his favorite handgun and began checking its chambers.

"Come now, Watson. You know that won't do you one bit of good against that creature!"

Watson eyed me thoughtfully for a moment. "Maybe. Harrys added a little something extra to the powder. You might be surprised at the results."

“Well then, so young Mister Houdini is up to more inventions, is he? I'd say it's off to explore the Fairy Way then."

I rose to leave just as Ms. Hudson came in with a tray of tea and scones. My stomach immediately yelled at me to sit back down.

I did.

"Surely the end of the world can wait until you've

had some breakfast?" She inquired graciously as the men started to move past the only man with some common sense now, me!

Watson was the next hooked by the scent. For some reason, he had been so busy in his mind with the idea of facing off the dread Hyde again that he hadn't gotten to paying attention to his nose yet.

Now he did. "My dear Ms. Hudson, are those raspberry scones?"

"Fresh from Paris." She admitted, setting the tray down on the table where Holmes had his work spread out.

Watson perked up. "Did you say raspberries, Ms. Hudson?"

"I did."

Watson scrambled to the table, moving faster than one would expect. I smiled. He had an extremely large affection for the good Ms. Hudson, but an even larger one for her scones. Especially raspberries. As did I, come to think of it.

Ms. Hudson poured tea for everyone, then handed them napkins.

I sighed after a bite of my scone. "I swear if I were to die today, I would leave this world a happy man indeed."

Ms. Hudson blushed. Watson's face darkened a touch. I had trespassed on sacred ground. He had staked out this woman for more than just a handy source of great-tasting scones.

"I didn't mean..."

She giggled and left the room.

"Extraordinary woman." Then I decided to play Watson a touch.

I watched her exit as if I would die and never see her again. All that time Watson was watching me like a hawk, his face growing redder. He had even stopped eating his scone.

Conan gave me a scathing glance. I knew what he was thinking and ignored it. Watson deserved a bit of teasing. If he wanted to remove his competition, he needed to speak up about his feelings for the good woman. Heaven knows I would have, had those feelings been there.

Conan cleared his throat. "I'm sure this has all been quite pleasant..." He emphasized this while looking at me sternly...and then continued, "But aren't we best being about looking at that wall? Hyde will pop up soon enough I suspect."

"Right!" Watson agreed, standing up, but shoving

some scones into his coat pockets as he did so.

I and Holmes exchanged amused glances, and then followed him and Conan down the stairs to pursue our adventure of discovery. I flung on my hat, as did Holmes his. Watson was already outside the door alongside Conan and heading for the wall when I and Holmes reached the porch.

For some reason, I paused for a moment. Something was bothering me, or perhaps it was a touch of premonition of what was to come. At the time I didn't intellectualize it. I didn't know how to put it into words everyone would understand. That's Harry's territory, not mine. Or even more so Conan's.

But something was telling me we just might have had our last meal together.

The Hateful Hyde

We reached the wall about two hours later. Not because it was so far from the flat, but because all of us were putting off what we were fearful of finding.

Evidence of Hyde.

I sensed a great disturbance in Conan's demeanor as we traipsed casually toward our destination. "Something bothering you, old chap?" I inquired.

He glanced at me. "Only that I keep trying to remember something that happened not that long ago. Something important. As if my very soul depended on it."

He dropped back further so the others couldn't hear his words. "Do you believe in reincarnation, Professor?"

"Absolutely. You're here, aren't you?" I laughed.

He didn't laugh. He gave me a pained expression, and then shut up. I touched his arm.

"I'm sorry. That was dreadfully rude of me. Of course, I do. Any sane man would. Ever since Einstein proved that energy can neither be created nor destroyed, that it is the essential essence binding all things in our universe, I've had to reconsider the ways of the India Islands more seriously."

"Oh?" Conan asked.

I waved my hand dismissively. "Oh, not that gibberish about thousands of personal gods. No, the possibility that we are born repeatedly, each time coming back at a higher plateau than the last. It makes a devilish amount of sense to me. Why would God go to the bother of creating all of this...?" I gestured at myself and him..."And then just wipe it off the map of the world forever. Incredibly stupid thing to do if you were God, don't you think?"

"I do. Considering my transition here from a dying body to a new one, I cannot deny such a possibility at all. No doubt it would be far easier for our God to do than shoot us off one by one as was done with me and go through all that balderdash when it wasn't necessary."

I smiled and gave him a warm pat on his back. "You do catch on fast, dear friend."

Conan nodded. "Madame Blavatsky teaches that as well. She is the one-woman spiritualist I have not been able to debunk. Now, in retrospect, after all, that we've been through, I no longer doubt her vision of the universe. Maybe, just a tiny bit of its interpretation. And even there I could be wrong. After all, any woman who can smoke cigars, drink me into an alley, and levitate her living room couch is something powerful and credible to deal with."

"So why the sudden question about it?" I asked, a bit at a loss as to his questions now.

"Because." He stopped. The others didn't notice or pretended not to. "Because I think I've been here before. Not this here. But here. Much like this one. Only different."

"How so?" I inquired out of curiosity. He was starting to stir up my imagination now. And perhaps, a reconsideration of the feeling I had but moments ago of dread.

"You, Holmes, Watson...the others who live here...they didn't live there. Only in my mind."

"Your mind only!" I exclaimed. "But how is that possible. Each one of us is unique and individual in so many ways. If we were part of your imagination alone, how could we have physical realities at all?" I teased.

"And that," Conan said as we finally arrived with the others at the wall. "That is what I shall leave greater minds than mine to discover."

I did not bother to help clear his mind at that time. He had made a splendid transition from his world to mine. I had made up my mind that once he crossed over,

I would never do a thing to shake his convictions. He had to discover the truth of his new life for himself first. And I knew, from what Harry and I had been talking frequently about, that Conan was like a bulldog when it came to seeking spiritual answers. Once he sunk his teeth into a question, he wouldn't let go until he had shaken the answer free.

Holmes and Watson stopped before the wall, which we had conveniently marked just to make sure the opening could be found again or at least its traces. No telling if it would stay or not. We had found others and they had vanished as quickly and mysteriously as they had appeared.

"I see nothing," Watson exclaimed and then put away several instruments he had been using to probe the wall.

I examined where he was looking. "Nor I. But that doesn't mean anything. Hyde doesn't always leave a clear mark. Or at least one we have been able to deduce."

Conan joined me. "Perhaps we are going about this the wrong way."

Holmes, who had been collecting samples from about the wall, top of it, and the walkway, looked at us. "Remarkable deduction. And on what do you base this conjecture?"

"It is called circular philosophy. I learned it from the good Madame Blavatsky."

I caught on then. "If it smells like a rat and spits like a rat and bites like one..."

"Then it is a rat." Holmes finished, rising to face us both. He nodded his head. "But you forget one thing."

"Which is?" I demanded.

"That we are not dealing with a physical entity."

"Quite the contrary." Conan broke in suddenly.

"What?" Both Holmes and I asked at the same time.

Watson watched the play among us silently, his eyes roving about as if making sure nothing was going to surprise us. He even felt something was off. Greatly.

"Einstein never said that energy couldn't take form, only that it couldn't be destroyed."

Holmes said nothing more. He turned his back on us in an almost rude manner and stormed away as rapidly as his feet could carry him.

Watson watched but did not follow.

He nodded his head. "I agree with you, Challenger. If Hyde has anything to do with this, then it is quite well concealed. But I suspect Holmes has something up his sleeve. For as usual he is ignoring us and pretending nothing is what it seems. But something else easily explained."

I'm not sure what has been explained in all my good friend Watson's journals about the fiendish creature. I beg your pardon if I may appear to be redundant or back-tracking in my retelling of the story. But there is a good Doctor Jekyll, who is affianced to the daughter of a prominent Baron. He has a family history of great charitable work for the poor and is honored by Queen Mary of Scots, as well as his compatriots. Along with that fame came notoriety for being a great healer and physician. And therein lay the crux of his great error. And our arch-nemesis!

Without knowing the good Doctor's story entirely, the rest of this story will not be quite so clear, or as feeling. It all began with an idea. Don't all great acts...and even sometimes the smaller? And he was an idealist of the first rank. Not even a bug could escape his benevolence, forcing him to step aside rather than step on one.

Was he a holy man? No.

Was he some kind of supernatural, spiritual being like the Golden Buddha? No.

Was he superstitious? No.

He was just an exceedingly kind man who one day in

his life decided to do something quite remarkable for the world; to help those who could not be helped. How was he to know at that time that he was making an error he would live to regret for the rest of his life?

That he was making a mistake that would have immense consequences.

Dark Revelation of Some Circumstance

It all started one day as he was returning from his office, tending to the poor he always sought to help on this special day. His heart was filled with well-being, knowing he had saved the lives of one baby, two pregnant women, and a street person who had poisoned himself with food he hadn't known was for rats.

Yes. It had been an exceptionally good day.

Somehow.

As he walked home, he passed one of the many dark alleyways that ranked London as one of the scarier places to be unescorted at night. He heard a sound, like clothing being ripped and horrible grunting sounds.

Not one to venture into dark places, or risk his life, something moved him to follow through in this case. He gripped his cane for protection in case he needed it and crept into the dark alley, waiting just long enough for his eyes to adjust. That was when his idea was born, inflamed into existence by what he saw.

One of his patients, a kindly older man dying of cancer, was dropped over a woman, her legs spread out beneath him. Her feet were trembling and shaking. What he could see on her face was utter terror. It was then that the older man, feeling someone was watching him, turned aside to look.

"You!" He cursed.

"Help me!" The woman screamed, her mouth free of the older man's grip for a moment.

Jekyll had thought to reason with the man. "Mister Banes, what has come over your good senses? This is atrocious and ugly, what you are doing! Let that woman go right this moment! I order you to!"

Mister Banes slowly stood up but kept a foot on the woman's chest. "Move dearie and I'll cleave your skull with my handy hammer." He told her, and for the first time revealed a deadly hammer with sharp prongs in his free hand.

"As for you, good doctor, I suggest you leave and allow me to continue my pleasures. Your skull is as easily adjusted as this fairy thing."

Doctor Jekyll was horrified at the man's comment and intent. Without thinking he rushed the man, and being much younger and healthier, he easily knocked the deadly hammer from Mister Banes' grip, and then smashed him across the skull with his cane, dropping him to the pavement.

The woman lay there moaning and sobbing, still

frozen in fear, not knowing if he was another horrible person just changing places with one less horrible, to torment her, or truly her savior. That night. He was her savior.

He laid his coat over her and helped her to sit up. He looked over at the older man. Then he grew alarmed. He let go of the woman and grasped the older man to turn him over from where he lay on the cobblestones of the alleyway. He pressed his ear to the man's chest. Nothing. He felt for a pulse. Nothing.

An Angry Resolution

He had gone immediately with the young woman to the nearest hospital and checked her in. He took it upon himself to examine her to make sure she had no serious injuries.

"Your honor has been destroyed, I fear," he finally told the young woman after he had finished.

She gave him a surprised look. "Doctor, I am ever so grateful for you saving my life, but I have had no honor for quite some time."

He thought back to the look of the constable he had stopped on his beat to help him. "Please help me get this young lady to the hospital at once. Her honor has been tattered and I fear her body as well."

He gave me this strangest look, which at the time I could not relate to the incident, so I just shrugged it off as police business. Now I understand.

She saw it on my face. She took my right hand and pressed it warmly. "Midnight Angels have no honor, dear Doctor. But they do appreciate it when they are given some kind thoughts occasionally. I will never forget your act of charity."

"I would do it again," he had stammered hastily.

Confusion Strikes

Rape is rape and brutality remains brutal, he thought as he finally arrived home. Elena was waiting up and immediately warmed up their dinner so they could eat together.

She winced once and he noticed.

She clasped her belly and smiled. "This is going to be a big one."

He rushed over to her and hugged her around her neck. "Have you given thought to a name yet?"

"I have."

"And?"

She smiled coyly. "Soon enough."

He knew best not to push. She had her mind made up but wanted to surprise him with the birth.

After they had lain in bed long enough for her to start gently snoring, he began scrutinizing his day again.

He could not forgive the older man, Mister Banes, for his actions, though he sought to understand them. How could a man dying of a disease eating his insides; a kind old man; one with a loving and generous family...how could he have committed such a heinous crime?

A Mission to Change the World

From that night forward, he spent his free hours devouring tome after tome of medical literature and psychological cases on rape and murder. He was trying desperately to get a handle on what he had witnessed and what he knew happened daily on the streets of London.

Still, finding nothing to explain the dichotomy of soul he had witnessed, he then turned to more esoteric works. Finally, desperate to solve this riddle and rid humanity of such horrid brutality, he began seeking out spiritualists.

He found one.

Madame Towers the Spiritualist

"Madam Towers?"

"I am."

She motioned him to step inside. "I have prepared everything for our little chat, Doctor Jekyll."

He gave her a startled look. "How did you know my name?"

She just smiled and shut the door, then guided him through a short hallway with beautiful pieces of art depicting flowers and angels. He felt mollified by them since there was nothing demonic or frightening to be seen.

So, when she brought him through what seemed a very modest and warmly decorated home to her office, it was no wonder he was surprised to see so many occult items arrayed about the room, including one of an Indian God, Ganesha, holding a baby in his hands.

"Don't be frightened, Doctor. My home is well guarded against evil spirits and those who would do us harm."

She motioned to a chair at a large round table, upon which were tarot cards and a crystal ball.

She smiled at him, but he could tell she was

surveying his face for reactions to the room and her words.

"I fear no harm, Madam."

"Good, please be seated."

She left the room while he continued to look about. Her bookcases were aligned with tome after tome of arcane literature, most of which he had no idea what they were about. Though he did spot a number by the incredibly famous Madame Blavatsky.

Madame Towers returned to the room with a small silver tray and two cups of steaming tea.

"I hope you enjoy tea."

"I do."

"I thought so," she said, again with that knowing smile of hers underlining her words.

She served him a cup and took the other.

He gazed at the crystal ball a moment as he lifted his tea, then promptly gasped. A huge eye was looking out at him.

He almost spilled his tea.

He recovered, then blinked.

The eye was gone.

At that point, he was almost ready to bolt for the door. He expected to find things he didn't understand, but he, like most of London, feared the darker magics and he wasn't so sure she wasn't a practitioner of it at that moment.

There were some in London who sought comfort and power through the Dark Arts. Black magic that tainted the soul. But she was not such a one. He knew that the moment she looked into his eyes this time. He no longer feared her. Something especially magnetic and warm exuded from her soul. It was as if he were gazing into the eyes of God if such were possible.

She sensed his surrender. "Seek no further."

He gave her a confused look. That wasn't at all what he expected to come forth from her mouth. Not even close.

"I don't understand. Seek no further for what?"

"That which your heart desires."

"My heart desires a lot."

"But this one thing it desires is like a wild man on a leash. It threatens to drive you forth across the world, never knowing who you truly are, losing that which has true meaning in your life."

"Nonsense."

Some things are not meant for man to do. Let alone undertake."

He bridled with anger for a moment. "I'm a doctor. Doctors heal. I only seek to heal that which is broken."

He glared at her for a moment. She said nothing. “If you can read my mind and heart as you imply you do, then you should know that I am not only determined but truthful in my wish for good.”

She sat there a long time; her eyes searching his, At the time he thought she was merely considering his need, but later he would realize quite the opposite.

She slowly shook her head. "Some journeys begin with the highest of hopes, the most magnificent of ideals, and tumble, darkened and scarred by ambitions that override the heart and soul."

"I am not such a man," he insisted, the naïve person he was. Certain of his moral grounds. His moral strength and courage. No one could shake him from what he stood for.

Again, a mistake. It is not others who loosen the sails of our downfall and expose us to the stormy waves of a violent sea of hopelessness and despair. No, it is our weak understanding of the true nature of life. Of soul development. Of what is real and good.

“No. I will never be such a man,” he affirmed, smiling proudly in his ignorance.

Maybe, had he been older, and had the wisdom to see the foolishness of his words, he might have been struck by his assertion, his arrogance. His self-development and moral caution might have warned him to avoid what came later: A future wherein he would be forced to face his self-debasement.

"They never are!" She finally said.

A Foolish Man

Her sad smile affirmed the words that had just left her mouth. He felt a chill settle in his soul, but his determination to know the truth he sought overrode any common sense he might have had otherwise.

He was driven like an addict to satisfy his cravings.

He looked at Madame Towers. She was a heavy-set woman, with twice the body mass of most her age, close-set eyes, but generous lips, and a kindly look about her, despite the eyes. But her eyes were the most powerful and demanding part of her. They seemed to look into a man's soul and weigh it. He felt uncomfortable in their gaze, but safe as well.

A contradiction to be sure, but one he could live with.

Her clothing, he noticed, was crisp and clean, even as her home was. Her office gave no hint of her ambitions, or even of her success. Unless one noted the crystal ball with the large eye and the portrait of Jesus hanging over the fireplace, that showed him not on a cross, but standing amid flames, his hands outstretched, a blaze of light pouring forth from the top of his head into clouds overhead where a gigantic eye watched and received the Light.

Something about the portrait caused him to pause in his considerations. Who was he to seek that which no other had been able to stop before him? Why did he have the hubris to believe that he was so clever and powerful he could heal the bestiality of his fellow man?

Then his inner self remembered the sounds in the alleyway, the cruelty in the older man's face, and the utter helplessness he had felt to resolve the issue in a sane way. He made up his mind: He had to find a cure.

She had been patiently waiting for his next words. As he had looked, he had weighed his soul's desire and found it balanced with good. He smiled at her.

"I am willing to take the chance of failing, for if I don't even try, then I shall surely have failed for certain," he admitted, a touch of melancholy in his voice. He felt more vulnerable at that moment, facing his mortality, his shortcomings than he had when threatened with death.

Madame Towers played with a wool blanket that kept her knees warm. It had intricate, occult symbols sewn into it in colorful swirls. She made as if to pluck a few threads off, and as she did so, the blanket began to come undone. Finally, she had pulled so many threads free that the blanket collapsed at her feet into a loose swirl of threads, no longer interlaced and woven into the shape of a blanket.

A smile touched her face, but she was not looking at him. Something, only she could see. Perhaps not.

She didn't look at him when she said, "Every action has consequences. There are laws within laws. Choices within choices. Are you willing to risk your very soul to save your fellow man?"

Faust is Born

She finally looked at him and he shrank inside himself, the look within her eyes was so powerful and terrible to behold. "Do you believe yourself to be a god among men that you are capable of doing that which must be done...at any cost?"

"I am not Faust!"

"He did not believe he was either," she retorted.

He stuttered back at her. "I... believe in the justice of my actions."

But he didn't truly. His ego surfaced as it does in most men caught in such a situation, having to face what might be a deadly outcome of their choice or choices. His determination was no longer a positive drive, but an addiction he had to satisfy.

She had seen it.

She nodded. The look in her eyes vanished. She reached over to the table beside her and poured two cups of tea. One for him and one for her, and then gave him a cup. She smiled. "What you seek is in Egypt. Alexandria. Seek out the legends there."

Her smile vanished. "What you find will propel you on a course that will affect many souls. May you bridge that which you intend and that which you do with a road of honor and courage. For you will need both to face what you have created."

She stood up and left the room. He was alone, filled with far too many, many thoughts, many of which made no sense to him at the time. He looked at the cup of tea in his hands and then set it down to leave.

He exited the home and walked several blocks, then had a terrible thought. *"I haven't asked her what to ask for in Alexandria!"*

He rushed back, but when he reached the block of her home, all he found was an empty lot. A constable was patrolling nearby, and he rushed to him. "Excuse me, constable."

"Yes, sir. How might I help you?"

"What happened to Madame Towers' home? I was just there but a few minutes ago, and now it appears to have vanished."

The constable gave him a look like he was mad, but then as if he were humoring an older man whose senses were failing him, he replied, "I think you might want to go to Earle Street and inquire there for her. They will surely know your answer."

As mysterious and vague as the reply was, he

thanked the Constable. "Safe patrolling, constable."

"I appreciate the thought. Good evening, sir."

"Good evening, constable."

The Constable smiled at him but said no more. He had met a lot of strange people on the streets of London, and this was just one more to file in his memories for when he had more time to consider the questions, he was asked…and more importantly. Why?

Doctor Jekyll rushed to Earle Street, thinking he would find the answer to his question there and the mystery of the constable's reply would be lifted.

But it wasn't.

Upon arrival on the street, the first thing he noted was that much of the street was fronted by a series of tall steel posts with pointed tops and a huge gate.

Over the gate was a large enough sign he could read it effortlessly, even in the new darkness of the evening: Earl Street Cemetery.

Madame Towers Home

He sought the entrance to the cemetery and almost stumbled into the Grounds Keeper who was attending to several fresh graves.

"Excuse me, sir. My name is Doctor Jekyll. I'm looking for a Madame Towers. I was told she lived here."

The Grounds Keeper gave him the look over as if doubting his sanity, but seeing the man be respectable looking, as well as of kindly manners, he answered in a guarded tone, "Yes. She resides here."

"Would you be so kind as to bring me to her then, my good man?"

The Grounds Keeper again looked at him as if he might be a bit off, and then nodded. He turned on his heels and made his way deeper into the cemetery.

After what seemed like forever to the impatient Doctor Jekyll, and a growing sense of alarm, the Grounds Keeper stopped. He motioned to a tombstone, and then kept on walking.

Doctor Jekyll stared after the departing man. "But I don't see her?"

"I doubt many do these days, Doctor." The Grounds Keeper replied, finally breaking into a burst of amused laughter.

"No need to be so simple about it." Doctor Jekyll remonstrated the fellow, who just raised a hand in dismissal and vanished deeper into the shadows of trees and tombstones.

Doctor Jekyll sighed and then turned to look at the grave. "Everyone's mad!" He finally stated emphatically, but then his eyes caught the name on the tombstone.

Not sure what he was seeing wasn't just from fatigue. He leaned closer.

The tombstone read: *"Madame Jasmine Towers. Her heart was in heaven and now she is as well."*

Holocaust

He felt his heart leap into his throat and leaned against the tombstone to catch his balance. He felt suddenly weak and ill. He was barely able to stumble to reach the street and luckily for him a horse and carriage were passing by. He hailed it and took it home, his mind lost in a holocaust of emotions.

The long way home was dark and dreary. His thoughts were even more so. His doubts were like a storm cloud about him. Had he gone insane?

The carriage stopped.

He paid the driver, and gave him a nice tip, then walked the short path to his front door. He paused before knocking.

The door opened.

Elena stood there in her nightgown.

He immediately rushed forward into her arms and burst into sobs.

Vision of a God

That night he tossed and turned, with little sleep coming his way whatsoever, while his dearly beloved Elena snored lightly as if nothing out of the ordinary had happened.

He found that both disconcerting and reassuring at the same time. At that moment in his life, he needed to be grounded in as much normalcy as possible.

But finally, before dawn, he fell into a deep and visions truck series of dreams.

He didn't know it at the time, but his wife feared for his life. A doctor even came while he slumbered and only told her he was suffering from extreme exhaustion.

And he was.

Of the spirit.

On the night of the fifth day, he had a vision of an exceptionally large tome with odd hieroglyphics on its cover. It showed an Egyptian god with his head facing both directions at the same time. One head was angelic, the other terrible.

He awoke from the dream, his body drenched in sweat.

He could sleep no more.

He leaped from his bed, barely taking the time to dress properly, and rushed from his home, giving his startled Elena only moments to give him a quick peck and he was gone.

Doctor Jekyll's Office

When he reached his office, his Nurse stood at the door speaking to a constable, her voice trembling with fear. "He hasn't been here in five days. His wife doesn't know where he is either. She's carrying his baby and I'm afraid it's been quite hard on her. Much more so."

The constable made a note.

"Is there anything we can do to find him? His life could be in danger."

She hadn't seen Doctor Jekyll yet. But he had overheard. At that moment he stood at a crossroads yet once more. He hadn't realized the impact his time away had until this moment. A twinge of fear for his wife's health and worry momentarily assailed him. But it quickly fled. She was fine. He had been with her. A lot to do about nothing.

"Ah-hem!" He cleared his throat.

The constable and nurse turned to look.

His nurse rushed forward, tears in her eyes, she hugged him. "We have been so worried about you. We thought something terrible had happened."

"Why would you think that?"

"Because you have been gone for five days!"

“I should have left a note. But I was in a hurry at the time,” he admitted.

Now he was lying.

One more doubt flared, but he quickly put it out.

“I’m glad you’re fine, sir. Nurse,” he said, touching his cap to her.

He left.

He entered his office the nurse hot on his heels. Immediately, he felt a flare of anger. Someone had put an absurdly large package on top of his paperwork.

“What’s this about?”

"You have two regular clients ready to see you and a third on his way."

"What is this package on my desk?" He demanded again, ignoring her words.

"It came for you just yesterday. Some woman, a very lovely sort with kindly eyes, came into the office and told us it was a present for you. She departed before I could catch her name. Why sir?"

Doctor Jekyll trembled with sudden terror. "What did she look like?"

The nurse told him.

He gasped, almost ready to faint. How was that possible? He hadn't even seen her until that night. How could she have known where he lived? And for that matter how could a dead woman have been here...in his office?

He hurriedly ripped the package open, his nerves on fire as he sought to figure out how this had happened and what it was.

His nurse hovered close but was wringing her hands nervously, thinking he had gone mad. He had, he thought.

And when he saw what he had in the package, the idea of him being mad wasn't so farfetched anymore. It was a book.

But not just any book.

It was the book.

The one from his vision.

The one depicts an Egyptian god facing two ways. One kindly face; one horrid and terrifying.

Doctor Jekyll wanted with all his heart to find a cure for the cruelty in man's heart. And there, almost falling into his lap, was the very book he had been seeking in his dreams. The one he was supposed to seek in Egypt, yet here it was, plain as day and delivered by a dead woman.

Impossible.

All of it.

And yet it was here.

It looked fragile, so he had to restrain himself from flinging it open at once to reveal its secrets.

But he held back. The impossible was made possible. The arcane made real. It shook him to the roots of his soul. But he hesitated only so much before...the moment's magic wore off and he scrambled to open the tome without damaging it in the process. He fingered it, his hand trembling.

"Nurse, please reschedule our patients. I will need some time to myself."

"Yes, Doctor." She replied and then withdrew, certain now that he had gone over the edge as he clutched the book to his breast as if it were a child to soothe and love.

She let out a yelp of fear as he suddenly brushed past her with the book, totally ignoring her, and exited the office, slamming the door behind him.

"Very interesting," Holmes noted.

Conan frowned. "I never wrote this fellow."

Challenger smiled. "Dear, dear Conan, just because you created this universe, doesn't mean you are the only one populating it."

Harry snorted with laughter. "And you surely didn't create me. My dad would have something to say about that."

Everyone laughed.

Ms. Hudson came into the room and refilled everyone's coffee cups, then set down a new platter of scones.

Watson came up a few moments later holding a tray of sandwiches.

Holmes smiled. "John has become quite the handyman of late."

Watson blushed.

Ms. Hudson gave him a peck on the cheek and then pinched it. "He's a keeper, this one."

Watson's eyes lit up and he followed her as she departed for the stairs.

"Watson!" Conan called.

"Yes, yes."

He looked back.

"The sandwiches."

"Sorry."

Watson returned and set the sandwiches down, then himself.

"Thought you were going with Ms. Hudson?" Challenger teased.

"I was. But then I realized if I did so there wouldn't be a single scone left by the time I returned."

Holmes chuckled.

Conan barked with laughter.

Harry came over and took one onto a small plate. "I agree with Watson on this one. We all know Challenger would love to hog them to himself."

Challenger sighed. "One can hope."

Watson gave his friend a friendly smile. "Don't worry, the reason she went back down is she has two more platters she's cooking."

He jabbed Challenger in the stomach. "She knows how many holes to fill in."

"I am not a hole!" Challenger roared.

Watson sat back down. "Keep telling yourself that."

Conan laughed. "He got you on that one."

Challenger turned on Conan. He was about to say something snarky but held his breath. He sat down at the table with the others as they ate and continued his story.

"Henry, Doctor Jekyll, fled his office and never returned."

Conan took a sip of his coffee and then raised an eyebrow. "I certainly would never have written a hero to do such a thing. Abandon his wife and child! Unheard of!"

"Oh, he didn't abandon them. He left them with more than enough funds to be taken care of while he was gone."

Ms. Hudson entered with the second tray of scones and set them down. She sat down.

"I overheard that. Money will never replace a good man's presence," she stated, her eyes on Watson while she said it.

Watson coughed and had to spit out part of his scone into a napkin.

Finished, he piped up, "Quite, quite, my dear. Wholeheartedly agree with you."

Everyone burst into laughter.

"What?" Watson demanded.

Conan chuckled. "I would write that."

Ms. Hudson raised an eyebrow. "I've read every one

of your books, you never have a female hero or show much sympathy for their plights."

Conan smiled, not offended at all. "Those were my first stories; since I've come here, they are quite different."

"Oh, then I'll have to pick up one of them."

Conan jumped up and rushed to his overcoat, plucked out a thick book, and plopped it on the table in front of her. "Thought you might like this one then."

She eyed him suspiciously. "You always carry your books around like that?"

"One never knows," Conan replied, keeping his eyes on the table as he reseated himself.

She turned it over. "The Baker Street Universe."

She smiled. "I like that title."

Holmes arched an eyebrow. "Quite presumptuous, isn't it?"

"Well, this is, isn't it?" Conan demanded, getting a bit hot under the collar.

"Yes, it is," Holmes replied. "Though the state of it leaves something to be desired at times."

Harry nudged Holmes lightly with an elbow. "Remember our last trip to Conan's world?"

"I do."

"You prefer to live there?"

Holmes considered it. "Not the way it was heading I wouldn't. I like the idea of a world where magic exists and science."

"Both can be treacherous," Challenger cut in, "Which brings me to the rest of my story."

The Hunt for Destroying Evil

Doctor Jekyll disembarked, his legs weary from the cramped cabin he had slept in. This was the tenth port city he was reaching now.

Athens.

He eyed all the sailing ships in the harbor, admiring their sleek forms, a part of him imagining the older times when Greeks had ruled the seas with their fast-growing ships.

"Sir?" A squeaky voice asked.

He turns to see a man with his name on a card. "Doctor Jekyll?" He asked this time.

Doctor Jekyll nodded.

"The Priest of Apollonius will see you now."

"Very good," Doctor Jekyll replied, following the man to a carriage waiting for him.

He admired the countryside as the carriage took a steep, rocky road carved from the rough cliff to the harbor. The sea was golden green. Clear, but golden from the sun and green from the row upon row of tall Olive Trees that leaned along the banks, flushing the banks with steep shadows and the waters with green reflections.

The High Priest of Apollonius

Angrily, he spits out words he would later regret at the High Priest, who remained unruffled by his outburst, but his eyes widened at the truth of the man he had received into the holy chambers of his office.

He rose.

"Doctor Jekyll, I fear you have wasted your time and precious resources coming here."

Doctor Jekyll rose and slammed a fist on the High Priest's desk, causing a cup of tea to bounce and spill its contents.

The High Priest noticed it, but again, seemed unruffled.

"You are a determined man."

"I am a driven man."

The High Priest nodded.

He turned his back to the doctor to look out over the Aegean Sea. "Many have sought the mythical division you seek."

"And some have found it?"

"What did you learn from the Rosy Cross?"

"That it was forbidden knowledge."

Doctor Jekyll made a weary face, wrinkled with

anger at the man he had spoken to, then looked at the High Priest again, who continued to keep his back turned.

"Nothing is forbidden."

"The apple of Eve was."

This time the Priest turned about, the hint of sadness touching his eyes and face. "The fall of man was of course, not by knowledge alone, but by his greed for it. The lust to have control."

Doctor Jekyll gave the man a thoughtful look. "I am not such a man."

The High Priest nodded, then sat down again. He opened a desk drawer, removed a cloth, and began wiping up the spilled tea. "That remains to be seen. Good day, Doctor Jekyll."

Doctor Jekyll spun about. "Give me something! Anything!"

The High Priest considered a moment, then nodded. "This ghost you spoke of..."

"Madame Towers."

"She gave you this book."

"The book of my vision."

The High Priest looked up; his eyes filled with a magnetic storm in them.

Doctor Jekyll backed up in fear.

“And yet you continue to pursue this dark vision and intend only good from it?”

“I...”

The High Priest rose and clapped his hands. Two tall men stepped into the office and nodded.

“Please see Doctor Jekyll back on his ship. If he is hungry, make sure he is fed before he boards. Good day, Doctor.”

The High Priest exited the room, a look of disgust on his face.

221 B Baker Street

"That must have crushed his soul," Conan uttered, a sad look on his face.

"I fear not," Challenger admitted, his voice subdued, which caught the attention of everyone listening.

"And the result of his hunt was not failure, or else you would not be telling us this tale," Holmes spoke up.

Challenger eyed his friend for a moment, then nodded. "Oh, he succeeded all right. Madness always finds a way. Through luck. Through the pity of others. But it always does."

Everyone fell into a kind of melancholy for a moment, then Conan sniffed the air several times. "Ms. Hudson, did you not take your last batch of scones from the oven yet?"

"Oh, dear!" She cried out and dashed for the stairs, with Watson hot on her heels.

"Please continue, Challenger," Holmes asked.

"The Doctor as you know sought the book at the Vatican, which was fruitless as he already had the only copy as he learned from the good Pope at the time, but he did gain further clues.

"And that led him to Greece?" Harry asked.

"It did."

"But surely he ran out of resources by then."

"He did."

Harry looked shocked for a moment. "Challenger, you sent him money, didn't you?"

"To my Eternal shame. Yes."

Holmes looked up as Watson came back into the room with a smoking platter of scones. Slightly burnt on their edges.

Challenger eyed them lustily. "Looks good to me!"

Everyone dug into them.

Ms. Hudson would have had a fit if they'd complained. It was their story that had betrayed her usual sense of duty.

When they were finished, Challenger smiled. "I won't bore you with the rest of the story. You are all aware of what happened next."

Conan made a face. "Blasted Hyde is what happened next. And I never wrote that Godawful creature, thank God!"

"Amen to that," Challenger agreed.

He examined the faces of his friends, then stopped on that of Conan.

"You never dreamed when you chose to come here

that you would become embroiled in such a monstrous case, did you?"

Conan shrugged. In my sick and older body, I might have found it taxing beyond relief, but now, I chalk it up to a good day's work."

Holmes smiled. "And if you hadn't chosen to come, we would have lost a good friend."

"Twice," Challenger said.

Harry nodded.

Conan smiled. "Then I am even more glad I chose to come. For before I was quite sure the greatest souls any writer could ever have given birth to were done with. But now…I find in this new world the opportunity to explore even more of your adventures than I had thought possible. So even if I did not write all your adventures, I am as pleased as if I had," he said, an eye on Harry, who grinned and nodded his head.

Holmes yawned. "I hope you don't mind. I usually like a good game of chess before I retire, but I fear the rigors of our work this past week have drained me somewhat."

He rose.

"Good night, Ms. Hudson, Challenger, Conan, Harry. Watson," he finished, a twinkling gleam in his eyes when he saw that Watson was holding Ms. Hudson's hand in his.

"Good night, Holmes!"

He left the room.

Challenger rose next. "Conan, I'll give you a lift home if you wish. Harry, you still have a late-night act to perform, do you not?"

"Yes, at the Globe Theater. I will be raising someone from the dead."

Watson laughed. "Good luck with that."

"I'll need it," Harry joked, then rose with the others to leave.

"Would you two mind dropping me off at the Globe?"

"Not at all," Challenger said agreeably. "Might we stay to watch the act?"

"It won't start till MidBells. Will likes to do the MidBells shows for the poor citizens who don't sleep during the night."

"That should be interesting," Challenger said, liking the idea.

They gave Ms. Hudson and Watson a nod and exited the room.

Watson turned to Ms. Hudson.

"I am no longer hungry."

"You shouldn't be. You ate half the scones, my dear Grumbly Bear."

He made a growling sound.

Holmes was partway back into the room, saw what was going on, and hastily removed himself, a huge smile on his lips.

Watson bit Ms. Hudson on the side of her neck and she howled happily.

The Ride Home

Challenger liked using a carriage. He had an electric car like most well-to-do men these days. But he preferred the company of his horse companions. They were friends to him. He kept them healthy and well-fed, and they loved him back in the ways that all horses do, with faith and trust and the occasional carriage ride.

He let his friends sit in the back, both nodding off as click-clack of hooves, the digesting of food and fatigue caught up with them.

He went back in his thoughts to what had happened again with Doctor Jekyll, his friend.

In his mind, he could see the letter the Doctor had sent him at one time.

Doctor Jekyll's Letter

"Dear Professor Challenger, I am at a great loss to explain the indignity I have so eagerly, but not very kindly, dropped upon my wife and family in the pursuit of arcane knowledge. Even though it might mean the salvation of humanity, I had inadvertently shredded any hope of a normal and loving life of my own."

Challenger clucked at his horses, and they turned right for him. He didn't believe in using whips or hard goads. Horses were noble and intelligent. They never denied him help or were stubborn if he was kind and fair to them.

Settled into the new direction, he let his mind drift again to the past and what had struck him as the sincerity of the man's emotions at the time.

Stains on the note. And it could be no doubt it was from his tears, the way the droplets had struck the paper.

Noting that sad moment, Challenger had taken a deep breath to continue. Doctor Jekyll wasn't sure if he was going to like what came next, but he must continue his pursuit of the truth. For himself. His loved ones. And for the sake of his friends, know as much as possible.

Challenger read on, "I have discovered a secret so dark and vast that I fear now for my very soul that it may be lost. It will give me the power over evil I sought, but I fear I have betrayed the very fountain of hope and love that has sustained me through so much...my dear Elena and child, who must be so tall by now."

Challenger felt tears coming to his eyes again as he remembered the next portion of the letter from his beloved friend.

"I have wept profusely like a woman who has lost her only child. The sailors have tried to console me with dance and music, but I would have none of it."

"Perhaps it was during those forty days and forty nights of the return voyage that I realized that I had been acting on evil impulses of my own."

Doctor Jekyll's Return

"Daddy, daddy's ship," his son yelled happily, waving as the proud merchant ship slipped into port and the sailors began throwing down the anchor and ropes to stabilize her.

A boarding ramp was dropped.

Elena clutched my hand tight.

"Don't worry, my dear, I'm sure he'll be quite happy to see you and a changed man."

I glanced at his son and smiled. "How could he not be with a beautiful son and wife to greet him after his long journeys."

His son, Robert, looked up at me. "Daddy's coming home."

I smiled. "He certainly is."

Doctor Jekyll appeared at the top of the boarding ramp, and I swear to this day I can't forget the look on his face when he saw his wife and the look, he gave the young youth standing next to her.

I had to stand back as he ran down the ramp and clasped them both to his breast, weeping with joy at the reunion.

221 B Baker Street

Holmes smiled. "I would be surprised if he acted any other way. The man is brilliant, but with a good heart."

Watson nodded. "Indeed."

Challenger took a sip of his coffee and eyed Harry, who was shuffling cards as he practiced a new trick to entertain his audiences.

Conan watched eagerly. He loved magic.

"Every day I see new magic here I am so grateful I made the journey to my new world."

I eyed him "You should; because if you hadn't, I would have had to come to heaven itself to drag you here."

He laughed, then he noticed I wasn't smiling.

"Oh!"

"So, what happened after that?" Ms. Hudson asked after wiping her eyes. She had gone quite teary after I described Jekyll's homecoming.

"I drove them home in my carriage and dropped them off.

It was not a week later that Jekyll returned to my home, where he spat out all his thoughts and research he had been consumed with. It was then that I also thought of a plan that might help him.

Harry eyed me sternly. "I thought he had given up on all that nonsense about splitting the soul."

I sighed. "No, never. He, much like our dear Conan here is quite a stubborn man when he makes his mind up."

Conan chuckled. "And rightly so, as most times my mind is quite correct."

Holmes nodded. "In that, I must agree. As part of your creation…" He gave us all a wink Conan couldn't see. "…It's only natural you would have quite an astonishing ability to intellectualize."

"Indeed so," Conan agreed, Harry, hiding a grin as Conan bought into Holmes's humor. "But please do go on, Challenger, you never spoke much about all of this before."

"Oh, there's much I don't talk about…like the time I went to the Mato Grosso and captured a living dinosaur and brought it back."

"You wrote about that," Conan corrected him.

"No, Conan, you…you wrote about that. I've never told anyone, not even you, what happened. It was one of the saddest times of my life and one of the most dangerous. I prefer to lock that memory safely away where all such dark things dwell."

I looked at Holmes. "I'm sure you understand, Holmes."

Holmes smiled.

Which meant he either did, or he had more to say but was keeping it to himself, or for a better time. Such is the nature of our good friend.

"Challenger," Harry spoke up. "Go on, I'm almost through doing my exercises and I'll have to leave soon for the theater."

"Very well," I said and did.

Challenger's Office

"The Sainted Pope of Alexandria could be your hope in this," I explained to young Doctor Jekyll.

The poor man gave me a confused look. I explained.

"He is not only a holy man but a learned person with three doctorates to his credit. He is also the most powerful man in all of Europe next to our dear Queen Mary of Scots and he has access to the entire library of Alexandria that had supposedly been burned to the ground at one time."

"You are telling me the library still exists?"

"I am and no one must know this besides you and me."

"Agreed," he said immediately. "You knew of this but never told me?"

"I had hoped, desperately at times, you might step away from this madness that has been consuming you."

He gave me a look of utter disgust. "Saving the world is something we do as doctors. How could you ever doubt I would be any different? You and your friends are always off doing something to serve humanity. Why should I not be as well?"

I looked away. He was right. How could I, even as his

professed friend, chide a man for that which I readily did every day with my Baker Street friends.

“That may be so, but one still must find a center in the middle of the insanity of our world. I would not have anything happen to you, dear friend. Nothing!”

He clasped my hands in his and pressed them warmly.

“And for that, I thank you with all my heart. But I must know more. Learn more. The world needs what I can give it.”

At that time, I feared for his sanity, and to calm him down and hopefully redirect his madness I offered a poor excuse. “I offer that great man up for your intellectual consumption now…but hesitantly…after my explorations in the Great Wall of China where there are many hidden rooms and chambers and tunnels that lead to sacred rituals and documents. Their country has been at the head of spiritual consumption long before the India Islands peoples."

“And?”

I looked him in the eyes. “The Good Pope often travels there for solace and meditation. It was there that I first met him and made friends with him. And why I also know that if any man can help you satisfy this…” I almost said madness…This quest, he shall be that person."

"Good, I shall leave at once!"

"But…" I spoke up, freezing him in his tracks as he made for the office door.

"But what?"

"You must take this as seriously as it is presented."

His face began to darken with anger.

I raised my hand.

"For the sake of your child and wife!"

He lost the anger and nodded. "I beg your forgiveness, I am so used to the idiots who ramble on and on about what they shall do for me, and then only mislead and misinform me."

He took my hands again. "But I trust you, Challenger. You would never betray a friend."

Impulsively, as the man tends even now, he swept me into a bear hug and began weeping.

At that moment, my heart went out to him. I still wasn't sure if I was helping or hurting him at the time, but the die had been cast and now I would find out if I had made the right decision in helping him further or not.

221 B Baker Street

Challenger eyed Conan a moment in thought. Conan broke his reverie. "I appreciate what you have done for me. I am sure he did as well. Good intentions are often rewarded with good outcomes."

Holmes and Harry exchanged looks.

Conan saw it. "Just because I have written of such times not always going the direction intended, does not mean this one should go wrong."

Challenger smiled. "Oh, dear Conan, ever naïve about so much. But we love you anyway."

Watson snorted. "How magnanimous of you, Challenger."

Ms. Hudson pinched his arm. "John!"

"Sorry, my dear, but humility has never been a trait of our dear friend her."

Challenger smiled. "Of which I am proud. For were I as humble a man as you, dear Watson, I would have married Ms. Hudson years ago and never brought a dinosaur home to London and caused all those terrible things. She would never have let me do something so stupid."

Ms. Hudson laughed.

Watson reddened in the face.

Holmes put a hand on Watson's arm. "John always does the best he can." He looked at all of us with great warmth. "As do you all. I consider myself blessed to have such a wealth of good friends."

Challenger nodded. "But to continue, Jekyll didn't make the same mistake this time. He immediately asked me for financial aid, and I quickly gave him the sum he requested, even though it was steep. But when I learned he did not intend the trip to be by himself, but with his entire family, this glow of warmth grew in my heart. Perhaps, his desolation had blossomed into something more wholesome."

Conan shook his head. He knew where Challenger was going with this story. "It didn't though, did it."

Challenger looked at his sandwich plate and shook his head. "Good intentions don't always reach happy conclusions."

Conan nodded. "Ever the truth. My father helped me understand that quite well when I received a stiff planking across my bottom for hiding mine once."

Challenger smiled at Conan's attempt at humor. Looked up. "But at the time I was so overwhelmed with him including his family in the equation, that I gladly loaned him the funds to secure passage, lodging, and food for the time he needed."

He gave Holmes and his friends a sad look. "I thought I was giving him a new lease on his life; a chance to rebuild his relationship with Elena and young Robert."

Challenger sighed. "How wrong I was."

The Merchant Ship

Doctor Jekyll held young Robert on his shoulders so he could wave to us as the merchant ship threw off its mooring ropes, drew its anchor in, and began edging out into the Thames.

" Bye-bye! Good-bye!" Young Robert kept hollering at us.

"I've never seen a happier lad than he was that morning."

"I agree," Holmes replied, a certain look on his face defying description.

"What?"

Watson looked at Holmes and chuckled. "Don't let him rattle you, Challenger. He just likes to look mysterious is all."

Harry wasn't so sure about that. He was biting his fingernails. He usually didn't do that except when he was quite worried.

I looked at Harry. "What's wrong?"

Harry glanced at Holmes, who gave him a slight shake of the head. Harry looked away. "Look, here comes Tesla and Edison."

They drove up in their new model electric car and

hopped out.

"Are we too late?" Tesla asked.

Then he saw little Robert waving.

Tesla did a remarkable thing. He took out a tiny blimp he had specially made with a message attached to its gondola. He spun its props and it buzzed to a tiny roar.

He aimed it at the young youth.

Elena caught the blimp and laughing, waved at Tesla, who waved back.

She waited until the props stopped, took the message from the gondola, then handed the now still blimp to young Robert, who clasped it to his breast, loving his new toy.

"What did you tell them?" I asked.

"Remember what's most important and you will find happiness no matter what happens or where you are."

Harry put an arm about his shoulders. "That was quite lovely."

"Thank you, I meant it."

Holmes nodded. "We all wish them the best."

He folded his hands behind his back which he was wont to do when he had something on his mind and walked off into the deepening morning fog.

"Even you, Holmes, had a smile on your face," before you left us that morning.

Holmes nodded, got up, and sat next to the fireplace again. He placed his lap blanket across his knees and then said, "But I fear you are leaving much out Professor."

"I am."

Challenger got up from the table, snatching the last scone before Watson could. He gave Watson a grin. Ms. Hudson touched Watson's knee and he bit back the bark he was about to unleash at Challenger.

"Thus, it was in the best of spirits all of us parted that foggy Monday morning. None of us expected what was to follow."

Conan eyed Challenger questioningly.

"Have patience, dear Conan. I'll be finished soon."

"Hope so, I have an appointment with a patient in an hour."

Challenger eyed his friend. "I didn't know you were doctoring again."

"Never stopped. Just don't talk much about it."

"What about your writing?"

Conan laughed. "With all the work we do as a team, you think I need the excitement of a story?" Conan shook his head. "Really, Challenger."

Challenger laughed. "I had to try, hadn't I?"

Conan smiled.

Holmes took his pipe and began refilling it with tobacco. He didn't light it though. He just put it between his lips. "I fancy you are leading to something quite uncomfortable to the lot of us."

Everyone in the room gave Challenger a questioning look. Challenger acceded to the point by nodding. "I fear you are not only right, but it disturbs me deeply to have to admit the mistake I made."

Watson laughed. "It's all right, Challenger. We all make mistakes. It's part of life and learning."

Challenger turned on Watson. "You will not like this mistake!"

Both Conan and Watson stiffened in alarm.

But Holmes just sat there watching and waiting for Challenger to finish. He already knew what was to come. It didn't take a genius to see that.

Challenger continued, "Jekyll met with the great Pope and was given unprecedented access to the Alexandrian Library, which was kept under lock and key beneath the Vatican and guarded by the most powerful warriors the Pope had. Once the Pope had seen the tome that was gifted the Doctor by the mysterious Madame Towers, he had immediately opened up all church resources to the good Doctor, helping him in every way possible."

Harry rose from the table and went to the windows overlooking Baker Street. He watched a moment as one of the huge merchant blimps passed overhead, burying the street in deep shadows until its massive tri-hulled shape moved behind the buildings.

"You let the Pope know he was coming, didn't you?" Harry stated, not asked.

"I did. And that was my second and probably greater mistake. I told the Pope, a dear friend of mine, that the Doctor could be trusted entirely with any available information."

Challenger kicked at the doorway entrance in anger, then spun about. "What have I done?"

Conan rose worriedly. "Easy, Challenger. Please finish your story."

Before he could, a loud pounding came from the front door below.

"Please let Constable Evans in," Holmes requested.

Watson ran down the stairs.

He flung the door open.

"Oh, it's only you, Constable."

Constable Evans took off his cap, and his mop of red hair fell out and flopped over his eyes. He shook it back and gave Watson a serious look.

Conan stood at the top of the staircase looking down. "It's Doctor Jekyll, isn't it?"

Doctor Jekyll's Lab

Doctor Jekyll drew the curtains shut on his view from his office window. The Thames flowed swiftly nearby, and its aroma of salt and sewage was quite strong at times, but it was refreshing when his mind was so tangled as it was now.

He looked at the vial he had cooking over a small Bunsen burner. It was at its lowest flame. He just started it. He was doing it slowly to give himself the chance to change his mind, but as he watched the black substance slowly start to boil and bubble, he knew he had already made his decision.

"I should let Challenger know what I'm up to," he told himself. "I need a second eye. A second mind..."

He shook his head violently. He would only prove to his friend that he hadn't meant a word of the contrition he had displayed before this discovery. That he was as unstable as Challenger had feared.

Only briefly did he think of his wife, Elena, and young son, Robert. It's as if they didn't matter anymore to him. Why that should have been if you had asked him, no doubt he would have said that wasn't his thought at all. But it was the truth.

***

He only saw one thing in his mind at that moment, the secret to dividing evil from a man and removing it forever.

"My son, the soul is pure energy. It takes whatever shape we give to it. Good or bad. Right or wrong," the Pope had confided to him as he eyed the huge tome that Madame Towers had gifted the doctor.

He eyed him. "You realize that once you walk this path, there's no turning back?"

"I do."

"That it might not lead to salvation as you think?"

"I do."

The Pope sighed deeply. "None have tried this alchemical experiment before and survived."

"I'm willing to take that chance."

"Your family?"

"I have left a huge provision for them." A lie, but the Pope didn't know that. Or did he? The way he looked into Jekyll's eyes, told him otherwise.

"They will be fine," he added.

"And you say this occultist..."

"Madame Towers."

"Yes, yes, that one. That she gifted this to you?"

"Yes."

The Pope's eyes narrowed. "That would be quite impossible as she had been dead almost a hundred years now."

Doctor Jekyll almost staggered at the insinuation hurled at him. "All the more miraculous and reason to follow my path. It is Divinely wrought."

"Some have called me the Golden Pope," he told Jekyll. "I prefer to think of myself rather as a man well educated in the art of telling the truth and dividing it."

Doctor Jekyll smiled. He knew he had won his argument but was waiting for the Pope to give him his final blessing so he could enter the archives and retrieve the forbidden formula.

"And I see in your face a man who loves his family deeply."

"I do."

The Pope leaned forward over his desk. "Then do not forfeit your soul on this quest. It is for God to show us the path to remove evil from our souls; not man."

Jekyll shrugged. "All things are of God, are they not? I was told you believed that."

The Pope finally admitted defeat and nodded. "I do. I cannot speak that to the masses for they would not understand the concept, but all my senior staff understands and abide by that understanding."

"Then you will help me?"

221B Baker Street

Holmes rose from his chair, threw his lap blanket on the couch, then strode to Constable Evans and took the message. He read it silently.

He turned to the others.

"A man's soul is in danger!"

He hurriedly threw on his cape and cap, slipped into his outdoor shoes, and hurried down the stairs with Constable Evans.

Conan stopped Challenger before he could follow. "I'm not Sherlock Holmes, but I fear for what we will find."

"As do I, dear Conan. As do I."

Challenger started for the stairs, then turned back as Watson flew past, snapping on his hat and coat. "Conan, I didn't mean for you to be involved in something so dark this early in your new life."

Conan grinned. "Good intentions..."

Challenger grinned back. "Indeed."

They rushed from the room.

Doctor Jekyll's Lab

Even as his wife was in the hospital preparing to give birth to their second child, Jekyll eyed the dark vial and its fumes rising slowly into the lab's air. "Forgive me, Elena."

He had sent Robert, his son, away with Tesla to see some of his inventions while he worked, and Edison was going to take Robert to the museum to look at ancient artifacts that children had left behind.

He was pleased with the details but felt some regret that he couldn't be with his wife. But he didn't want to worry her. He had told her he would meet her at the hospital as soon as he took care of a new patient suffering from a dreadful disease that was eating their flesh away.

She had believed him.

He hoped she had.

But now as he clasped the extremely hot vial to swallow its foul liquid, he wondered if he had only been kidding himself. Her eyes hadn't looked like she understood at all.

He forced a smile on his lips. "I'll make it up to you, my dear Elena. I swear it," he told himself and then tossed down the formula that would free him of all evil.

Ryan Street

Challenger growled at himself after reading the message that had sent Holmes running for the hundredth time.

"In case..."

Conan put a hand on Challenger's arm. "Do not beat yourself up, my friend. He's probably fine."

Holmes stiffened in the front seat of the police car.

Conan didn't like that at all.

He turned to his friend again. "I'm sure young Jekyll was just trying to get us to come and help him not do what is so dangerous."

"I wish I could believe that." Challenger sighed.

Watson, seated to Challenger's left shook his head. "A fool and his..."

"Stop!"

Watson shut up, but Challenger got the point.

Conan sighed and looked away. This world was so much more complicated than the one he had left. But even so, his new life with his beloved wife and a chance to write more and even do doctoring again...made it all worthwhile. But this new aspect of it, dividing a man's soul in two, splitting off evil? It seemed diabolical.

Doctor Jekyll's Lab

"AIEEEEE!" Doctor Jekyll screamed as he threw the empty vial against a wall, shattering it and sending pieces of sharp glass into the air.

He rushed to the curtains and ripped them free, growling like an angry beast as he did so.

He looked at his hands. Hair was spouting on his palms. His fingernails were turning into claws.

He rushed to his mirror and looked.

His face was hideous and bestial.

It was not the face of a normal man anymore. Maybe not of even a living man ever.

"Noooo!" He cried out and shattered the glass with a fist.

Then the formula reached its full strength inside his body. He began shivering violently. He became so hot that every inch of his body began to perspire, and then he began to freeze, his teeth chattering loudly in his mouth.

He threw himself against his lab tab and overturned it. In the process, he heard his right upper arm break. He tumbled to the floor and thrashed about, smashing, and kicking. His right foot broke, then several of his left ribs broke as he hurled himself against an overturned leg of the heavy table.

That was the moment that Holmes and his friends broke into the lab.

Jekyll looked at them, his eyes wet with tears. "Forgive me, my friends, for I have sinned!"

He howled like a madman for a long time.

Challenger started to run to him. Holmes held him back.

"Holmes!" Conan cried out.

"Back, back!" Holmes commanded.

He had seen what they had not. Jekyll's body was starting to glow a brilliant red at its edges and the glow was expanding. It was quite subtle, but Holmes knew the nature of what Jekyll was doing. So did Harry.

Harry put himself in front of the others.

"Holmes?"

"Let this finish. We can do nothing until then."

Harry watched in horror, as did the others.

Jekyll howled one last time and it sounded like every bone in his body broke at the same time. At once a radiant evil red form burst forth from his broken body and stood over it.

Jekyll looked lifeless, like a broken doll.

"Dear God protect us!" Watson cried out.

Challenger had his long gun out and fired without thinking.

The bullets passed through the hideous red glowing creature.

Its huge black eyes stared at him, and a grin grew on its evil face. "Challenger!" It hissed. "You will be first!"

"Who are you?" Holmes spoke up.

The creature eyed him. "I am that which everyone wishes they were."

Harry's right fist lit up a bright blue.

"What are you?" Holmes insisted.

"I am Hyde!" It flung itself at Challenger.

Harry interjected himself and flung up a glowing blue hand. The force of the light caused the terrible creature to howl as if in great pain.

It flung itself back, then turned about and dashed for the windows.

Harry was muttering a spell to destroy the creature when it smashed into the nearest. The window exploded outwards as if driven by a solid body.

The creature vanished.

Harry threw himself out the door and dashed to try and find it and destroy it.

Watson and Conan followed.

Challenger dropped to his knees beside Doctor Jekyll and bowed his head. "He was a good man."

But he wasn't dead. His eyes fluttered open. "I saw its thoughts. Save my wife!"

Challenger grabbed him. "From what?"

"My evil!"

Jekyll fell back.

Challenger looked at Holmes. "Save her, Holmes. She's at the Saint Marymount Hospital."

Holmes ran from the lab.

Challenger gently lifted Jekyll into his arms and cradled him like a child. He wept as he said, "What have you done, my dear friend?"

A long pause as he clasped the man closer to his chest.

"What have I done?"

Saint Marymount Hospital

Nurse Biddy tucked a blanket over Elena's baby and her.

"Thank you, nurse."

Nurse Biddy smiled. "Don't worry, I'm sure the good doctor will be here soon."

"I'm not."

She eyed the sweet girl in her arms and smiled. "I have an angel in my arms. How could I worry?"

"Just wait until she gets old enough to attract boys, then ask yourself if you still think she's an angel," Nurse Biddy said, then laughed.

Elena smiled.

Nurse Biddy turned to exit the room and then froze.

Outside the opened door stood something straight from hell. Its reddish glow filled the room and the hallway with a bright red glow.

Its ebony eyes were so huge they seemed to be burning charcoal.

Nurse Biddy screamed.

It passed through her body, and she stopped screaming as every single cell of her body was sucked into the horrid creature, draining her of all her life force in an instant.

She collapsed to the floor, just a sack of flesh now.

"No!" Elena cried out.

Her baby woke up and began to cry.

"You are mine!" The creature told her.

"What are you?"

"Your husband."

Elena screamed.

A passing doctor came into the room.

"What's going on...?"

Hyde spun about and entered his body. The man's eyes lit up a huge black color and he eyed Elena. "I have a gift for you, my love. For our child."

Elena tried to get up, but she was too weak.

The possessed doctor grabbed the foot railing of her bed and pulled it towards him, then he began rubbing with the bed, shoving it towards the windows behind the bed.

Holmes and Watson burst into the room. They saw the man pushing the bed and immediately went for their weapons. The man kept pushing and shoved the bed through the window glass and frames until it dangled halfway out.

Elena stopped screaming. She brought her baby to

her breast so it couldn't see anything and talked sweetly into its ears. "I love you."

The doctor smiled at Holmes and Watson. "Those cannot harm me!"

Watson fired, then Holmes.

The man gave them another smile, and looked at the bullet hole in his chest, unable to see the one in his skull above his eyes.

He fell backward onto the bed.

It didn't fall free.

"Hurry, Watson. We must pull the bed back," Holmes cried out.

They rushed to reach the bed.

The dead doctor sat up and gripped both sides of the window frames and grinned at Holmes and Watson.

"Come closer and I'll shove the bed the rest of the way."

Holmes and Watson stopped.

"What do you want?" Holmes asked, hoping for some kind of chance to stop what was about to happen.

"I don't want anything."

The man put both his feet on the room's floor and slowly stood up, letting go of the window frames.

"You must want something, for God's sake," Watson

demanded.

Hyde examined Watson for a long time. “No, I have everything I need.”

He spun about and flung his weight on the front of the bed.

It broke free from the window frame and flew outwards over the Thames.

Seagulls flew past, not slowing, but veering off so as not to strike the bed.

Then it dropped from view, leaving only the skies and a deathly silence behind in the room.

Gateway to Fairie

Twelve days later, Holmes and Watson stood at the gateway to Fairie once more. Conan and Challenger stood watching as Holmes pressed a hand to the wall and frowned. "Nothing."

"You feel nothing at all?"

Holmes eyed Conan. "Nothing."

"Let me try!" Challenger roared and pushed to the front. He slammed his hammy right palm against the wall. His face went from disappointment to dismay, then he turned to give his friends a look of utter resignation. "This is impossible. Only this morning it was quite warm."

Conan put a hand on his friend's arm to help calm him down. None of them were the same since the horrible death of Elena and her child.

As to Doctor Jekyll.

Conan shook his head at the thought of that man and the burden he carried now. He had been like Icarus who had strived to reach the heavens on wings of wax and plunged to his death when the wax melted.

"Dear Challenger, sometimes the equity of our lives does not sum up to that which we desire."

Watson said nothing. He had been in such a situation so many times with Holmes by now, that even the darkest of situations was to be expected.

And handled.

Such was life.

Such was fate.

Such was man's free will.

And those of Fairie.

Not that they could blame the blokes for wanting to shut down their gates to London. It wasn't like they didn't have enough monsters on their side to deal with.

"Holmes?"

Holmes glanced at Conan, then looked away. He had no thoughts on the matter.

Yet.

Challenger sighed. "What it means is we must give this more thought. And I suspect Holmes is already hot in pursuit of those very exact thoughts."

Holmes glanced at Challenger, his face unreadable as he folded his hands behind his back and walked off, leaving them to conjecture what came next.

221B Baker Street

Conan sat next to the window overlooking Baker Street, a thoughtful look on his face.

"This is all so new, so exciting, but..." He turned to look at Watson who sat near the fire alongside Challenger, who was nodding off, obviously quite tired.

Watson smiled faintly. "Taxing."

"That too."

Watson glanced toward Conan. "We can't help what happened to Doctor Jekyll any more than we can help what happens to any soul who chooses to make such decisions."

"I suppose," Conan sighed. He looked outside again. "But how anyone in such a remarkable world can choose such a dark path when they are such a bright soul..."

"...Is what makes us each unique, dear Conan," Watson explained.

Harry sat at the table dealing cards, to the table, then flipping them one by one and watching them climb his arm, pass behind his neck, down his other arm and slip into his other hand, all nicely stacked. "Cheer up, Conan. You haven't seen anything yet."

Conan glanced at his new friend. "I hope not. What

I've seen so far has been more frightening than my passing into this world from my death bed."

Challenger snorted, then rubbed his eyes and nodded. "Believe him."

Watson laughed. "Don't worry, Conan, it can only get better from here on."

"But Hyde is loose!"

"Well, there's that," Watson agreed. "But we'll deal with it. We always do."

"How can you guys be so positive about all of this..." Conan said, then searched for the right words. "...Insanity!"

"Welcome to the Baker Street Universe," Harry greeted with a grin.

Conan glared at him.

"No, really," Harry insisted.

Conan sighed, then folded his hands behind his back much as Holmes might do. He turned again to watch over Baker Street. Even now after so many months had passed since his transition from his Earth to this alternate Earth, he was still enthralled by its uniqueness and its terrors.

How could anyone with even a grain of intelligence not be?"

Portals to other worlds.

Fairies.

Jungle Lords.

Dinosaurs.

Zombies.

People that are made from pure energy.

It was just as amazing as it was baffling, this world. He jerked from his reverie when a huge shadow crossed several buildings, then one of the new Tesla-powered blimp ships with a tri-hull and glaringly bright lights swept overhead. Below, a mono-cyclist shot past with his steam engine puffing white smoke behind it.

"This world is..."

"Remarkable," Harry finished for him.

"No, it's home," Ms. Hudson declared as she entered the room. She walked to the table, carrying a huge platter. On it were two steaming pots. One of coffee. One of tea. A small silver bowl of sugar. One of cream. Spoons and forks. And a huge plate of steaming freshly baked scones.

"Strawberry as requested," she said, her eyes on Watson.

But his eyes were fixed on the scones.

He jumped up to help her set the platter down.

She giggled.

Challenger and Harry exchanged amused looks.

"I wonder what Holmes is up to?" Conan asked, sitting down at the table, as Challenger also came to sit.

"Knowing Holmes, he's likely to be puttering around with his chemicals," Harry started.

"Or burning up brain cells on trying to figure out this portal mystery and its connection to Hyde."

"As for me," Watson declared, handing out napkins to everyone, then sitting down. "I am pure of an earthlier mind."

He put a hand over Ms. Hudson's as she sat next to him. "Thank you, dear."

She smiled.

He let go and began forking over scones onto his plate.

Challenger reached over to stop him. "Leave some for Holmes!"

Ms. Hudson giggled. "Oh, I made a whole plate for him. He won't be left out."

Holmes never came out of his room as they ate their simple repast.

But the room was warmed by their gentle chatter, as much as by the hearth fire, which Harry stoked with a wave of his hand, causing it to renew and strengthen, chasing away the cold vapors of the evening wind that was beginning to embrace Baker Street outside.

Light silver flecks began drifting like tiny fairies across the view. Snow falling. Christmas was near yet again.

As Conan sat with his new friends, he pondered the mystery of the wall and Hyde's connection to it.

Watson, however, gave it no further thought. His attention was solely on his next scone, which he promptly reached for with his fork and lifted to his mouth to eat.

Conan shut his eyes and relaxed.

It had been a long day.

His whole body shook violently for a moment and then his awareness was consumed by a sense of lightness, and he found himself exiting his own body and fluttering above the room, where he hovered for a moment, watching his new friends eat and talk with each other.

Then his eyes caught notice of a glowing point of light that erupted in front of him. At first, he thought it was the fireplace, and then as the light widened, it became a tunnel of light.

Standing within it were some he knew.

Some he had known quite well.

But they were dead!

And these were those that had never lived in his world.

He felt an embracing warmth grasp his body, closed his eyes, and allowed himself to be sucked into the radiant light before him.

Never Ending Story

I pray you will allow this small disturbance in the major story I have been revealing. It will finally unwrap that one last knot of confusion that may have still been troubling you to this point in time.

So, for those of you who have waited patiently for the entire story to unfold and come to closure, I must relent, but with a kind warning. This story will never end!

But now, back to what happened after Conan went into the white light.

I was there with him when it happened.

In that life and this one.

Here is what happened.

I stood beside my dear friend Conan's bed, watching him along with his dear wife as the man struggled to hold onto his last breath.

Now you as well as I, dear readers, know the length and breadth of his life and of my choice to sustain it. You have tasted the wonders he now lives on because of my intervention on his behalf, but you also can see the gift he was given and the promise that we all have held out before us as we face closure of our own lives.

I could not grieve for my friend as he passed away,

because unlike his dear wife, Jane, he was not facing dark oblivion or life in hell as so many believe so wrongly. No, his life goes on dramatically in an alternate universe. One where all men such as he can live their lives and fulfill their dreams in a manner never possible in this one.

Is it any wonder then that instead of being sad for him, I was elated?

He had this peaceful look and his eyelids fluttered as if he were observing something. A smile touched his lips, and he felt relieved such as I've never heard before, and then as if we were part of some kind of pre-arranged rehearsal his eyes opened, bright and cheerful as if he had just received a round of applause. He smiled warmly. "The game's afoot!"

He grasped his wife's hand and gave her a look like none I've seen before. "You are wonderful!" He told her.

She burst into tears when his hand went limp; his eyes froze in their position, staring off forever. He let out this great sigh of contentment and I swear for a moment I saw him rise from his bed and look at us. First at me with a smile, then at Jane with the sweetest and most loving of glances that a human is possible of giving.

A great tunnel of white light opened before him. Standing in that tunnel of white light were Sherlock

Holmes, Watson, and Harry Houdini, their faces radiant with smiles and an unbelievable warmth.

They gave him a warm embrace and then glanced back at me, nodded, then turned to walk deeper into the light, which began to fade.

I looked back at the bed where now all that lay before us was an empty shell of the great man he once was here in this world. His good wife cried out and clutched at him. I touched her shoulder gently. She looked at me with tears in her eyes. "Is it true? Have you come to take him on greater adventures?"

"My dear, dear Ms. Doyle, don't you see? I already have!"

I hugged her for a long time, and then when her sobbing stopped, I stepped back.

"We'll meet again," I told her with a smile.

I turned on my heels and the portal had opened once more, but this time she as well as I could see it. I felt a great relief as I stepped into it. I knew Conan was safe because the portal was back; but now I, the brave, but now wary Professor Challenger, was a touch unsure if my journey would be a return home or another place I would prefer to not reside in just yet.

But as I stepped into the light, I felt the warmth of

acceptance and love that I'm sure Conan had. I feel relieved. *His journey and mine here are done!* I thought with contentment as I saw my friends waiting for me at the other end.

I turned around and glanced at Ms. Doyle.

She smiled.

Yes, she could see me and where I was going.

Good!

I knew in my heart of hearts I had done the right thing that moment. I am a somewhat arrogant man at times, and even at the last feared I might be biting off more than I could chew, and all would not turn out as I had planned.

But a much firmer hand than mine had lent its strength to this endeavor as it turned out. Harry, who had opened the original portal, had not opened the one that I and Conan returned through.

I gave Ms. Doyle a warm smile and a nod.

Her face seemed to grow brighter and brighter as if a divine point of love had just opened into the universe.

And I knew at that moment, even as she, that we would both meet again. *Soon enough she would be able to join us as well,* I thought,

Then the light closed the veil between our worlds.

I stepped out of the portal to be greeted by my friends who waited for me in the Baker Street Universe.

And the one who had turned the tide of my fear to the triumph of a new life with fellows I will always cherish to my dying days: Professor Challenger.